T0272976

SIXTEEN

Auguste Corteau

SIXTEEN

Auguste Corteau

Etruscan Press

Etruscan Press
Wilkes University
84 West South Street
Wilkes-Barre, PA 18766
(570) 408-4546

 Wilkes
University
www.etruscanpress.org

Published 2019 by Etruscan Press
Printed in the United States of America
Cover design by Carey Schwartzburt
Interior design and typesetting by Aaron Petrovich
The text of this book is set in Mercury Text G3
First Edition

17 18 19 20 5 4 3 2 1

Library of Congress Cataloging-in-Publication Data

Names: Kortåo, Augoustos, 1979- author, translator.
Title: Sixteen / Auguste Corteau.
Other titles: Dekaexi. English
Description: First edition. | Wilkes-Barre, PA: Etruscan Press, 2019.
Identifiers: LCCN 2018012569 | ISBN 9780998750842
Classification: LCC PA5622.O755 D4513 2019 | DDC 889.3/4--dc23
LC record available at https://lccn.loc.gov/2018012569

Please turn to the back of this book for a list of the sustaining funders
of Etruscan Press.

This book is printed on recycled, acid-free paper.

To Puppy – Love of my life.

I would like to extend my profoundest gratitude to Robert Mooney and the rest of the gang at Etruscan Press for making this dream of mine come true.

SIXTEEN

Auguste Corteau

PART ONE

Allegro Antisovietico

CHAPTER ONE

"Then you, too, must be out of your mind, Comrade Samoilenko!" Sretensky's face went purple, the eyes swollen, the nose twitching like the snout of a hog in heat. Alexei Mikhailovich Samoilenko flinched, though he knew this moment of brutality was only a show. Here was the formidable Sretensky, dread seizing him tighter with each new defection. The man actually believed that one piece of music could bring down an empire! Sretensky's panic was visible even in the way he collapsed into his wing chair, and in those shaking hands with which he poured himself another tumblerful of Stoli and lit a Brazilian cigar.

Sretensky's first puff sent him into a fit of coughing that he silenced by downing the vodka. For a long moment the two remained silent, staring at the space between them. No telling what strategies the Colonel was grappling with, but Alexei felt sure of his own thoughts; the memory of lighting up his first Gitanes, smooth, sleek, delicious filtered beauties, while sitting for the first time at *Les Deux Magots* under Uncle Petya's inscrutable gaze.

Here I am, he thought, backstabbing Uncle's memory, making an ass out of myself, and in front of an ass!

It wasn't as if he'd gone to the authorities on his own. He'd never think of such a betrayal! How could he deface the legacy of a great artist and imply that Uncle Petya's life and music, which were the subject of a book it took Alexei ten years to pen, was somehow an attack on the very Party which he had served so well?

You mean to say, comrade, thought Alexei, the erstwhile great artist sonata-ed when he should have serenaded? Dirged when he should have allegro-ed?

And yet, there was no denying certain facts. The empire was crumbling, and something, someone, must be blamed. So now the Party felt compelled to order the scholar-nephew to provide an "expert" opinion on the matter and swear, here before Comrade Khrushchev's beleaguered right-hand man, that he would divulge to no one the subject of these dealings.

How does one diagram a miracle? It was certainly beyond the thirty-year-old musicologist and biographer Alexei Mikhailovich.

Sretensky's glare and the smoke of his cigar, thicker with each desperate puff, made it imperative that Alexei offer some modicum of knowledge that might solve this baffling national crisis.

Taking a deep breath, Alexei said, "Polkovnik Sretensky, regardless of these preposterous rumors which, allow me to stress once more, I do not in any way believe, one should keep, I believe, a cool head about the matter considering the late Comrade Rabinovich's long standing and heartfelt dedication to the Party and—"

Sretensky banged his fist on the desk, cigar ash blizzarding around him. "Rabinovich. Rabinovich! I'm sick and tired of hearing that Jewboy's name..." His voice trailed off.

Sretensky's loss of nerve gave Alexei heart. When the Colonel raised his head, the panic in his eyes made Alexei almost feel sorry for him, faced as he was with a situation that was arguably preposterous.

It was indisputable that the Great Father's recent demise still hurt more than Stalin's former subordinates cared to show. Alexei, though he'd never been a particularly dyed-in-the-wool apparatchik (of course, he had revered Stalin, as every sane citizen would) often experienced pangs of terror and sadness at the thought that their venerable Leader no longer walked this earth. It was a visceral feeling, yet unreal. We're both stricken mourners, Alexei reflected.

"Colonel Sretensky...?" Alexei ventured in a timid voice.

But his inquisitor had regained his composure and cut him off with a raised hand. "Are you certain there are no recordings of the blasted thing?"

"No, Colonel Comrade—to the best of my knowledge, there aren't." But he wondered how true that was.

"What's that supposed to mean? You don't know? I thought the two of you were thick as thieves! You're not absolutely certain?"

"Actually, Colonel, sir, although Comrade Rabinovich and I were indeed quite closely associated, he adamantly barred me from any part in the rehearsals of his last symphony." This exclusion had wounded Alexei almost as much as Uncle's passing. Alexei did clearly recall seeing the rachitic sound engineer, Panteleyev, lugging his equipment into the closed auditorium, followed by the sixteen members of the string orchestra. How could he admit knowledge of this without also admitting that he hadn't been able to locate a single tape of the recording or any trace of the people locked behind those doors? This had been Alexei's most harrowing regret for the past months: that those fifteen men and two women had vanished without leaving the slightest piece of physical evidence, save for their three performances.

This was not only an infuriating mystery, but one that could prove disastrous. Being the last known link to Rabinovich, Alexei had been frequently pressed to reveal the whereabouts of *Sixteen*'s possible recordings, the musicians and the sound engineer. With each innuendo, he had insisted that despite scouring the countryside and the composer's archives, his searches had been fruitless. Now, standing miserably within the overheated confines of the KGB headquarters under the inquisitive eyes of its most merciless bloodhound, the risk he was running became as real to him as a hand gripping his throat. It was entirely possible that if the suspicions about *Sixteen* could solidify into concrete clues, then his sincere desire to be of aid to the Party would mean nothing. He'd be promptly whisked away to Siberia.

He took a step towards Sretensky's desk. "Before we rush to conclusions," he said, "allow me to remind you once again of Comrade Rabinovich's firm stance in all matters concerning Party loyalty and adherence to the rules and principles of Socialist tradition. The '*River*' alone—"

"Comrade Samoilenko," spat Sretensky, "If I hear the fucking *reka aforizm* one more time, I'll put a bullet between those bushy eyebrows of yours." Yet the threat was flat.

Words out of a toothless mouth, thought Alexei. In a halting monotone, Sretensky continued, "What we need to bear in mind above all, is that our great nation should in no way fall victim to old wives' tales or stupid gossip. The sacrifices we made to save the world from that son-of-a-whore Hitler still weigh heavily, and there are no lengths to which the imperialist swine won't go to undermine and destabilize the power, peace and prosperity of our glorious Soviet Republics. So we cannot—" his bulging eyes challenged Alexei—"we cannot be jerked around by suspicions about some dead composer's ghost! Don't you see how outrageous it is to even allude to such a thing?"

No more outrageous than appointing a barbarian like you as art censor, thought Alexei.

Balancing his cold cigar on the rim of a crystal ashtray, Sretensky shuffled the papers strewn across his desktop. "We have reports of former citizens becoming traitors overnight. There seems to be a pattern linking these heinous acts of sedition with the Party-approved performances of *Sixteen* in Moscow, Leningrad and Stalingrad." Raising his head, he noted the sour look on Alexei's face and resumed rummaging. "Of course, assumptions that there could be a connection between the concerts and subsequent occurrences are fucking tripe. I mean, for the love of God, there must have been at least three thousand people in the combined audiences, and the number of traitors is nowhere near as high!"

Not yet, Alexei thought.

"It's just that you can never tell what these artsy-fartsy faggots and their bourgeois entourage are up to now, can you? If we'd left it to artists to defend the country, we'd all have met the same end as the Polish Jews! It's not the first time we've picked up a correlation between so-called 'artistic freedoms' and high treason. We'd have to be stupid not to notice that most of the bastards defiling our Republic are shameless intellectuals, immoral queers and elements of corruption. If you ask me, we should have sent the lot of them packing to Siberia long ago, with your dear Rabinovich first and foremost. But I will return to the facts. You still claim no knowledge of this symphony being recorded? And you also claim that you haven't been able to contact any member of the orchestra? Not a one of them?"

"Not for lack of trying."

"But how is that even possible? It says here that they are all a bunch of old farts! The oldest, this double bass player, is ninety-two, for fuck's sake! You're telling me a man with one foot in the grave can just bypass all our security measures and vanish?"

"I honestly don't know."

Sretensky gave Alexei a disdainful look before nodding toward one of the leather chairs facing his desk. Alexei sat down at once. Alexei watched the sour cigar roll off the desk and drop onto the thickly carpeted floor.

The Colonel shoved the papers into a folder. "It is possible that all this is nothing but a combination of imperialist propaganda and muddled counter-intelligence. It goes without saying that whatever is causing these disturbances, they by no means pose a threat to the sovereignty of our Union. Even as we speak, Comrade Khrushchev is ridding the Soviet people of the poison that ruthless members of the police have been feeding them for far too long."

Alexei nodded eagerly. The thought that the poison in question had been, until a few months ago, Sretensky's own bread and butter never crossed Alexei's mind.

The Colonel continued. "The guilty party behind these occurrences will be tracked down and dealt with. However, it goes without saying that the Party demands your absolute cooperation and discretion in all matters concerning this... oh, let us call it an investigation? Though it's nothing nearly as definite yet. Do I make myself clear?"

Alexei nodded.

Because," Sretensky went on, "although I personally find it ludicrous to ascribe such superstitious power to any piece of music, we must not downplay the importance of Comrade Rabinovich's legacy. But what is even more important, and a point I'm afraid you've missed for all your intimate knowledge of the man, is that your master wasn't, isn't and never will be your exclusive possession. He's not inside that box of yours, let me tell you. Rabinovich's work was about—Comradeship! Rabinovich was all about comradeship! Socialist concord and the betterment of the Soviet world! So lighten up, boy. Try to concentrate on your job, and your duty toward the People's Party. I mean, when you think about it, you and I both listened to this thing, right? We were at the fucking premiere! And I don't see either of us fleeing the blessed land of our Father and Teacher!"

And with this feeble attempt at levity, Sretensky extended his hand and forced a smile onto his flushed face. Alexei had no choice but to shake his hand, though the Colonel's parting remarks had struck a painful chord.

He's not your possession. He's not inside that box of yours. But he's not your possession either, nor am I for that matter, thought Alexei. And as for the premiere, you were most likely snoring away the vodka that's eating through your brain like so much acid.

Leaving behind the spill-your-guts fluorescence and the we'll-sweat-it-out-of-you radiator of the Colonel's office, Alexei slunk past the Lubyanka Square guards and was swallowed by the frigid night air. Thin snow had been falling for ten days, coating the streets with a treacherous icy crust. It seemed not so much a meteorological phenomenon, as a punishment from the heavens. As if God, loathed by the Marxist creed and loathing its adherents in return, had metamorphosed into a vast crystallized corpse that was covering the faithless in snow.

Alexei wrapped the threadbare scarf tightly around his throat and buried his gloved hands in his pockets. This would be his first winter without Rabinovich, although technically there had been those four weeks in March; but at that time Alexei had been stunned by grief so immense that it couldn't be described as actual living. So this was the overture to a life-time of solitary snow. Across the way, children were skipping down Maroseyka Avenue, screeching off-key some song that Uncle Petya had churned out years ago for a sentimental film.

Never again will Uncle Petya listen to such singing, nor draw a sharp breath in the cold, Alexei thought: Which was shameless melodrama, for Uncle Petya abhorred children, and bitched about the cold. Alexei laughed as he remembered the layers of undershirts, sweaters and overcoats Rabinovich bundled himself in, until his thickened arms projected out from his torso.

Unfortunately, as Alexei had come to realize, life was a minefield of such endearing minutiae. Although some people dismissed memories because they were too painful, others hoarded, clinging to the flotsam of spent days until the emotional toll threatened to smother them. No matter how hard he tried to concentrate on his work, Alexei was constantly ambushed by lethal fragments of Uncle Petya. They crept up on him like a multitude of lamenting spirits. Alexei was powerless against this pain. Pain had become his sole possession. Pain was his fortune and his legacy, his sustenance and his companion. Yet this self-inflicted violence of remembrance cut through his flesh and mocked him, conjuring all the things Uncle Petya would never see or feel again, reminding Alexei of the delights and horrors that had been stolen from both. Death, it turned out, was nothing but a relentless pickpocket.

Even if he weren't so keen on self-torture, how could he overcome a death so cruel? They said that suicide was more painful because the victim snatched away part of the survivors' souls, through the constant remorse of having done nothing, even if nothing was to be done. How could one ever hope to recover from a loved one's suicide when the death itself was inextricably tied to something as ubiquitous as the cold?

Of course, the propaganda office reported to the world that the composer's death was due to "acute myocardial infarction brought on by chronic coronary disease." This was plausible enough since Rabinovich was in his early fifties and smoked like a chimney. So "the singing heart of the Russian people," as a one-time chairman of the Soviet Union described Rabinovich, had officially passed away peacefully at his home, as any law-abiding nicotine-addicted Communist ought to; and moreover his death had occurred (in yet another corny touch the press couldn't help adding) mere hours after the Great Gardener's own demise, as if the two great men were somehow linked.

Alexei, however, was one of the few to learn the bitter truth. He'd harassed the quaking bureaucrats at the morgue, threatening to blab to anyone who'd listen, until they disclosed the facts. And ever since, he'd been wondering whether he wouldn't have been better off not knowing. Would he not have been even the tiniest bit happier had he believed that Rabinovich perished from an insidiously weak heart?

The truth was that at shortly after three in the morning, on Friday, March 6, 1953, Rabinovich took a hot bath while fully clothed. Then, wearing only drenched corduroys, a dripping cotton shirt, and no shoes, walked to the Gorky Kul'tury Park, a distance of three kilometers, in below-zero temperatures. There he collapsed on a park bench and died. He left no note. According to the autopsy, Rabinovich suffered from no serious illnesses and, besides a discolored liver and a blackening of the lungs, was in perfect health. The deceased, the doctors concluded, had succumbed to exposure. The coroner's aide was a kindly old man in a foul-smelling rubber apron. He had taken pity on the weeping Alexei, who wasn't allowed to view the body, and told him that Rabinovich's face looked peaceful in death and that as soon as the body had begun to thaw, the autopsy room had filled with an elusive fragrance. The old man described it as "pleasantly bitter-smelling, like wood, or some exotic plant." Alexei recognized the description as Uncle Petya's favorite vetiver foam bath salts. Alexei immediately regretted talking to the old man. The olfactory element of the vetiver scent added to the harrowing vision of Uncle Petya lying butchered on the coroner's slab made the awful scene even more real.

Alexei, childish collector of memories, had finally decided to disregard the imagery of the morgue and the lies of the authorities. Instead, he'd conjured up a scene of his own: wandering the deserted streets of Moscow on the night of March 6, he came upon Uncle Petya before the Party vultures had the chance to spirit his body away. At first, he'd cast himself in the role of Uncle Petya's savior, rushing him to the hospital with a severe-if-not-lethal case of frostbite and a nasty cold. However, his guilt grew unbearable. So he settled for the tragic version of the tale, where, shaking and crying, he came upon a motionless Uncle Petya, slumped across the park bench, forever free from the pains of this world.

Despite not being able to resurrect Uncle Petya, Alexei wasn't entirely powerless in this waking dream. He could sit beside his master, put his head on the frozen shoulder and let his tears soften the rigid shirt. He'd hug the dead man, burying his face in the still chest before collapsing on Uncle Petya's lap. Alexei fantasized that the warmth of his tears and the vigor of his embrace would magically melt the icy crust that shrouded Uncle Petya's body. Alexei would press his face against the damp clothes and breathe the blessed vetiver emanating from the beloved body like the myrrh rising from the relics of Saint Dimitri Solunski. Then, Alexei would kneel and thaw the poor wounded feet with yet more tears, and finally he'd lie down in the frost, looking up at Uncle Petya's inverted smile, and he'd smile too, like a child awaiting a treat; for what a treat it would be to die at Uncle Petya's feet and be with him forever!

CHAPTER TWO

The most soothing thing about death is its infectiousness; the poison of its stillborn fruit. When pain, love and regret will cease. This is the glory of dying—the unrivalled sense of all things coming to an end. Because, if such a merciful nevermore truly exists, one can hope for some quiet; no more the loudness of existing. One should respect death for its finality, welcome the gift of its silence, and never disturb or question it. Take the damn thing already. It was always meant for you.

– Pyotr Anastasevich Rabinovich, *The Aphorisms*

Alexei didn't need to read these lines, for they were etched into his soul, along with Rabinovich's other bitter pronouncements that constituted *The Aphorisms*. However, like a man absently stroking a pet that perches on his lap even while his mind races, so too, did Alexei's fingers mechanically brush over the cover of Rabinovich's famous tome as he sorted through the jumble of papers on his desk. Only when his eyes rested on the book did Alexei make the connection. For all Sretensky's bureaucratic obtuseness, the man had driven the nail home. Alexei was acting as though Rabinovich were still his exclusive possession. The way he clung to Uncle Petya bordered on the

possessiveness of a devout ignoramus. *Worship God enough
and He'll be all yours.* And yet, how else could one behave
when dealing with a man of such great import? How could he
not ritualize the years he'd spent in Uncle Petya's company,
even to the point of making his earthly belongings into holy
relics? It was true that this slender volume was Alexei's Bible.
Often he tucked it into his jacket pocket like an amulet that
dictated the beating of his heart. He was irritated that the
book was read by thousands, that it wasn't his alone. *The
Aphorisms* was the guidepost that had shaped his sense of
morality, honor and integrity.

And how obscenely I have strayed from its teachings, he
thought, dejectedly perusing crossed-out paragraphs, some
typed and others handwritten. The project that had consumed
Alexei was far from respectful of Uncle Petya's opinion on
death. Alexei was disrupting mortality's sacrosanct silence by
violating the stillness. What was worse, this violation would
benefit no one, least of all himself. It could, in fact, destroy
him. This he feared above all, having witnessed up close the
Party's ugly face.

The Aphorisms was an assortment of two hundred and fifty-
six brief texts, ranging from sophistic dictums and abstruse
reflections on the human psyche to paragraphs of introspection
and bursts of free verse. The language and tone of the book
implied that the author had dabbled in Presocratic philosophy
and was also familiar with Marx and Freud. One might view
The Aphorisms as an erratic diary, since the chapters often
included allusions to the author's personal life. Or it might be
read as a bleak document of unforgiving times.

Clearly the author's frame of mind was choleric. Lenin had
somehow gotten wind of the book and had mentioned it in a

1921 edition of his famous *What Is To Be Done?* Despite the fact that Rabinovich's book made no reference to the Bolshevik Revolution, Lenin described *The Aphorisms* as "a brilliant, if brutal, portrait of the hardship awaiting mankind until the shackles of class oppression are forever shattered by a global Revolution" in a footnote. The shackles of class oppression had persisted longer than the exalted leader hoped, and the greatness of the Russian people's destiny remained debatable. Yet these passing mentions had earned Pyotr Anastasevich Rabinovich the first half of his immortality.

Rabinovich was eighteen years old when he privately published *The Aphorisms*, and a mere twenty when his name, owing to Lenin's mention, came to the attention of the ever-mistrustful Stalin. At the time, the General Secretary was attempting to downplay Lenin's insults in *Testament*. A hush-hush meeting with the young author was speedily arranged. Had this interview not pleased the General Secretary, Rabinovich could have disappeared without a trace, like a snowflake clutched in an angry fist.

Rabinovich not only survived but went on to receive an honorary degree at the Moscow State University. Then, in 1925, Rabinovich became one of the first recipients of the Lenin Prize. It was only natural that so much Party-approved fuss would cement the youth's reputation. Seemingly overnight, Rabinovich became a popular idol, an *enfant-sage* hero of the people. Even academics, though privately rejecting his book as a hodgepodge of bourgeois babblings, were forced to hail him as one of Russia's most gifted thinkers. After such a portentous launch into fame, a life of wealth and success were readily available to the young writer. Rabinovich never wrote another book. Instead, the vocation which was to earn him the second half of his immortality had been the means by which he'd seduced the volatile Stalin during that first audience. It was an art even more open to interpretation than literature: the art of music.

The Aphorisms and his subsequent career as a composer were the two obstacles facing any biographer of Rabinovich.

First, although Rabinovich severely criticized his own youthful opus, it was impossible to ignore the importance of this solitary publication in his life. *The Aphorisms* was the budding of his prominence and had enabled Rabinovich to evolve into a hugely popular composer while still in his twenties. But to place too much attention on the book was tantamount to condoning the composer's enemies who implied that Rabinovich was no more than Stalin's puppet. Alexei knew this could not be further from the truth. For all his state-sanctioned laurels, Rabinovich behaved toward the Party and Papa Ioseb with smiling complacency. There was no denying the astounding popularity of his music, with new recitals and recordings sprouting around the globe. Therein lay the second rub: what did Rabinovich truly think of music? The sole aphorism devoted to it was more perplexing than revealing. Rabinovich had posited, "Is music immaterial, if matter is required in order for sound to be created and transmitted? Is God immaterial, if a human brain is needed to conceive of him? And might we then dare think (dare hope!) that music is no invention of humanity but something that transcends if not precedes it?"

From the scraps of information concerning the composer's early years, Alexei eventually attributed Rabinovich's musical inclination to his family. His father, Anastas, had presumably been a wealthy, sophisticated man of Jewish extraction, while his mother, Ekaterina, hailed from an equally prosperous family of Ossetian landowners. As an only child, Pyotr had grown up in a highly encouraging environment, which nurtured his inherent gift for languages and his diverse creative streak. It stood to reason that, in that long-ago cornucopia of childish delights, there had to have been a piano and perhaps a music teacher. But all of this was mere conjecture. Despite Alexei's probing, Uncle Petya rarely rewarded his curiosity with anything firmer than snatches of memories and bursts of impersonal reminiscence. From these sparse remarks Alexei had tried to assemble a story. Displaying an uncanny intuition, Rabinovich's father had renounced both his Jewishness and the greater part of his estate shortly before the Bolsheviks' coup, justifying this gesture of munificence as a token of his gratitude toward the proletariat, the men and women whose toil had helped him accumulate all this wealth over the years.

Then again, this could be a fanciful fabrication by Uncle Petya. Having been born just before the psychotically suspicious documenting of his homeland's people, Rabinovich's true origins remained shrouded in mist. Depending on his mood, his mother was either the daughter of moneyed Jews who had rejected wealth and religious tradition to elope with a penniless *moujik* or else a fallen woman from a family of serfs who had given birth to an illegitimate child. At times, both his parents were "Orthodox zealots," "Bible-thumping Christians" or "enlightened atheists." At round-table discussions attended by Party officials, Rabinovich's parents morphed into zealous Marxists.

Not even his date and place of birth were verifiable. Thus tonight, Samoilenko was faced with a biographer's worst nightmare—a puzzle of journal jottings he despaired of ever solving.

One of the few things Alexei did know was that in 1920, the still-unknown Rabinovich, a self-taught pianist who earned his living as a silent-film accompanist, was approached by the eminent composer Alexander Glazunov at a screening. Glazunov had been intrigued by the young pianist's improvisational flair and invited Rabinovich to join his composition class. Glazunov, well-known for his sound musical judgment and generosity toward fledgling talent, listened as Rabinovich played one of his own compositions. When young Pyotr was finished, Glazunov lumbered to his feet and played Pyotr's piece, embellishing the left-hand part while pincering a cigar between his left index and middle finger. To Rabinovich he said, "It's a wonderful tune, but your pianistic skills, the pedaling—everything, really—even your posture is wrong. So despite being a damn good melodist, there's no hope that you will become a composer in any meaningful sense of the word."

The young Rabinovich didn't mind being told his technique was hopeless. He'd received the praise he was craving from the corpulent composer. He'd been called a maker of memorable tunes. After all, Rabinovich never intended to join the ranks of contemporary masters like Stravinsky or Rachmaninoff. Years later, when his list of compositions included sonatas and quartets, symphonies and operas, cantatas, film scores and oratorios, Uncle Petya still described himself as a songwriter. Two years after that auspicious encounter with Glazunov, when *The Aphorisms* had elevated him to an altogether different plane of fame, the melody he'd played for Glazunov became the basis for the song "Soar High, Tender Feather." It was one of three songs he composed for Meyerhold's production of *The Seagull*, and this one, lamenting the death of a child, deeply stirred the hearts of millions of people.

Although the later years of Rabinovich were well-documented, his initial rise from obscurity into stardom remained unknowable. It was as if Uncle Petya's ghost, having denied Alexei access to his enigmatic swan song, was now barring his way to the starting point. Uncle Petya seemed to be whispering, "Back off, dear boy. You were never invited back there."

"*Moy angel*," said Faina, a glass of red wine in her hand.

Alexei's feet had carried him blindly and deposited him on the stoop of the home they shared. The old woman's voice touched Alexei's troubled spirits as if a devoted dog had placed a paw upon his knee. He smiled as she crossed the carpet, noiseless in felt slippers, and placed the wine next to his ashtray before laying her palm upon his head. For a minute, mother and son gazed into one another's inner lives. Their sorrows radiated and overlapped.

How old and worn-out she looks, Alexei thought, this woman I still remember as a beauty.

Faina's eyes momentarily strayed to his overflowing ashtray in an unspoken rebuke. Catching that glance, Alexei might have been annoyed that he was still living with his mother, but he couldn't help it. Uncle Petya's place overawed him, and the State didn't permit bachelors to have apartments all to their own. Maybe Faina was having the same thought, and wondering which would hurt more—to have her baby snatched away by some woman or to die knowing that he'd be all alone, without a soul to love him half as much as she did.

Nodding at the wine she said, "I warmed it up just the way you like it, my angel," before leaving him to his work.

For the moment, work was no longer possible. The maze of jumbled facts, myths and intentional distortions that made up Rabinovich's story, to be memorialized in Alexei's *Pyotr Rabinovich: A Life,* was daunting. Alexei's concentration had been shot by his mother's use of his pet name: "My angel."

Angel was the name given to Alexei's father at his christening. Grandson of a Bulgarian priest and son of an equally religious Belarusian farmer, Angel had been devout until swept into the storm of the Revolution's fanatical church-loathing. Angel had not merely renounced his religiosity but, terrified of being labelled a non-Russian reactionary, had his name legally changed to Mikhail—the archangel's Hebrew name being the most Soviet-friendly alternative to his given one. Yet one's name is not something one can shed, like hair or skin. Sometimes the potent syllables leave their mark forever. Indeed, Alexei's father, though renamed, had retained his angelic qualities. He was a meek and affectionate man, yet strong and protective of his family. The old name might be gone, but Faina had kept her husband's flame burning. Alexei's mother had also been a pious woman of religious stock, and she, too, had been forced to cast off all outward manifestations of devoutness. She'd met her beloved as Angel in 1915, before the world came tumbling down. He had truly been her angel and had even given her a baby seraph to love, whose existence made her heart glow despite the creeping darkness. Although she'd never again called her husband by his Christian name, and even though the years of worshipful devotion to the Party had gradually stifled the daily prayers, candles and the lightning-quick crossing of oneself, the Angel of her youth was never forgotten. When Mikhail Samoilenko perished from abdominal cancer in 1939, Faina resurrected the winged spirit in a motherly endearment.

Alexei's mind drifted to the directives he'd been brought up on, the rules so ingrained he didn't perceive them as suppression. For what did Marx, Engels, Lenin and Stalin demand of him? Only that he turn his back on a seemingly naïve yet insidious religion which had resulted in the oppression and the extinction of millions of people through the ages. Despite all the rigors of unbelief, Christianity ran in Alexei's blood. Religion had been the haven and the solace of his family for decades. His parents and grandparents had knelt before the Supreme Being and gone so far as to attribute their very kindness and lovability to the Lord's beneficence. So what if there weren't a God? What if this ancestral devotion, albeit meaningless to him, had been meaningful to them? And what if all the accumulated faith, the collective fervor of belief, the worship of empty eidola and barbaric totems, had actually created a God? People still practiced religion across the Soviet Union, even if covertly, and Alexei had been one of the lucky few to travel abroad. To this day, Alexei recalled coming upon the *Pietà* as he entered St. Peter's Basilica and thinking, How could this be wrong? Often an echo of that question would resurface. How can so many people be nothing but misguided fools? Over the years, the piety evicted from his parents' souls had surreptitiously imbued Alexei's own. He wanted to be a faithless, fearless Soviet citizen—the kind of man who trampled on the fallen icons of demolished churches like so much gravel—but the older he grew the harder this became. Now even more so. A Godless universe precluded the existence of an afterlife, and no afterlife meant never seeing Uncle Petya again.

This was as unthinkable to Alexei as his own extinction.

It was a quarter to ten by the time Alexei retreated to bed, feeling edgy and afraid. Another day gone to waste. He lit his last cigarette of the day. His gloominess seeped beyond dysphoria over the whole *Sixteen* affair and the daily angst of dealing with his classes and money worries. It spread to questions about his purpose now that Uncle Petya was gone. Was it to write a book on Rabinovich? Ha! By the time the censors were done with it, the biography would be no better than the rest of the pulp already vomited by the Party musicologists. His draft so far was too painful to read, a caricature, really. It didn't come close to capturing Uncle Petya as the man that Alexei knew him to be.

Did he know Rabinovich at all? Gripped by panic, Alexei bolted upright and lit the bedside lamp. Next to the photograph of his father's kindly face, Uncle Petya beamed at Alexei.

How beautiful Uncle Petya was in this photo! How sweet, this wide, heartfelt grin, breaching the face of a man who smiled so rarely. And this because it was I who took the picture, Alexei thought. For it was true that Uncle Petya had worn this luminous smile only in the presence of Alexei or his mother.

"Still up, my angel?"

Alexei gave a start and crushed his cigarette out in a saucer. Faina, in her sixties, was increasingly suffering from insomnia. Ever the devoted son, Alexei worried her sleeplessness was but a prelude to a greater affliction which would seize her as stealthily as the falling of the night. "I'll sleep when I die!" she would say, laughing at his pillow-wrinkled face when he came upon her in the kitchen, rolling dough at four in the morning. The thought that his mother's body, sensing its end, kept her awake to make better use of her decreasing time was unsettling. So here came Faina, to perch upon her son's bed, and soothe him. How light her touch as she cupped his cheek with one hand! As she took the saucer from the nightstand her gaze lingered on the photos of the two dead men. But instead of uttering the typical Russian widow's sigh of "*Oy, Misha...*" she addressed Uncle Petya, his smile reflected on her face.

"Ah, Comrade Rabinovich. God rest your kind soul!"

Shocking Alexei, she made a cross before the photo three times before turning off the bedside light and leaving him in the dark. Alexei's eyes remained wide open. To invoke God and make the sign of the cross, after... How many years was it? He couldn't remember. Wasn't it what he would do if he weren't too embarrassed by the backwardness of the gesture? Didn't he often, when no one was around, close his eyes and press his lips to Uncle Petya's photos just as old women secretly kissed the icons of Jesus, the Holy Virgin and the Saints? Uncle Petya had cared and provided for mother and her son like a saint. How long before some fresh hell forced them to hide this photo as well, and cease all overt displays of affection toward the deceased?

Alexei recognized that he was going too far into this nightmare-spinning. Rabinovich was still too firmly a part of the establishment to be overthrown. For God's sake, he was the only artist besides Mayakovsky to have received so much praise from Stalin! Now that Stalin was no more, Uncle Petya's posthumous fate was in the hands of bureaucrats with inscrutable agendas.

What if this idiocy about *Sixteen* grew out of proportion and overnight Rabinovich became an enemy of the people? What would happen to people associated with the disgraced composer? What would happen to his precious Faina? The first thing to do would be to remove all of Rabinovich's photos. The wrong photo on your living-room wall could easily earn you ten years in prison without the right to correspondence. Shuddering, Alexei recalled Uncle Petya telling him about a well-known method of neighborly extermination. "Try this with someone you don't particularly like," he had said, removing a dusty hardcover from a crammed bookcase. "Just cut out this photo of Trotsky and paste it on the neighbor's wall while he's out queuing up for condoms, and then call the secret police on him. The guy will find himself building a lodge for the Abominable Snowman of Irkutsk before he knows what hit him!"

Such was the astonishing power of perishable matter—of paper, of the flesh and bone and hence Alexei's need to cling to this portrait of Uncle Petya like a drowning man on a piece of driftwood. The better to fight Sretensky and the Furies of the *Agitpróp*. Evil music! The idea was nothing but a hateful smear campaign. Alexei, his eyes growing heavy, ran his fingertips across the photo. The glass was cool to the touch, yet Alexei let his fingers rest upon it until it acquired the warmth of memory. "Comrade Rabinovich, God rest his kind soul!" Faina's words rose in his ears. To an outsider, the words might have seemed oddly formal. However, Faina couldn't very well refer to their benefactor as "Uncle Petya." After all, Rabinovich wasn't Alexei's real uncle, nor had they ever been related otherwise.

However, as the first Aphorism stated, *Amor, ergo sanguis.*
Love is thicker than blood.

It was during his first few months as Rabinovich's amanuensis that the tender moniker was born. Alexei could still recall the afternoon they'd first been uttered.

They'd been sitting in the composer's study, listening to the historical Busch recording of Beethoven's last quartet. Rather, Rabinovich was seated at his desk while Alexei hovered across from him trying to memorize each note emitted from the worn record. Rabinovich had told him a number of times to take a seat.

"You may even hunker down on the floor if you're so awestruck by my presence though I must warn you, I never let the cleaning ogre into the study, so you'll really be sitting on a plush layer of what I'm told is mostly defunct skin cells. Your disrespectful buttocks will be effectively lying on top of my dead body."

This was still in the early days when Alexei found it difficult even to exhale in the same space as the Master. The thought of being so close to Pyotr Rabinovich, of having the hallowed composer perform dozens of improvisations on his 1828 Bösendorfer piano in daily private concerts, was too much. It felt like a fantasy that was so intense it was almost sensual, a dream so arousing it made him self-conscious, as if he were constantly sporting an erection. Incredibly, the man he had venerated for years was his boss, assigning him the privileged task of notating, revising and often even orchestrating works. But this wasn't the half of it. For the same man would regularly treat Alexei to dinner and press on him pocket-wrinkled wads of money whose weekly sum amounted to nearly twice what Alexei earned in a month of teaching composition at the Moscow Conservatory. He gave Alexei credit, insisting that Alexei's name be printed in concert programs and mentioned in articles covering premieres of new works. Within a couple of months, Alexei had risen from a former underpaid nobody to a minor celebrity in musical circles. The Master had even suggested that Alexei join him on a trip to Prague for a performance of some early Rabinovich gems that the two of them had reworked the previous week.

On this particular day, the Master had an unexpected treat of yet another magnificent tea. Its small sachets contained ground black tea leaves and the tiniest morsels of caramel. Rabinovich always took his tea without sugar and extremely weak. It was nothing more than hot scented water, which Alexei brewed for him in the apartment's roomy kitchen. Soon the Master was sharing this stock of rare teas more freely with Alexei. Alexei, in turn, had adopted the shameful habit of barely dipping the sachet into his own cup, and then stashing the moist packet in an envelope. Later, at home, he re-brewed the purloined tea bags for his mother.

As the quartet dragged through the third movement, and Alexei was picturing Faina happily sipping her *chay caramel,* the Master groaned.

"My God! This is interminable. I marvel at your ability to remain in an upright position after so much blather." Rabinovich gestured dramatically at the empty chair. "Take. A. Fucking. Seat. Your hovering's making this worse, and we have important business to discuss."

Alexei forced himself to sit still while the Master turned the volume down.

The Master sniffed his visage into a cunning smirk. "I couldn't fail to notice that, as of late, you've become a trifle redolent. Today I'd venture that you smell of...wait...day-old bergamot, am I right?"

Alexei blushed on the verge of collapsing in an apologizing heap. Instead of announcing that his worthless hide was fired, the Master threw his head back and roared with laughter. "You thought I'd never notice, didn't you! But seriously, why didn't you just ask for some? For the love of God, just take as much as you want. I don't even like tea. I only drink it to dissolve the gunk in my lungs, courtesy of these vile Soviet cigarettes! I mean, this stuff is God-awful. You'd really be doing me a favor if you removed the whole nasty batch."

"Comrade Rabinovich, you're too kind," Alexei said with a forced smile.

"Nonsense!" He waved away Alexei's dithering gratitude. "In fact, would you mind if I ordered my Party goon to take care of the rest of your mother's eatables? I throw away most of the things they bring me. Last week it was frozen snails. Disgusting shells filled with the petrified mucus. So, if you'd care to have a crap-load of fancy comestibles delivered to your place, say the word."

The prospect of having all their groceries handed to them as a favor from the Party made Alexei dizzy. Mama wouldn't have to haul around all those heavy bags on her own! Nor would she have to queue interminably in subhuman temperatures. But he knew accepting this offer was impossible. Faina didn't want to be either envied or disliked by the neighbors. "Thank you, it is out of the question. Mother would think it most inappropriate. You know how old people are..."

"Perfectly well, as I'm turning into one myself."

"I didn't mean..."

"Oh, hush! You don't have to be constantly on tiptoe around me. I'm not 'Comrade Rabinovich,' not to you. Loosen up, call me 'Uncle Petya.' I'm not Stalin's henchman, that bloody Beria, I just happen to write smashingly popular songs. And this songwriter, is sick and tired of this noise!" With that he turned the record player off, dragging the arm so violently that the needle made a hair-raising scratch on the vinyl. "Why, oh, why is respectable music so goddamn unsmiling? These days, people can't spare the time and effort that an hour-long orchestral work demands—not when there's even the merest chance for actual entertainment lying around. When you've just clocked in a twelve-hour day at an eel-skinning factory, the concert hall just can't compete with the movie theater.

Now, the average drudge in 1820 had virtually no choice when it came to having fun. Nailing your ass on a seat for three hours of decent music was preferable to having a staring contest with the family cow back home. But music, if one ever hopes of being serious about it, has to be enjoyable—and that may mean enjoying a good cry!"

CHAPTER THREE

Alexei's uncomfortable meeting with Sretensky was on December 22. December 23 was uneventful for most people around the world and might normally have gone unnoticed by the Russians. The year, however, was 1953 (*annus horribilis mortis Stalini*), and on this day the Party announced that Lavrentiy Beria, long-standing Politburo dignitary and chief of the secret police, had been executed for charges of treason and terrorism.

That morning's *Pravda* was almost entirely taken over with this story. Employing the full arsenal of epithets available in the Russian language, *Pravda* buried Beria under a pile of insults until his carcass was metaphorically reduced to ashes. The populace seemed relieved to be rescued from the thug who had overstayed his welcome. Seated on a tram, Alexei might have shared in their relief, had he not been scanning the paper for references to Rabinovich. His eye lit on a single-column opinion piece on the last page.

The article, "Is Any Art Ever Truly Safe?" had been written by some Party ass-kisser with the uber-Soviet pen name of Melor Melorovich. The name was a double iteration of the acronym that stood for Marx-Engels-Lenin-Oktyabr'skaya-Revolyutsiya.

Melorovich was reporting on "rumors of an unprecedented number of bourgeois agitators secretly plotting to disturb the peace of the State by fleeing straight into the arms of the West or instigating defection through carefully planned methods of brainwashing." This menace, the article stated, had been "summarily thwarted by intelligence agencies." However, the officials were still unclear as to "the precise instruments of anti-socialist contamination," and there was talk among them "of a high-profile individual belonging to the artistic community, whose long-standing bonds to the Party had placed the person, until now, beyond suspicion."

Comrade Acronymovich recited a list of famous artists whose affiliations with anti-Soviet concerns had been exposed in the past. The question that concluded the piece—"Can the people of the Soviet Union ever be without the shadow of a doubt secure from the morally corrosive element that is often the bane of artistic creation?"—was the *coup de grâce*. Alexei was ashamed to belong to such a country while a staccato of terror along his spine urged him to make a run for it.

He was certain that this article and yesterday's interrogation were related. The irrational thoughts that there might be a grain of truth in the hack piece he'd just read and that a burgeoning epidemic of defection linked to *Sixteen* was afoot raised the tempo of his terror. Alexei was confident the writer had no idea that *Sixteen* was the regime's new enemy. Otherwise, the reporter would have included Rabinovich. Alexei concluded that there had been no irreparable damage to Uncle Petya's reputation. Not even Stalin could have cooked up such an absurd conspiracy! A twelve-minute tuneful *sinfonietta* at the epicenter of mass brainwashing?

Alexei didn't plan to twiddle his thumbs while idle composers and illiterate bureaucrats concocted more lies and accusations. He had to act before this hogwash got out of hand.

Pre-emptive damage control was called for. He must overcome his morbid trepidation of Uncle Petya's apartment and ransack the place for clues. To muster the audacity, Alexei had to remind himself that this was all Uncle Petya's fault to begin with.

Uncle Petya had doggedly prevented Alexei from witnessing the creative and technical process leading to the work with which he'd secretly planned to bid the world adieu. The first Alexei had ever heard of *Sixteen* was when Rabinovich had invited him to attend the premiere in their box at the Leningrad Philharmonic auditorium. At the time, Alexei had intended to interrogate Uncle Petya diplomatically about his recent remoteness, his solo journeys abroad, and his composition and orchestration of a complete work without Alexei's help. However, once they'd taken their seats, he'd been so happy to see Uncle Petya that he had jettisoned his planned inquisition. Then the lights dimmed, the strings plunged into the opening. The music was so ravishing, so bewitching, it felt to Alexei that his whole being was tingling like a tuning fork.

Nearing his stop, Alexei tucked the newspaper under his arm and crossed the narrow aisle of the rocking tram. Strangers cursed as he careened into their knees. Disembarking, he joined the pedestrians slouching along Nikitskaya Ulitska. Alexei wondered how he, who lived and breathed music, could ever have believed that a composition could be used as a subliminal delivery system. For God's sake, the country was still nursing its war wounds, not to mention the lacerations following Stalin's death. Not even a year had passed since the world's violent upending, and purges such as Beria's demonstrated the mountainous uncertainty with which the Soviet Union was coping. Even if this instability devolved into an epidemic of terror, the Politburo would surely have to come up with something more convincing than a catchy tune.

Alexei had assumed his rigid teacher-face upon entering the Moscow Conservatory, but his confidence wavered as he stepped into his classroom. If Stalin was officially treated as a contaminated glacier that had to be defrosted, what would stop the Party from going after that other frozen corpse—Stalin's favorite composer? If music was condemned as the art of the modern-day Lucifer, the popular Rabinovich could easily be turned into an Antichrist. And if such a moment arrived, would Alexei be able to pit himself against the mighty Party?

To betray Uncle Petya would be to strip himself of all that Alexei held honorable. He would be unworthy of missing Uncle Petya, and the life of regret that would follow would be its own Gulag.

Professor of composition Alexei Mikhailovich Samoilenko sat at his desk glancing at his pupils' exercise sheets while twenty male would-be composers filled the room with chatter. Not one student exhibited the slightest hint of originality. Glancing up from the pathetic counterpoint sheets, Alexei exhaled the bitter sigh that is the leitmotif of professional misery. As Uncle Petya had once said, while trashing *How the Steel Was Tempered,* "How marvelous the acoustics inside Ostrovsky's head must be!"

Alexei knew to keep Rabinovich out of his work at the Conservatory. Alexei was the target of widespread rancor among his stiff-necked colleagues who were jealous of his personal relationship with Uncle Petya and his acquisition of a teaching position at the age of twenty-seven. His students were also resentful—balking at learning from someone barely five years their senior. While Uncle Petya was still alive, Alexei had reported these backstabbing pupils to the disciplinary board.

Now, with the fifty-minute period stretching desert-like before him, Alexei was seized by the helplessness he'd felt on the tram. He was about to address their poor performance in the exercise, when one student, not bothering to raise his hand, blurted out, "Comrade Samoilenko, what's the deal with Rabinovich's *Sixteenth*?"

The ambusher was his most troublesome student, Stepan Grigoriev. At twenty-two, Stepan was six-feet-two-inches of densely packed brawn topped by a handsome face dominated by deep blue eyes. If the question had been voiced by another pupil, Alexei might have deflected it, but with Grigoriev he had a hard time even clearing his throat assertively.

"I...um...well, I fail to see how this pertains to your assignment, Comrade Grigoriev."

"Oh, it doesn't," Grigoriev said, grinning. "Just curious, is all."

Don't take the bait, Alexei told himself. But then couldn't help asking, "And what is it you're so curious to know?"

"Is it true that all copies of the score and all recordings of the work have been suppressed by direct order of the Party?" Alexei's shoulders clenched in a fighting stance. "Is this the shit that's been keeping you from submitting an assignment that doesn't look like it was written by a deaf five-year-old? Because if so, you should know there's not an iota of truth in the garbage you're spewing."

"Then why were there only three performances in total?" Grigoriev asked. "And how come it's not playing on a loop on the radio as one would expect from Rabinovich's ties with the regime? What is it about this piece that's gotten everyone tied up in knots?"

Alexei's jaw stiffened. "If you don't wish to be kicked out on your ass, you had better quit this gossip-spreading at once."

Then a mousy brown-noser with thick glasses and atonal inclinations, shot his mouth. "I couldn't agree more. What's there to talk about anyway? My father's cousin, who attended the Leningrad premiere, said the whole thing was barely twelve minutes long. Not even a proper symphony. Just a chamber group of strings which hurried through a few themes, all in the same key, without any development to speak of. A total rip-off."

At this disparagement, doubly odious for being delivered from the pedestal of juvenile ignorance, Alexei raged. He imagined himself for several murderous seconds pouncing on the rat-faced, two-bit Schoenberg and shoving the bungled homework down his throat.

Instead, with a twitching smile, Professor Samoilenko countered, "Same-key motifs are the lifeblood of Russian music, be they traditional folk songs like those that have inspired the celebrated work of Comrade Tsintsadze, or musical miniatures such as abound in the work of Tchaikovsky. As for chamber ensembles, one has only to think of Prokofiev's *Classical Symphony,* or for that matter, Rabinovich's own symphonic rendering of 'Suliko,' which so pleased the Father of Nations."

Intoxicated by what felt like a win against collective idiocy, Alexei would have gone on hectoring the students if his eye had not fallen on his desk. With horror he realized that Grigoriev was this accursed inquisitor's namesake, his full name being Melor Vasilievich.

This coincidence abruptly evoked an equally arresting pair of eyes and a body of sinewy perfection: his dear friend Vittorio, whose laughter came hurtling into Alexei's memory, interrupted by his disbelieving gasps of *"Non ci credo!"* as Alexei, also laughing, tried to convince his friend that the Soviet people were so desperate to conform that they named their children with communist acronyms. Alexei imagined that laughter echoing in a Spartan seminary that had vowed reticence centuries ago. Silence? Commitment? Chastity? Vittorio must have made these promises to the Church with his fingers crossed behind his back.

He was unaware, as Vittorio's laughter faded, of what a terrible mistake it was to wear his heart on his sleeve in front of the class until it was too late. Grigoriev didn't miss a beat.

After a half-hour of desultory instruction, Alexei retired to his musty, cupboard-sized office and locked the door. Sitting at his desk, he twisted like a man wearing a new suit from which a careless needle worker had forgotten to remove the pins. His suit, however, was old, and its yielding fabric accommodated his lower body's movement as he squirmed rhythmically in his seat. At such moments, Alexei valued his unpopularity and was thankful for his secluded, fourth-floor office.

The agitator was Alexei's left hand. The same hand with which he notated, smoked and ate. There was something wicked in Alexei's abandonment to the steady motion, one that could only take place in the seclusion of his office. Not at home, of course, with his mother conscious of every sound. Nor in the consecrated ground of Uncle Petya's apartment. On and on he gave in to the shudders and winces of pleasure brought on by fingers thrust inside his unzipped trousers to stroke and arouse the anatomy he rarely glanced at, the appendage he repressed even in thought and which, except for Faina's maternal ministrations in his first years of life, no other hand had ever touched.

Although later he was always ashamed, Alexei was willing to bear the aftermath—so savage was the relief afforded him, so sweet the shivers of release from the despair of frustrated desire. He obeyed the bidding of his flesh, knowing that unless he did, the pent-up carnal poison would spread to his mind, rob him of sleep, threaten his very sanity. Sometimes he even had to take a break from work to relieve himself; otherwise, his concentration was shot.

Shameful, too, were the images that flooded his mind during the minutes he spent trapped by physical need. In the darkness they flitted in a fever, his imagination now grasping, now releasing a fragment of a remembered face, the curve of a stranger's body glanced furtively on the street, a shifting amalgam of beauty as witnessed in books and museums, all merging in the fusion of lust. For a moment, the forms settled, perhaps becoming Vittorio or some other man whose memory produced this firing of hidden nerves. Today, it was that bloody fool Grigoriev, and at the heated invocation of his name, a surge of craving more savage than fury made Alexei's blind groping hurt so much he gasped.

As he drew near the moment of discharge, Alexei knew that he'd be twice distracted. The first halt would be Rabinovich, whose picture was the sole adornment of Alexei's desk. The photograph of Uncle Petya in his early twenties was face-down while Alexei beat off, but it was never entirely out of mind. In the snapshot, the young Rabinovich was a creature of spectacular beauty. Alexei had encountered the photo long before he'd ever met Rabinovich, and it had been the younger man, the stunner, whom Alexei often saw when gazing at Uncle Petya. In these private moments, the contemplation of that youthful face always caused him momentarily to cease his frenzied tugging. Inevitably, as he resumed the task, the specter of a man who'd been as dear to him as Uncle Petya would interrupt him a second time. The beloved face of Uncle Rodya, his actual kin, would manifest; and the faces of these two would compel Alexei into a profound sadness even as he climaxed.

Rodion Alexeevich Samoilenko had been the first to bring fame and honor to his family. Two years younger than Alexei's father, Rodya had been the epitome of Slavic allure from cradle to adulthood. His image was worthy of a Bernini pagan god, with his thick, spun-gold mane and eyes like miniature lagoons. Although six feet tall, Rodya had exhibited a precocious gift for dance. This was evident in the folk dancing in his school's calisthenics class. Alexei's grandparents had enrolled him in the Saint Petersburg Imperial Dancing Academy at the age of five. By his early twenties he'd already been dubbed "the tall Nijinsky," with the divine Vaslav being Rodion's fellow alumnus and dear friend.

Uncle Rodya's art nurtured Alexei's own. Rodya had given Alexei his first piano, after seeing his four-year-old nephew hammer out a song he'd learned by ear on the family's old upright. Despite Alexei's parents insisting that the piano was already too extravagant a gift, Rodion had paid for the child's first piano lessons at the Conservatory. This ended Mikhail's tacit hopes that his son would succeed him in the respectable profession of accountancy. Alexei often reflected that his entire life, with all its wealth of pleasure and experience, was a debt owed to Uncle Rodya's selfless love and to the faith he'd shown in Alexei's talent. It was as if Uncle Rodya had intuited a similarity between them. It was impossible not to draw further painful parallels.

If Alexei had been asked as a child, he would have professed Uncle Rodya to be a far greater knower and lover of women than his own father. This mastery of the female cosmos was obvious in the way women fussed about him. Faina adored her brother-in-law and spoke of him with unrestrained pride. Whenever Rodya visited, she'd whip up sweet semolina pie, his favorite dessert, and would listen for hours to his flamboyant small talk. There would be stories of Rodya's glamorous life of the stage and accounts of his extensive travel abroad, a vivid monologue that led to a stream of hushed disclosures mixed with obscure grown-up gossip about his celebrity friends. The female devotees were apparently endless. Ballerinas, actresses and orchestra girls sometimes missed their cues from gazing too intently at Samoilenko's gossamer-clad body leaping across the stage.

In little Alyosha's mind things were quite simple: Uncle Rodya was a woman's man, just like him, whereas his father was a man's man. Alexei knew instinctively that Papa wasn't pleased about the amount of time he spent at the piano. Mama, however, was positively ecstatic. This bond of mutual adoration also mirrored Uncle Rodya's relationship with Alexei's grandmother, who had been infatuated with her second-born. Alexei's father used to joke, a trifle bitterly that whenever she spoke of Rodion, Katya Angelova's spit turned into honey. By the time of her death in 1922, Katyusha was convinced that the greatest thing to have ever happened to Russia was her son's latest performance at the *Bol'shoy Teatr*. Despite this maternal and public adoration, which seemed to shield him from all that was evil, Rodion abruptly vanished from the world's stage in the late 1930s. Though never spoken aloud, there was only one explanation for his disappearance: He had been secretly killed and his body disposed of in an unknown location. Since these were the years of vanishings without abductors, of killings without murderers, of survivors without a loss to mourn or a body to bury, Rodion seemingly evaporated without outside assistance. His uncle's unknowable fate had sealed Alexei up, bequeathing him an inheritance of silence. Ah, silence—the lovemaking sound of the lonely, the whispered song of the perspiring palm.

How maddeningly unfair it had seemed to Alyosha. Then he'd been terrified. If something like this had happened to Uncle Rodya, why, then, had Papa managed no more than a hasty handshake whenever Rodya's many male friends came along and afterwards meticulously avoid them? Alexei found his father standoffish, especially since he enjoyed nothing better than being coddled by these affectionate men, who were as warm and funny as Uncle Rodya. The one he'd liked best, the kindest and funniest, had been Vladimir or, as Rodion's dearest, closest friend had insisted Alexei call him, Uncle Vladko.

Rabinovich's predecessor as a self-appointed uncle, Count Vladimir Ivanovich Voloskonsky III was a smallish, thin, red-haired and bearded devil of a man, a famous dancer well before the Revolution. He had since relinquished his title and the vast majority of his family's estates to become one of Russia's most famous choreographers. Vladimir had first set eyes upon the young Rodion Samoilenko in a Paris Opera production of Bartók's *The Miraculous Mandarin,* a *succès de scandale,* because of the designer's daring costumes. After publicly declaring Rodion "an angel whose heavenly grace makes up for the wings so cruelly clipped," Vladimir and Rodion became inseparable. From then on, Rodya starred exclusively in productions choreographed by Vladko, who being older and well-connected in show business, took on the unofficial role of Rodion's manager and spokesman. No one initially seemed to mind the pair's increasingly strong bond; however, in 1937,

Rodya decided to move into the former count's magnificent, secluded dacha in verdant Shchyolkovo. Vladimir's home was more of a mansion than a dacha: a grandiose white limestone building with a sprawling estate. It was the sole remnant of the Voloskonskys' ancient, renounced glory, which had survived the Bolshevik scourge. Rodion's life-altering decision had caused an irremediable rift between the Samoilenko brothers, one marked by bitter remarks and hushed husband-and-wife conversations, with ten-year-old Alexei, dreading this sudden coldness, glued to the door. The cohabitation had seemed not only natural but positively wonderful to Alexei. Uncle Rodya and Uncle Vladko were sharing this grown-ups' version of a hidden treehouse, and Alexei couldn't understand why Papa had described the situation as "sick." Furious with his father for banning him from the uncles' country home, Alexei seethed with unspoken rage. Sick? Uncle Rodya was anything but sick! Sick people had a fever, they were frail, bedridden or lying in some hospital. They smelled of medicine and sour old-man sweat, like *Dedushka* had before he died. Whereas Uncle Rodya and Uncle Vlad were the living image of health: vibrant men who traveled the world and threw parties and had fun as no sick person ever did.

One morning, shortly after Alexei's eleventh birthday, Uncle Rodya had knocked at their door before sunrise. Now he did look sick: his lean frame had withered to a worrisome thinness, his ever-ruddy face was pallid, and a ghastly greenish bruise had turned his left eye into a slit. Despite her distress, Faina had made an effort not to cry. Uncle Rodya tried to joke about his frightful state, dismissing the bruise by claiming that last night he and Vladko had gotten into a "bar-squabble" with some "rough characters." Mikhail was palpably itching to berate his brother for his carelessness, but in the end he'd kept silent, retreating to the kitchen to boil some tea for everyone while Faina tended to Rodion's wound, pressing a dishcloth wrapped around a chunk of ice against his swollen cheekbone.

Things seemed to quiet down until Alexei, fighting tears, had asked after Uncle Vladko. To everyone's horror, his uncle had buried his ruined face in his hands and dissolved into violent sobs, saying over and over: "He's gone! Gone!" Alexei really began to bawl, and Mama had to soothe him, saying, "It's okay. Uncle Vladko will come back. He's just off on some unscheduled trip, you'll see." Wiping his eyes, Uncle Rodya confessed he was thinking of going away, most likely to Paris, where he had many friends who could put him up.

That morning was the last time Alexei ever saw his uncle. At first, Alexei's parents used the imagined flight to Paris to explain Uncle Rodya's absence. There were unconvincing claims about unscheduled trips, time-consuming projects and spells in some faraway countryside. Alexei soon saw through these lies. Mikhail could stand no more. Ignoring his wife's tearful pleas, he'd gone to the commissariat to inquire about his brother's whereabouts. It and a second visit had been fruitless. Then, Papa, in only his underwear, had been dragged away by armed goons in the middle of the night and held for two terrifying days of questioning. Rodion's name was never mentioned again, not even by his mother, who was soon carried off by metastatic silence. Young as he was, Alexei learned a valuable lesson: even if love was not a sickness, to surrender to certain kinds of love fared you no better than a terminal disease.

This rumination wasn't helpful right now. This feeling threatened to soften up things below the waist. Alexei ground his teeth, squeezed his eyes shut and gave himself over to his mind's pornographic eye, not stopping even when Grigoriev and Vittorio were succeeded by a glimpse of Uncle Rodya in a skintight black leotard. The moment of reward came with an almost cyclonic force, squeezing out of him a moan much louder than he intended. When he finally opened his eyes, the first thing he noticed was a drop of semen had escaped the edge of his carefully placed handkerchief and stained the knee of his left trouser leg like a thick, glistening teardrop. Goddamn it.

There was a sudden sound of footsteps in the hallway. He hurriedly zipped up, so overwhelmed with fear that the pain of a stray pubic hair catching in the metal teeth didn't register. Alexei sat transfixed until the footsteps moved away. His mind turned back to nine years before, when a similar set of footsteps had come to a halt outside his classroom, and Rabinovich had knocked on the door of his fate.

Could Rabinovich have chosen him back then not solely for his still-fledgling musical skills but because he'd been driven by some other ineffable affinity? Alexei had often pondered the troubling depths of this question, though nothing had ever caused him any doubt as to the chasteness of the intimacy shared with Uncle Petya. But still, one had to wonder why a man so blessed with talent and renown had chosen to lead such a doggedly celibate life. Could there have been some lost, forever-mourned Vladko in the intensely obscured past of Pyotr Rabinovich? And how was one to dwell on matters denied a public dwelling?

Alexei examined the soiled trouser knee; the stain winked at him, moist and refusing to fade.

CHAPTER FOUR

I'm being followed, Alexei thought as he hurried through the chilled darkness on his secret journey to Rabinovich's apartment.

In the past fifteen years, Alexei had endured a number of square-shouldered tails, first as a relative of Rodion's and later because of Rabinovich, a "prime target" for corruption by the West. Each time was as disturbing as the first. There was the hulking physique of the professional hound, the fixed predatory gaze and the panic of never knowing why the shadow was following him. What knowledge did he harbor? What counter-revolutionary crime had he committed like a treasonous sleepwalker? The unspecified guilt churned foully in his gut.

This pursuer's apparition raised the hair on his neck. Not even one's home was safe from this human evil. If Alexei got up to pee at four in the morning, and if Faina happened to emerge from the dimness of the kitchen at the same time, speaking his name in surprise, her benign silhouette was enough to make him cry out in fright.

"What other species, sexual or territorial, challenge notwithstanding," asks *Aphorism* XCIX, "experiences such a deep, irrational yet overwhelming terror by suddenly coming upon one of its own?"

Alexei hadn't always been so philosophical about these pursuits. When he first noticed he was being followed back in

1938, the thought of being liquidated by the State had filled him with terror, producing erotic nightmares where his pursuers were naked. This changed when Rabinovich, no stranger to being tailed, took Alexei into his confidence. According to the composer's cynical reassurances, these prowling men, despite their menacing appearance, were an aggravation but nothing to lose sleep over. "They're just like pigs after some treat," he'd said. "A cucumber, say. Now their trainer has told them you may be hiding a juicy *ogurets* on your person, and so they can't help sniffing after you. But if you haven't slipped a fucking cucumber in your pocket or up your ass before leaving home, there's nothing they can do to you."

Alexei had to take Uncle Petya's word for it. The Master had been systematically followed ever since Lenin's praise put him in Stalin's crosshairs. He'd been trailed to ensure that, despite his popularity, he wasn't being disloyal to the new Party leadership. He'd been trailed because his growing songwriting fortune made him a defection risk. Later, Rabinovich had been trailed when he returned three days early from a trip to the United States where he performed before President Coolidge, despite the fact that he'd found America too vast and populous. This was to establish whether his public dislike of the enemy's homeland was sincere or if he'd loved the place so much he had become an undercover spy for the U.S. Finally, in the last decade of his life, Uncle Petya had been followed by stalkers multiplying "like foot fungi, but worse-smelling." So it was only natural that Uncle Petya had become immune to the sight of the interchangeable thugs that followed him everywhere—so much so, that sometimes he'd lose patience and hurry over to introduce himself. In the summer of 1949, Rabinovich and Alexei had flown to Australia for a concert, and the haggard man who'd been tailing them couldn't keep pace. Uncle Petya had stopped dead in his tracks and pointed at the wretched guy, who'd frozen at being singled out so easily. "Just look at the miserable son-of-a-bitch! This inhuman heat is boiling the vodka in his veins!" Uncle Petya had crossed the street and stretched out his hand. The gray-faced man was glued to the spot. Rabinovich shook the rigid hand and introduced the poor soul to Alexei.

How easy it had been to rid himself of fear when Uncle Petya was walking by his side and joking about things no one else would dream of treating as a laughing matter! Alexei longed for that contagious cockiness that came from being the protégé of someone who behaved as though he were invincible. That balmy Australian afternoon couldn't be further away from this biting winter night as Alexei tried to outpace the giant on his trail and escape the glare that burned like a bull's-eye on his neck.

What colossal stupidity was this last-minute decision to visit Uncle Petya's apartment a day after being grilled by Sretensky! This was precisely what a panicking conspirator would do—scramble back to the scene of the crime to destroy what damaging evidence he could. When he'd reached this foolhardy decision back in his office, it had seemed the only sensible course of action. Rabinovich had kept him in the dark about everything pertaining to *Sixteen*. The fact that the composer had pulled the whole thing off all on his own was the root of the mystery. Alexei knew Uncle Petya would never have been able to complete an orchestral work without his help—not even a twelve-minute string symphony that was all exposition and no development. A rather sloppy orchestrator who relied on the musicians he chose to work with, Rabinovich had become even lazier in the last years of his life. Their usual workday consisted of him hammering away at some old or new earworm on the piano, and Alexei jotting down what he could catch of the music and assuring the Master, who often got frustrated with his own declining dexterity, that it was neither shit nor the fruit of unconscious plagiarism. There was only one way to explain *Sixteen*'s manifestation: Uncle Petya had entrusted the music's transcription to an unknown third party. Alexei had immediately realized that at the work's premiere, though at the time he'd tried to evade its horrible sting of betrayal. There weren't many suspects for this ghost orchestrating, since not a single page of score had ever appeared. There'd been no music stands and no conductor that night. The sixteen members of the orchestra tore into the ravishing music by memory. Either those elderly men and women, none of whom Alexei had ever seen before, had helped the Master along during the closed-door rehearsals, or Rabinovich had magically completed a score himself.

In a fit of jealousy, Alexei imagined that Uncle Petya had turned to a different arranger because he'd lost faith in Alexei's skills. This fantasy was petty torture, as he cast a series of potential composers who might have wormed their way into the Master's trust behind his back. That wall-eyed Dmitri Dmitriyevich was always anxious to curry favor with the Party. Or that Stravinsky-wannabe Prokofiev, the ever-mediocre orchestrator whose own last symphony had been a chamber work. The real Stravinsky was out because Rabinovich loathed him. Sibelius, a dear friend back in the '20s, had long ago fused with a leather armchair by the fire. The backstabber might even be some Conservatory floozy! A younger version of Alexei—some starry-eyed queer too inept to handle winds but shrewd enough to make off with the Master's last score. However, if any of these scenarios had been true, Uncle Petya would never have been so cruel as to rub it in by making Alexei attend the premiere by his side. If anything, Rabinovich had been unfailing in his kindness until the bitter end.

Picking up his pace, Alexei shoved all the rehashed conjecturing out of his mind and tried to concentrate on what little he knew as fact. It all came down to a single piece of pertinent knowledge.

On November 2, 1952, Uncle Petya had called him late, long-distance from the sound of it, to say he'd decided on an impromptu trip in order to gather material for a new opera. Alexei had been surprised that he hadn't been invited, but he'd managed to sound encouraging. In the middle of December, the same thing happened again, and Alexei found out about the trip only after the Master returned a week later. When hearing of the final jaunt that had taken place, Alexei decided to quit acting like a spoiled brat and show some respect for the creative privacy a genius like Uncle Petya was entitled to.

Yet Alexei was unable to stop speculating, because another stone-hard fact was that Rabinovich had never liked opera. The man could barely sit through one without nodding off or sneaking away during the intermission. He couldn't imagine Rabinovich spending a whole month on operatic research, much less on attending performances without Alexei to wake him up when the lights came up and nod discreetly at the drool the Master ought to wipe off his chin before they made their stealthy getaway.

Another possibility was that Rabinovich had undertaken these mysterious travels alone because they'd been somehow connected with the enigma of his personal life. All the more reason not to behave like a spurned lover. Such nonchalance was unforgivable in hindsight, but back then Alexei hadn't known that Rabinovich had less than two months to live.

But what if Rabinovich had known? Until now Alexei had chosen to believe that Uncle Petya's suicide had been a momentary madness. Alexei remained firm in this belief so as not to drive himself mad with guilt.

A freezing gust of doubt rushed in. What if the two last things Uncle Petya ever did—make music as a final burst of life then destroy himself—were linked? The timing of his suicide could hardly have been coincidental, and Alexei never bought the public explanation that Rabinovich had been "unable to live in a world without Stalin." This meant that Uncle Petya had known the chaos Sixteen would provoke, and had excluded Alexei from every step of the music's birth in order to protect him.

You can't be serious, rebuked the voice of reason. All the musical hocus-pocus bullshit aside, how could you say that Uncle Petya left you all alone to protect you?

No sooner did Alexei raise this inner protest than the footsteps behind him grew louder. There was another lighter foot keeping pace and, over his shoulder, Alexei saw a second glowing cigarette tip and the bulk of a second man striding alongside the first.

Alexei broke into a run. Bolting down Nikitskaya past the Biblioteka Lenina, he crossed Mokhovaya and penetrated the northern side of the Alexandrovsky Garden. He zigzagged between the trees and kept to the darkest stretches of the park. At the Borovitskaya Tower, he set off east toward his intended destination while the footfalls continued behind him.

Despite the cold, Red Square teemed with people: couples were out on evening strolls, ancient vendors hawked blini and beer, mothers pushed babies bundled up in their buggies, soldiers rigidly patrolled the Kremlin and the homeless slumped in doorways. Alexei merged with the throng, chuckling as if he'd finally won. A daredevil giddiness filled him, this fearful mouse who still had managed to outrun vicious cats by running up a tree and disappearing into its dense foliage. This feeling carried him as far as Lenin's Mausoleum, where it dawned on him that cats were born climbers and the branches of trees were often thick with mouse-fed owls.

Was he so stupid as to think he'd evaded the legions of the People's Commissariat for State Security? The human sea around him could well be swarming with more agents following him from a distance. His every movement seemed laden with danger, and by the time he reached the Museum, so did every single thing around him. Every Moskvitch rushing down Nikolskaya was transformed into the vehicle of his fatal abduction. "Oy, Mama," muttered Alexei, "Faina!"

Obsessed with protecting Rabinovich and this doomed circumvention, he'd forgotten what his downfall would mean for poor Mother. Not bothering anymore with a circuitous route, Alexei found his way to Tverskoy Boulevard. When he reached the pair of lime trees framing the ornate front door of Uncle Petya's building, he snuck inside like a thief, the keys barely leaving his pocket.

Sixty-four Tverskoy Boulevard was a glaring oddity of socialist hierarchy with its Art Deco splendor including striped wallpaper, burgundy carpet and gilt sconces; the foyer alone was downright imperial. The elevator, softly aglow across the hallway, was a spacious golden cage which allowed passengers to marvel at the stone-and-marble innards of the building as it spilled out shafts of light upon them. Rabinovich used to call the elderly contraption Starik Kirill, after the Grand Duke who'd escaped the Bolshevik scourge. Alexei pressed the top floor button, and with its usual clang of resolve, Old Kirill began his long ascent.

A red glow greeted him in the silent apartment's vestibule. It was shed by one of the several identical lamps the Master had favored, their shades a bright hue of carmine. The same color was found in the Persian rugs, the rows of leather-bound books on the shelves and the various ornaments and souvenirs scattered about. Strindberg said that red was the color of the soul. This particular lamp stood on the narrow table that held a bowl of spare change, an extra set of house keys and the sporadic mail Rabinovich continued to receive. Alexei inspected the apartment, making sure everything was in place and trying to accustom himself to the bizarre fact that he was the proprietor of the sprawling penthouse.

The inanimate world around him oozed memories as if he trod upon a huge sponge. Alexei constantly had to look away, armoring himself as the concerned proprietor. Everything seemed to be in order. The floors were spotless and the furniture dustless, kept so by the same Georgian cleaning lady Rabinovich had designated as his private Nemesis, a tight-lipped woman "beastly enough to frighten portraits into facing the wall." Alexei had always treated her gratefully, since she, too, had looked after Uncle Petya, regardless of being on the Party's payroll to do so. Surely this beautiful shrine would have fallen into decrepitude without her. Alexei had no illusions about the apartment's tidiness. Long before the trouble with *Sixteen* arose, as early as when Uncle Petya's body was found, a horde of NKVD agents would have scoured the late composer's residence looking for clues that might explain why Rabinovich had resorted to the highly anti-Soviet act of taking his own life. Party snoops were sticklers for appearances. To leave the place ransacked would imply that there was cause for concern, which would cause yet more concern through the admission of vulnerability.

Now for some snooping of my own, thought Alexei, standing outside the double doors of Uncle Petya's study, from which the key protruded. Part of him insisted that no matter how thoroughly he searched, it would all come to nothing. Wasn't this the voice of his own reluctance to disturb the Master's most private space? Out of the dimness of his thoughts emerged a memory, or was it a dream, of Uncle Petya raising his eyes from the disorder of his desk to ask Alexei what the day was. Saturday, Alexei had answered.

"Really? When did I last leave home?"

Alexei had to count out the days on his fingers. "Monday?" he had ventured at last.

"Jesus Christ!" Uncle Petya exclaimed in disbelief. "Did I die or something? Am I really here, or am I haunting this place?"

Now, smiling to himself, Alexei turned the key all the way.

If only it were so.

The last time he was in the study, Alexei hadn't really been there. Rather he'd entered as if in a fiery, blinding cloud of pain. Delirious with loss, he'd tried to piece together the chaos of Uncle Petya's suicide.

Great shadow-birds had soared among his disordered thoughts, shrieking the hidden message of the Master's self-destruction. A belated reaction to the horrors of the Holocaust, that was how death snuck up on him! Rabinovich had never once alluded to the genocide; his very Jewishness was no more than conjecture. Terminal illness, cancer, tumor-riddled body. That had to be it! Hence, the sudden solo trips abroad: Rabinovich seeking a cure that didn't exist, then renouncing the gift of life before it grew too poisoned with agony. Wouldn't Alexei have perceived some indication of all the pain endured? While he sought proof of those echoing cries, Alexei had reiterated the Master's order to the silent, expressionless housemaid: she wasn't to set foot in the study.

The conscientious cleaner had apparently heeded his command. The dust on every surface was the same that had accrued in Uncle Petya's lifetime. The tips of the cigarette ends crushed into the overflowing, acrid-smelling ashtray still bore the invisible mark of his lips, and the dull, sebaceous spots on the keys of the upright piano were the lingering trace of his fingertips. Lowering himself in the Master's leather chair, Alexei gazed across the windowless space.

The short, slim bookcase contained those books Rabinovich had loved dearly. Alexei had read most of those books, although some of them were too mystifying to be truly appreciated.

The wooden file cabinet had been Alexei's hard-won addition to the study. Its three drawers held the assembled archive of the composer's complete list of works. This collection was largely the fruit of Alexei's years of diligent notation, orchestration and completion. Among the archive's real treasures were rescued sheets of Uncle Petya's lifelong struggle with transcribing onto paper music that was incandescent in his mind.

Alexei's eyes rested on the horrid Picasso that hung prominently on the nicotine-stained wall. Executed in a purposefully slapdash manner during the painter's celebrated infatuation with Stalin ("Though to be fair, Gertrude Stein had a thicker mustache," Uncle Petya had once commented on the donor of this questionable gift), it depicted a naked, squatting woman with a bovine heart suspended from a cord whose hook pierced the woman's inflamed, protruding labia. Underneath, inscribed in the same red ink as the drawing,

Picasso had transcribed (his Russian touchingly misspelled) one of the few poems contained in *The Aphorisms,* and the sole one that Rabinovich had ever set to music:

> Once upon a time, my heart was red.
> It is still red. It will be red the day I die.
> And red will rest the blood, the fury silenced.

Alexei found the poem too mournful for pleasure; however, in the '20s the Party had exploited the befittingly Bolshevik recurrence of "red" and turned the poem into a widely popular ear sore, faithfully performed each year on October 25 by military bands whose clamorous incompetence was only rivaled by the crowds that bellowed out the lyrics. As to why Picasso had chosen to illustrate the poem with such pornographic incongruity was a mystery best left unfathomed.

Before his unforgettable first visit to the Tverskoy Boulevard apartment, seventeen-year-old Alexei had imagined it discreetly populated by portraits of Rabinovich, ranging from the artfully photographic to the regally pictorial. What was art if not a memorial to the artist's self? To his surprise, he'd found no fireplace-crowning oils or rigid studio headshots among the clutter adorning the walls. Marx, Engels, Lenin and Stalin, those bulwarks of the Revolution and staples of Soviet wall-filling, were conspicuously absent. Only three small framed photos graced Uncle Petya's home. The first was taken when photographs still bore a grainy resemblance to paintings. At its center, a woman slept among the roots of a tree, her tranquil face resting on folded hands while dappled light played upon the gossamer of her voluminous gown. It was instantly apparent this was Rabinovich's mother—so stunning was the resemblance. That such an intimate memento hung in plain view might come as a surprise to many, but not to a mama's boy like Alexei. Next to this hung a photographic recreation of Schubert in his final bedridden moments, a token of Rabinovich's worship of the Austrian *liedermeister*.

The last photo broke Alexei's heart. He was its subject, and Uncle Petya had taken it in 1947, while the two of them vacationed in New York as guests of Consul-General Lomakin. The black-and-white Polaroid captured Alexei dozing on a lavish bed on the consulate's third floor, summery light bathing a slumbering frown.

"But why all these sleepers?" Alexei had asked.

Rabinovich seemed to lose himself in thought. "Because our truth is only revealed when we don't know ourselves," he finally replied. "Either that, or I'm a complete pervert."

Really, though, Alexei thought, truth is the ultimate pervert. That sullen, impersonal virtue held everyone to its own delusions.

Ten minutes later, his excavation of the top two drawers had resulted only in a paper cut and a heap of useless miscellanea, including paid bills and completed tax forms.

The only find was equally unrelated to the pressing *Sixteen* business, yet Alexei couldn't help spending a few moments grinning at the oblong piece of paper. It was no small thing to be holding a million-dollar check made out in your name.

The year was 1933, and by then sentimentalism had long completed its victorious invasion of the talkies. The Soviet film industry wasn't going to miss out on such lucrative fun, and so, while continuing to demonize Hollywood as purveyor of bourgeois propaganda, socialist realism appropriated Western schmaltz and began to produce its own maudlin historical dramas. Female factory workers, after being extravagantly brutalized by some lecherous White Guard villains, got their happy endings in the arms of dashing Red militia fighters. And since such movies require mawkish soundtracks, Rabinovich was happy to oblige, churning out dozens of mushy scores and lovelorn songs, many of which became instant and heavily uddered ruble cows.

Enter Cole Porter, who, fresh from a year of songwriter's block, roams the Continent, looking for inspiration. During his sojourn in melancholy Prague, he falls in love with a song he hears on the radio. The Russian tear-jerker moves him so tremendously that his creative juices flow anew. The song is called *"Dayte mne vashu ruku"* ("Give Me Your Hand"). Porter pens off an effusive fan letter to its composer, secures its foreign adaptation rights, composes his own whimsical lyrics and, along with the soundtrack for a hit romantic comedy starring Claudette Colbert called *Sweaty Palms,* goes on to win the Academy Award for Best Original Song.

This provoked a minor furor among the more patriotic members of the industry, since the song's original composer, credited in the film and thus a co-winner of the Oscar, was some Russkie by the name of P. Rabinowitz.

The misspelled Rabinovich wanted no part of this win. Despite its popularity, he considered the song an offensive bastard. He refused to travel to the States to accept the award, a decision much applauded by *Pravda* as a proud Communist act of contempt for capitalist institutions that stops short of saying "We shit on your two-bit prizes."

However, the shunned statuette managed to make its way across the Atlantic and, traveling via diplomatic circles, finally reached Rabinovich. The composer was so incensed he threw the Oscar in the trash, from which it was rescued by the cleaning lady, sparking a cycle of hostilities that lasted nearly twenty years, during which the Oscar was regularly retrieved from garbage cans and used as a bookend, paper weight or doorstop by one enemy party until it was trashed again by the other. The trophy was eventually sold in 1941 to Ignatiy Zhukov, a billionaire expatriate and Rabinovich enthusiast, for the astronomical amount of one million dollars, the check for which the composer deposited, torn into pieces, in the same litter basket. Six years later, following Zhukov's tragic death by an enraged male emu during a safari, his attorney discovered the outstanding payment and issued a second check, this time in the name of Alexei Mikhailovich Samoilenko, to whom it was presented as a birthday present by a delighted Uncle Petya. After reviving his assistant, Rabinovich decided to hold onto the check so that Alexei would not "spend it all in one place."

Alexei sighed as he returned the check to its nest of paper. Those mythical dollars were never truly his. It was just his name on a piece of paper, of no more actual value than Rabinovich's last will and testament that transferred ownership of the apartment to Alexei. His earthly lot, including the freedom he enjoyed, was his only so far as it wasn't required (and revoked) by the Party. All that belonged to him was the paper cut he'd been sucking on during these reminiscent moments.

The bottom drawer was more forthcoming. Leafing through a thick pile of more hoarded junk, Alexei came upon another photograph. Its existence was a curiosity, for despite the surprising number of cameras Rabinovich had owned, there were no albums, no loose snapshots, not even films to be developed among his effects. It was as if Uncle Petya had belonged to a tribe who didn't believe in fixing life on paper.

Alexei had never seen this photo before, but it was clear that the woman depicted in fuzzy profile was Ekaterina Rabinovich. The flimsy dress she wore was the same as in the photo hanging on the wall, as were the numerous rings that bedecked her fingers, the thick gold chain around her neck and the tortoiseshell comb holding her abundant hair. What made the photo even more special was the fact that in this one Uncle Petya, alarmingly young and handsome, and smiling as Alexei had never seen him smile, stared into the lens, his head reclining on his mother's lap. Returning Uncle Petya's gaze, Alexei felt a pang of filial rivalry. He wished he, too, possessed a photo like this: one that captured his love of Faina and the pure, boyish happiness he still felt in her physical presence.

Sixteen's potential association to Uncle Petya's mother had been the first course of private inquiry Alexei had embarked on. There was the numerical connection. Years ago, while sharing a bottle of bathtub *tsuica*, Rabinovich had revealed that "dear old Katyusha" had been a child bride of twelve when *"Dedushka* auctioned her off to the wealthiest bidder" and sixteen when she gave birth to her only son. Then came the dreaded seventeen, the February Revolution and an outbreak of epidemic typhus in the Petrograd environs, which carried off more than seven hundred people, Mrs. Rabinovich among them.

But to define *Sixteen* as an esoteric work of mourning was going too far on too little. No matter how the photo wrenched his heart, Alexei knew it was his own unmeasured love for Faina he was assigning to Rabinovich. No, even this phony suicidal fancy was a misallocation of pain to explain another, unknown pain that had eluded his loving attention—that Uncle Petya was stronger than he. Uncle Petya had proved this by ending it all, whereas Alexei would go on wallowing in loss as he now wallowed in the poignancy of its photographic monument.

Slipping the photo in his pocket, Alexei stood to have a ruminative smoke. "Stop behaving like a sentimental fool and think!" he barked at himself. A secret panel in one of the walls? Some hidden compartment in the desk activated by a switch hiding in plain sight? A strongbox, perhaps, disguised as a... What? Rabinovich was the single most forgetful person he'd ever known. The Master's distracted mind could never store safe combinations or the location of an intricately operated hiding place. Even if he had owned such a cache, Alexei would have known about it, since he'd be the one required to unlock the damn thing while Uncle Petya looked impatiently on, fiddling with a matchbook and toying with the thought of setting the house on fire if "tiresome Alyosha" didn't hurry up already.

Alexei looked into the frame of the piano. Nothing but strings faded into darkness. Since the lid was raised, he leaned over the stool and played a quick arpeggio, but stopped abruptly, flinching at the dissonant whine of a high F. Gazing sadly at the upright Petrof, he recalled Rabinovich mentioning a beautiful 1628 Amati some collector had bequeathed to the Conservatory and how painfully the precious violin had screeched upon first being played. "It's not disuse that does it. Any old instrument is more than its neglected material," Uncle Petya had mused, drawing deeply on his cigarette before crushing it into the ashtray. "It's the sorrow of lying untouched. They go out of tune just like an old man's voice grows hoarse from too much loneliness."

Only one place left to look. An obvious place, yet one Alexei hadn't gone anywhere near since that unthinkable time, when living felt as hard as treading among ruins. Back then he'd told himself he didn't need to search the file cabinet. The truth was that he feared the desolation it would bring to look at the music Rabinovich and he had created together. Those folders, blessed with the Master's genius, seemed like so many rows of orphans in their cots whose sleep he couldn't find it in his heart to disturb.

It was pure arrogance to think that he'd fathered Uncle Petya's music because he'd provided a written record of it. Looking through the cabinet's top drawer, Alexei couldn't help smiling at the thought of what a difficult and negligent mother Rabinovich had been toward his own musical offspring.

Only the moment of conception seemed to make him truly happy. It was that tiny rift in time when his wondrous mind grasped at its own lambent magic and gave birth to a melody that haunted him until it flew out of his fingertips and sparked the piano to life. As soon as it was out in the world, Rabinovich instantly grew wary of his musical newborn. Hands hovering above the keys, he'd stare into the emptiness just moments after the joy of creation. He'd turn to Alexei with the questioning eyes of a mother silently inquiring of the doctor. Is it supposed to look like this? Does it seem deformed to you, too? Unless Alexei managed to convince him that the music was worth keeping, that he should give the kid a chance, Uncle Petya would condemn it to the nether world whence it had been plucked, muttering disgustedly as if discarding a useless mass of afterbirth.

Nowhere was this vicious self-derision more evident than in Rabinovich's attitude toward his youthful compositions. It was understandable to a certain point. Youth is but the embarrassment of getting to know oneself, a process even more onerous for one who has attained fame while still in his early twenties. Rabinovich had long struggled with musicians and conductors, with fans and critics. Seeking the simplicity of song, he'd stumbled into siring a work that was to hound him with its two-edged popularity.

Leafing through its folder, Alexei laughed out loud at the memory of the month-long fight he'd had trying to convince Rabinovich that it would be an "unforgivable shame" for the score of the composer's first fully fledged symphonic composition to exist only in unauthorized secondhand versions.

"It's nothing but goddamn Stalin farting through the bullhorn of my own incompetence!" Or so the rant would commence, before escalating to a literal brawl, where they'd yell at each other. Rabinovich would break Alexei's pencil in half, lest his disciple write down a single note. Based on a poem by Akaki and set to music by Sulkhan Fyodorovich Tsintsadze, both eminent sons of Stalin's native Georgia, the titular "little soul" and its tearful, nightingale-wanderings pleased the General Secretary like no other, especially since he was on one of his cultural-policy-altering nationalist moods. When Rabinovich bullied the orchestra members into improvising along with him during the half-hour orchestral piece and invited Stalin to the premiere, the General Secretary not only attended, but joined the standing ovation. Stalin loudly demanded that the symphony be performed again. One week later, he awarded Rabinovich his first Order of Lenin, personally pinning the badge to his breast in a private ceremony. No photos of this had survived because, according to Uncle Petya, on that day Stalin had been awakened by the excruciating pain of a rotten molar. The abscess had disfigured the left half of his face.

"Both I and that fucking pestilence of a symphony became synonymous overnight with ass-kissing and not the figurative kind. Oh no! But the actual act of sticking your face into the crack and brown-nosing it for all you're worth. People all over Russia use the very word while wagging their asses on all

fours, begging 'Yes! Yes! Suliko, all nice and ready for you!'"
Alexei remembered this particularly graphic part of Uncle
Petya's diatribe word-for-word, since at the time it had given
him an unwelcome hard-on.

Dare he go deeper, past the folders containing the scores
of Uncle Petya's numbered symphonies, to the void that lay in
the back? What good would it do, other than stoke the pain
with the sight of the cenotaphic folder?

Sixteen's cream-colored folder was empty, labeled in
absentia by Alexei while Rabinovich was away on his last
puzzling trip abroad. Though he had managed to extract little
more than the title of the work-in-progress during Uncle
Petya's phone call, he expected that upon the composer's
return life would go on as usual. The Master would be lunging
at the piano, and he bustling to keep track with the music's
unstoppable flow.

Deep in the drawer, Alexei's fingers closed around the
upper edge of the folder and paused for a moment to indulge
in the magical thought that it would reveal a sheaf of pages,
the music of *Sixteen* written by Uncle Petya's ghostly hand
or infinitely better, a long, affectionate letter of farewell, the
suicide note he ought to have found and never did.

Blinking away tears, he pulled and felt the folder's weight
resist. He backed away with a sharp intake of breath, his heart
thudding as if his fingers had just grazed the feathers of a
visitation.

He'd made a mistake, surely. He'd miscounted and scared
himself. Why did his heart keep up its frenzied beating as he
approached the cabinet again; why did the vestigial beast in
him raise the hairs on his neck and make his hands grow numb?

A few dazed seconds later, Alexei found himself holding
something that shouldn't be—a slim, once white, French

volume of *Aphorismes,* published by Gallimard in 1929. The yellowed pages were uncut, the spine still smooth. Its presence in the study was an aberration of Rabinovian laws.

This is how Alexei knew that he was right.

They'd been working hard on a string trio for the better part of the morning when the cleaning lady had knocked on the door, slid it open without waiting for a response and, after exchanging a vitriolic look with Uncle Petya, dropped a thick parcel on the desk, muttering that it had just been delivered.

"Did you hear the doorbell ring?" Rabinovich asked Alexei, holding the brown-paper package next to his ear. Nothing was written on it, and the string holding it together was loosely tied, so that the objects inside shifted visibly. "Because I keep expecting that Hydra to hand me a home-made bomb one of these days."

The parcel contained something even less welcome and much more explosive: six complimentary copies of *The Aphorisms,* likely sent to the author by some well-meaning soul in that mammoth book monopoly either new on the job or oddly ignorant of the strict no-communication rule concerning this particular writer.

Instinctively stepping back, Alexei counted the seconds until the meltdown. No compliments, remember. Just pretend the package never arrived. Create a distraction. Fetch him a cognac, drop the ashtray on the floor, pretend you're having a fit of renal colic.

But Rabinovich stood and, holding the books under his arm, stepped out of the study without a word. Honestly fearing a fistfight with the housekeeper, Alexei hurriedly followed and found Uncle Petya in the living room feeding the books to the fireplace one by one.

This chilling act of self-hatred had stayed with Alexei, and he knew that the book he held now, surreptitiously inserted into the folder by Uncle Petya during his last days, was a clue related to *Sixteen*, deliberately placed where only Alexei would find it. The fact that it hadn't already been found by the secret police was either indicative of sloppiness in their investigation, or it meant that *Sixteen* was still a low-priority case.

The trouble was that Alexei's French was patchy at best. Rabinovich's teaching method had consisted of forcing Alexei to read one novel per week, aided only by a dictionary and discussing the book with him *en français*. Although Alexei could plod through a relatively accessible text, his spoken French resembled the pause-filled speech of a stroke patient.

Still, this was one book Alexei knew by heart. Fingers forked, he probed the yellowed page, hoping to find a margin note, a clue written in a hand so cherished he could reproduce it impeccably. The pages were pristine. On the last, his eyes wandering wearily over the final aphorism, Alexei sensed that something was off.

The passage in the middle of the page was wrong, as if an alteration had been made by the author, which, in the case of Rabinovich, was equally impossible.

Then he noticed the number: CCLVII. It took a few seconds before Alexei completed the conversion.

An extra aphorism. Of course! Alexei tore the bound pages free and dropped into Uncle Petya's chair, grabbing a pencil and placing the book before him while his mind spun.

"As the...randomness of all my misery and happiness was once...contained in the unique...snowflakes that, melting together, created me...so should the answer to my every mystery be sought out...amid the...unmelting snow I left behind."

Alexei could have spent several hours trapped inside the loop of these lines, but suddenly his conscious brain was violently wrenched to reality by the loud ringing of the desk phone.

In the seconds needed to tuck the book into his pocket and pluck up the nerve to bring the receiver to his ear, the tidal wave of terror he'd fled by hiding in Uncle Petya's apartment came rushing back. He saw again the goons, the idling car and the path that led to Faina waiting in vain for the sound of his key in the door.

He hadn't expected a woman's voice, much less one so warm. "Is this Comrade Alexei Mikhailovich Samoilenko speaking?" she asked. Admitting a ray of hope into his heart, Alexei confirmed that it was.

"Please hold the line," the operator cooed. "Comrade General Secretary Khrushchev will now speak to you."

CHAPTER FIVE

A lexei stood in a rustic den facing the stately rump of the ruler of the most powerful nation in the world. Moments before, Nikita Sergeyevich Khrushchev had greeted him with a vigorous handshake. Now he addressed Alexei from a sideboard while pouring what sounded like generous drinks. In the gloomy light, Alexei squinted at the General Secretary's abundant hindquarters and concluded that the dimness was calculated. It was intended to evoke a legion of shadows poised to pounce at the slightest threat. The trick was wildly successful. Alexei was beside himself with fear.

To distract himself, Alexei devoured the General Secretary with his eyes, noting every detail. For starters, Khrushchev wasn't as tall as photographs made him seem, but that had been true of Stalin as well. Power worked as slyly as elevator shoes. Then, there was the General Secretary's attire. Alexei had expected a drab double-breasted suit and tie or, if the purpose was to terrorize, the decorated uniform of Lieutenant General. Instead, Khrushchev wore a pair of chinos and the elaborately embroidered *vyshyvanka* of the Ukrainian national costume. Was this the leader's favored mufti when away from the Kremlin, or was it a prop to put the Ukrainian Samoilenko at ease? The effect was transfixing. Staring at the stitch-work shimmering like a thousand insect eyes, Alexei felt as if his host were an entity endowed with Protean powers, made palpable by its human incarnation. That had also been the case with Stalin. During the ten minutes that Alexei had spent in the presence of the Leader and Teacher, he'd struggled to discern the Soviet people's God in the short, overweight and ailing man with a withered right hand. Yet, Stalin had terrified Alexei—as Khrushchev did now. Alexei reasoned that a leader so unprepossessing, who had yet managed to climb to the highest echelon of political supremacy was far more formidable than one blessed with natural magnetism. Surely that had been the source of Napoleon's and Hitler's spell on the masses.

"Comrade Alexei Angelovich Samoilenko, welcome to my humble abode." The mention of Alexei's original patronymic was enough to dispel any notion of genuine hospitality. He was as welcome in the remote dacha as a fly would be in a spider's web. Khrushchev didn't acknowledge Alexei's feeble reply but rather poured their drinks. He hadn't yet been asked to take a seat. He stood, nailed to the thick bearskin rug, pricking his ears at the voice that came from the dark.

"We hope you appreciate," the General Secretary said, words separated by the purposeful clinking of glass on glass, "that although you are by no means a dignitary deserving special treatment, you have so far been afforded the respect befitting a man of achievement. Rest assured that, seeing as we're no spoon-fed aristocrats, we're not in the habit of extending such courtesies to citizens regardless of their devotion to the Party. Therefore, you should view this meeting neither as an official interrogation nor as an inconsequential conversation. Because, Comrade Samoilenko..." and at this point all sounds except Khrushchev's voice ceased, "the matters we have summoned you to discuss are of the gravest national and political significance, and your attitude toward them will determine whether the aforementioned civility you, and those close to you, have been enjoying is going to be prolonged."

This thinly disguised threat was followed by a moment of silence. Then came the steps as the General Secretary took both glasses and, turning, approached Alexei. The drink in the cut-crystal glasses released a slight peppery aroma. Alexei remembered the scent from formal dinners he'd attended in Uncle Petya's company, where he'd sipped a heady vodka distilled from hot peppers. This exclusive spirit and the tumblers holding it blatantly contradicted Khrushchev's denouncement of aristocratic leanings. Alexei noticed that the General Secretary held the glasses close to his torso, in a silent warning. Reach for this drink and your hide belongs to the Party and its whims.

In truth, Alexei didn't have a choice; he had to reach for the glass with the humility expected of him. The fear that invaded every inch of Alexei's being made him suddenly crave the vodka as a miraculous elixir. So take it he did, thus officially signing off his ass to the Party, whose property (let's not kid ourselves) it had always been.

The upper half of the General Secretary's pudgy face remained rigid, while his thick, spit-gleaming lips stirred subtly, in the ghost of a smile.

"Good." He took a hefty swig, and gripped Alexei's left shoulder with a dog-owner's pride. "It's most pleasing to see a young man remain unflinching in his devotion to the people's cause. I believe it was your mentor who wrote, 'Dedication is the hands and feet that hold society upright.'" Alexei ignored the General Secretary's misquote, salivating over his drink but afraid to take the first sip. Khrushchev continued. "Yes, dedication is very important. It is the cornerstone of every trusting relationship. Because, you see, only two things may become of the trust and loyalty of the Party you've so far enjoyed—they can either be honored, valued and reciprocated, or..." and downing the rest of his drink with a shiver of pleasure, he added, "they can be drastically and permanently revoked."

Khrushchev's was a supreme authority whose will could smite Alexei as easily as God could smite Moses. Yet Alexei was convinced that while Moses stood on those steep rocks, facing his fearsome Lord, the prophet had secretly felt a volcanic surge of dizzying human pride, and while kneeling to burden himself with the precious Tables of the Law, he kept thinking, "We are so far apart. You so powerful and I so weak, that it would be meaningless to destroy me. Besides, you need me, or else You would never deign to speak to me at all. Do all the burning and not-consuming You wish. Deep down I know there is some part of the Creation that even You do not understand, and maybe, in all my puniness, I can help explain this mystery to you. So long as that stands, so long shall I remain alive."

They sat in opposite chairs, their outlines merging in the cavernous gloom. Alexei was clinging to the dwindling effects of the exquisite vodka, knowing he'd never dare to ask for a refill. Khrushchev was rooting in his pockets, an unlit cigarette dangling from his pouty lips. Alexei's lighter burned a hole in his left pocket, but he was afraid of the General Secretary taking offense at such an intimate gesture. With a final grunt of exasperation, Nikita Sergeyevich fished out a matchbox and struck a match. In the seconds it took his palsied hands to align the trembling flame, Alexei took in the room: a haphazard jumble of rustic furniture, interspersed with a hodgepodge from every known corner of the Soviet States. His gaze roamed over a heavily ornamented brass samovar; loom-woven kilims on the walls (depicting what was probably farmers, or Stalin, or Stalin as a farmer); a vitrine the size of his two kidnappers combined; atrocious examples of traditional painting and pottery; a balalaika next to a duduk; and an ornately carved table covered with a white sheet that reached down to the floor. This was strange. Alexei had seen such old, yellowed sheets used as dust covers in rarely visited country houses, but one would expect the ghostlike clutter to have been cleared away before the General Secretary arrived. The house was probably some remote country dacha which served as a meeting place and a repository for souvenirs and artifacts caught in the wake of General Secretary Khrushchev's official wanderings across the country. Alexei guessed that the fireplace remained unlit on purpose, so that no far-seeing, evil-intended eye could guess that the dacha was inhabited. He wondered briefly about the time. By now, Faina would be rushing to the front door every time she heard the elevator's distant whirr. For once, Alexei regretted having adopted Uncle Petya's hostility toward wristwatches. "Time is too arbitrary a concept," he used to complain, "and I am far too important to bow to its whims. Let time accommodate me instead, and fuck it if it doesn't. Same as it's gonna fuck us all sooner or later."

Khrushchev inhaled greedily on his cigarette. The clove-scented smoke that filled the space between them was so mouthwatering that Alexei imagined reaching across the table to tear the imported cigarette from the General Secretary's lips. Then Nikita Sergeyevich leaned toward him and delivered another warning. "Needless to say, Comrade Samoilenko, that whatever information we choose to share with you is for your eyes alone, and should, therefore, be treated accordingly.

What I am about to disclose is a matter that may turn out to be of tremendous importance in relation to national security and peace among the socialist nations. This is a matter of life and death—your own included."

Fear wiping away all thoughts of vodka, cigarettes and his own mother, Alexei nodded passionately. From years of dictation, he had memorized most of the General Secretary's superfluous threat.

"Yes, Comrade General Secretary, of course. I understand completely," he babbled.

But Khrushchev, a man used to subordinates, soldiers and commissariat underlings replying to his questions in the same manly tone he used, cupped his hand around his ear as if he hadn't heard a word. "Do I make myself clear, Samoilenko?"

"Yes, sir! Comrade Khrushchev, sir!"

"Good. That is good to know. We truly hope that you prove to be the decent young man we take you for. It was high time we had this little conversation, since you are one of the persons, perhaps the only person, most closely involved in this...unfortunate situation." A calculated pause. "Surely I don't have to explain to you, a Soviet citizen who has been exposed firsthand to the poverty, the inequalities and moral degradation of the Western world, why the Soviet Union is forced to safeguard its citizens from the venomously corruptive influence of the West? One often hears young men, reactionaries mostly who have already been infected by the poison disseminated by the capitalist spies, raising the issue of unrestricted freedom of movement. Why, judging from the clamor that the worst of them are capable of generating, one would think they were living in a prison instead of being the privileged natives of the sole state which truly protects its citizens' fundamental rights. You have had a taste of the so-called 'capitalist wonder.' You have witnessed with your own eyes what a cesspool of terror, oppression and despair it really is. And though most people believe that we have managed to keep the specter of another global conflict decidedly at bay, the bitter truth is that there is still an increasingly widespread war waged night and day around the world. 'Liberalism.' 'Civil rights.' 'Free trade.' All targeting our Soviet Union. Once a nation as tremendous in size as it is in power falls prey to such unrelenting global attack, the first and most exigent course of action is to ensure the safety of its own people, so that they can continue to lead their lives in peace, protected from the enemy who lurks just across the borders."

This paean to Soviet superiority was entirely unnecessary for one claiming to be pressed by a staggering disclosure. In his travels abroad, Alexei had seen what he had seen. He also knew that for the majority of his compatriots, the thought of setting foot in the West was as far-fetched as a journey to the moon. They'd no more question the inviolability of the Soviet borders than they'd think of questioning gravity. Alexei had never felt in any way confined. Thanks to Uncle Petya, he had visited this "cesspool of oppression and despair." Sure, he'd seen indigent people during his time abroad, but nothing like the earthly Hell that Khrushchev had just depicted. As far as Alexei was concerned, all the politicians he had ever known were like children in this aspect—they all loved to boast about their own superiority and curse their enemies. To them, peace, war, prosperity and wholesale death were all one big competition.

"I trust that Sretensky has filled you in up to a certain point about the disturbance we are faced with." Alexei mumbled assent. "The thing is, we suspect that whatever this may be, it's escalating. Even if an approximation, the numbers mentioned in the intelligence briefs are indicative of a bloody mess. And, of course, you're aware that all the evidence we've managed to assemble so far points to your mentor Rabinovich and his final composition." Alexei stared into the dusk, too petrified to nod. "These are dangerous waters we are wading in, Alexei Angelovich. This wave of insurrection may very well end up pulling our very homeland under, and no one is safe until we determine the exact nature of this. Well, why mince words at this point? This conspiracy. And as the honorable comrade we hold you to be, you must put your loyalties to the test."

What loyalties was the General Secretary alluding to? Which part of my life and soul is at stake here? Alexei wondered. Before he could gather his thoughts, before he even had a chance to move the fear-tightened muscles of his brow into a frown, the General Secretary pressed a switch on a length of cord, and everything was suddenly inundated with violent brightness. The effect on Alexei was like that of a hare loping onto a country road suddenly caught full-face into the headlights of a truck. His eyes instantly narrowed to slits against the painful assault of zillions of photons. The lamp-lit murk and the cold fireplace had been part of the theatrics, for through the dazzle Alexei saw that all the windows were boarded up with metal shutters as impenetrable as vault doors. Having delivered the finishing touch with aplomb, Nikita Khrushchev was revealed as a man who held the power to summon the light of life or the darkness of death in an instant.

While Alexei's eyes recovered, Khrushchev had taken a couple of thick folders from a low table next to his chair. He perused the contents of the one on top. "Tell me," he said. Removing a large glossy photo from the folder, he held it for a moment aloft and then dropped it on the coffee table. "Have you ever seen the man in this photograph?"

Alexei immediately drew back with a loud gasp. It was the frail, emaciated, almost saintly carcass of an extremely old man, his jaws toothless and sunken, the scant hairs on his scalp and chin like weeds sprouting around the mouth of a freshly covered grave, the skin of his eyelids like bruised parchment. Despite the distorting horridness of death, there was something familiar about the elderly corpse. "Was he..." Alexei said, choking on the words as he fought back gagging. "I believe he was among the... the members of the group which performed..."

"Correct. He was indeed one of the musicians who performed Rabinovich's..." Here Khrushchev quickly consulted the file he was holding to get the number right "Sixteenth Symphony. Or is it plain Sixteen? Well, no matter. Now tell me, have you ever been in contact with this man? If you've ever so much as exchanged a word of greeting on the street, I want to know about it."

The question was easy, but Khrushchev's gaze made it difficult to answer. Even if Alexei had casually run into the old man over the years, how could he possibly remember? "No, sir, Comrade Khrushchev. I've never worked with or spoken to this man in my life."

"And yet it says here that he took part in all three performances of this... Sixteen thing. Which begs the question. How is it that you never met this man in your life, as you claim, despite being Rabinovich's right-hand man, as you yourself profess to have been?"

Alexi realized that this moment and the way he handled it, was the one that would determine his fate. Clearing his throat, he repeated what he'd been forced to admit many times over the past weeks. "Comrade Khrushchev, I am sorry, but Comrade Rabinovich, for reasons which are also outside the scope of my knowledge, didn't include me either in the composition or in the subsequent rehearsals of—"

Khrushchev silenced him with a wave like the beginning of a backhand slap. "And how about this?" The General Secretary, visibly angrier, tossed another black-and-white photo on the table. Mercifully, this one depicted a living person. It was an old woman with thick tortoiseshell glasses and hair as white and voluminous as spun sugar. Alexei struggled momentarily to dredge up any memory of the aquiline nose, the fuzzy, pursed upper lip. "Yes! The cellist!"

"Correct again. I gather you have had no personal contact with her either, is that right?"

"I only ever saw her once, on the night—" Another annoyed wave of the thick-fingered hand. The General Secretary was clearly not a fan of verbosity outside his own. As the highest-ranking bureaucrat in the country, he knew that to be allowed to ramble freely is to relax. He clearly intended on keeping Alexei on his toes.

"Would you care to explain again to me just why these two people, who you claim are perfect strangers to you, were among those entrusted by your friend Rabinovich with this his last...piece? Weren't the violoncello and the double bass players he'd worked with in the past up to the challenge? Or did this matter never arise between the two of you either?"

"I'm afraid it didn't, sir."

This time the General Secretary looked up from the files, his beady eyes two slits through which Alexei could glimpse a world of barely suppressed anger. "You mean to tell me that, after so many years of working so goddamn closely with Rabinovich, the man didn't share any facts at all about this symphony and its three goddamn public performances?"

"No, comrade, sir. Actually, I wasn't even invited to any of the rehearsals."

"Is that so?"

"Yes, sir, Comrade Khrushchev."

For a long moment, Khrushchev went on rifling through the files in resentful silence. Then in a flat voice, he stated, "The old man's name, since I suppose you don't know that either, was Joseph Abramovich Tisharenko. Aged ninety-two. His occupation was musician, though he retired in the thirties for health-related reasons. Still your good friend Rabinovich managed to drag him out of the coffin and make him part of the gang without your knowledge. As to the woman, the cellist," (the word uttered as though playing the cello had suddenly become a loathsome bourgeois depravity), "was Yelena Kotowski. Born in 1875, retired in 1941. Well, your boss sure liked them ripe and shabby now, didn't he? What sort of composer does this, anyway? Who would willfully trust his work to the hands of pension-sucking old geezers?" The question was rhetorical, so Alexei didn't even exhale. "Of course, the choice of collaborators was entirely at the discretion of the late Pyotr Anastasevich, and hiring moribund old farts would, in different circumstances, be perfectly harmless in itself. I mean, sure, why use the fully capable orchestra the State provides when you can scour the old folks' homes, recruiting their most senile patients instead? It's their funeral if they kick the bucket in front of the audience! Or maybe Rabinovich wanted to pay some sort of homage to centenarian fiddle-strummers. Hell, he was planning his own permanent retirement, right? Neither of them was of Russian origin to begin with. Why, you're not quite Russian either, Samoilenko, and so far you've kept your nose clean, or so your record shows." Here Khrushchev forced his lips into a terrifying smile. "No, what's unequivocally suspicious about Comrade Rabinovich's intentions in collaborating with these individuals is the fact that both of them, despite their advanced age and ill health, were arrested days after their last performance in Kiev while breaking the law."

"Breaking the—"

"Oh, yes! You wouldn't have thought so, judging by the looks of these two, would you now, Samoilenko? And up until the night they were last seen, taking a bow at the end of the concert, both had been model citizens, utterly beyond reproach. And then, just ten days later, both were arrested for suspicion of high treason!"

"High treason?" That kindly granny and that human fossil? Would they be physically capable of high treason? It can't be. This is sheer madness.

"Oh yes, Samoilenko," Khrushchev went on, grinning at Alexei's astonishment, "and I daresay that, had the motive of their criminal acts come to light at the time of their arrest, your dear Rabinovich would have been arrested right along with those two!"

Alexei was in a state of shock. Khrushchev paused to light a cigarette whose tip caught with a flare. "Joseph Tisharenko. Apprehended on March 14, a few miles off Sorokoshichi, shortly after having illegally crossed the Belarusian border. On foot, no less! Resisted arrest, spat at the officers and cursed at them, howling, 'The blood of Babi Yar is on your hands too!' During his subsequent questioning, the suspect confessed that he had been on his way to the aforementioned ravine in Kiev where the Nazis slaughtered his entire family in 1941, including seven children. The man was clearly delirious from physical exhaustion. He was taken to Chernobyl for further interrogation as well as for the treatment of a severe case of frostbite. Both feet were amputated. He died two days later from a combination of renal failure and pneumonia brought on by exposure. Exposure," he said, with a malevolent gleam in his eyes. "Does this ring a bell?"

Alexei was in no position to gather his thoughts, let alone voice any sort of answer. "And now onto the lovely *gospozha* Kotowski. Let's see, then. Apprehended early in the morning of March 13, while attempting to cross the Yenisei River, at the confluence with Lower Tunguska. She was trespassing on military soil, specifically an area adjacent to the Turukhansk Gulag. When the guards at the gate warned her to proceed no further, the old biddy screamed that they couldn't stop her, that she wanted to be reunited with her husband. Interestingly, Kotowski had been a widow since 1931. The men rightfully presumed the woman was mad, wandering all alone as she was in the farthest reaches of Siberia. Still, they had a job to do. So they fired a warning shot, but to no avail. Kotowski kept on walking, until suddenly she collapsed in the snow. Never regained consciousness. The coroner's report once more specifically stated it was death by exposure. Among the personal effects of the deceased the authorities found a highly incoherent letter addressed to the Soviet Communist Party, in which she denounced the State as a legion of villains and murderers who had assassinated her 'innocent' husband. As to Witold Kotowski's so-called 'innocence,' his file mentions that he was arrested way back in 1930 and charged with high treason for collaborating with a Trotskyite faction. He was executed a few months later, following the outcome of a fair trial, along with a group also found guilty of collaborating with subversive elements of the same ilk.

"Now, though no one at the time thought to connect these two incidents with the suicide of your good friend

Rabinovich, you have to admit that the cause of death is a striking coincidence. Killing oneself by exposure. You don't see that very often! However, those were dark days for the Soviet Union. The arch traitor Beria and that fool Malenko were about to hand us over to the Americans on a silver platter. Every branch of the Politburo was either in a state of moral decay or placed on national alert. Of course, nobody had the time to scrutinize the deaths of two elderly musicians. Not when Stalin had just died! Even your mentor's suicide had been linked to the demise of the Father and Teacher. Who would have thought how far such a presumption of loyalty was from the truth? Anyhow, the cases of Tisharenko and Kotowski were deemed isolated, random occurrences. Until just a couple weeks ago, when national security agents and border control officials became aware of events which had been going on for quite some time. I gather you know what I'm referring to?"

"The defections, Comrade Gene—"

"You're damn right the defections!" Khrushchev banged his clenched fist on the arm of his chair, raising a puff of dust and silencing Alexei as if he'd fired a gun. "You know how many defections have been recorded over the past eight months? Ten thousand, one hundred and two! And we're not talking cases of attempted defection. There are even more of those! And even this is an estimate, which doesn't take into account those who failed to return after their authorized stays abroad had expired. You realize what a blow this is to the Soviet Union? To the Eastern bloc as a whole? The same outbreak of dissent has been spreading across the majority of our allies' countries as well! And all of a sudden we have the *Cominform* giving us hell for allowing an international conspiracy to germinate under our very noses! The secret police can scarcely deal with our own traitors, proliferating like bloody germs with every passing day, and now here comes that idiot Gomulka bellowing on the phone about the wave of defections that has seized his goddamn Poles. He's convinced they're all in cahoots with us to bring about some half-baked Soviet conspiracy! And just when I've managed to calm that cretin down, the phone rings again, and now it's fucking Zápotocký, screaming bloody murder because his own secret police have been chasing mobs of people trying to cross the Czechoslovakian borders. He believes they're all secretly under the influence of Soviet agitators! And then it's the turn of that bed-pissing little wimp Nagy, whining that Hungary is threatened with collapse by some fucking radio transmission which he claims originated from a pirate radio station in Moscow! And you know the common denominator in each and every case of this bloody mess, don't you, Samoilenko? Because this is serious, deadly serious. Goddamn throngs of people driving the radars over at border control insane! Surely you must know by now what these criminals had been doing right before dropping everything and becoming single-minded traitors, don't you? Surely you've heard the rumors, read something in the paper. We have every single Soviet satellite state crawling up our ass to get to the cause for this shit storm!"

Khrushchev's display of naked rage, like a monster tearing off its clothes and baring its deformed body, had a curious effect on Alexei. He was frightened, but the fact that the General Secretary held him personally responsible in lieu of Uncle Petya somehow conferred upon him the invincibility of the departed. Even an enraged tyrant can no more strike the dead deader than he can grasp in his shaking hand the music that is so offensive to him. And music was the second reason Alexei didn't feel nearly as powerless as Khrushchev's ranting intended. When all was said and done, the man before him knew nothing about music; otherwise, he'd never have deigned to ask for his help. This turned Alexei into something akin to a doctor urgently summoned to an irascible patient's sickbed.

Foam at the mouth all you like, old man. In the end you'll have to listen to what I say. All Alexei had to do to remain calm was to avoid Khrushchev's glare and focus on the imperfections of the man's skin, the furrows across the General Secretary's brow, his deeply etched crow's feet and the liver spots on the back of his wildly gesturing hands.

"When the first reports started to arrive by the dozen," Khrushchev went on, rapping his fingers on the folders that were resting on his thighs, "we were all convinced that it had to be related to Stalin. There were enough self-proclaimed Stalinists who'd love more than anything to destabilize our great country by showing, as the Jews of America have been saying in their mendacious rags, that the mighty Soviet Union, without the steering of our beloved Father and Teacher, was crumbling. Oh, I'm certain there are people who would love to see this happen, for we are currently engaged in a brutal war. But as to the manner and the propagation of this conspiracy, at first the NKVD was at a loss. All the known printing presses and every legal broadcast, as well as all personal correspondence of known foreign agents operating undercover, were placed under the strictest possible scrutiny—but still, not a thing. And then some low-rank Politburo pen-pusher came up with this statistical analysis whose findings, he claimed, couldn't be coincidental." After one swift look at the paper on top, he resumed his monologue. "In his urgent report, this know-it-all said that among the roughly three thousand people who attended your friend Rabinovich's last concert, there had been eleven hundred defections and attempts at defection recorded by the police. The number was worrisome, but not enough to force us to declare a state of national emergency. We'd known all along that the artistic crowd had always been one of our most tireless enemies at home. We've all been hunting down imperialist propaganda disguised as art for decades, and this has taught us that all artists are essentially cowards, people incapable of ever posing a tangible threat. All this until our European friends began to panic, and increasing reports began to arrive, mentioning for the first time a fact that could no longer be disregarded. So now, you must tell me yourself: Do you know of any existing radio transmission of this symphony that has been broadcast over the past nine months?"

Alexei replied that he had no knowledge of any such transmission, stating his denial of the fact as convincingly as he could. He was telling the truth, after all. Uncle Petya had always been fastidious when it came to concert recordings and live broadcasts. He'd never allow either until the work in question had first been successfully performed abroad under conductors of the caliber of Stokowski, Toscanini or Mitropoulos. Though he couldn't exclude the possibility of some bootleg recording circulated among Rabinovich aficionados, Alexei was positive that Uncle Petya would never have allowed a live broadcast of *Sixteen* to be made with just three performances of the work—especially as it was one he had scored without Alexei's assistance and thus one he was bound to have felt even more self-conscious about. Alexei felt so certain of this that he made a display of self-assuredness by lighting his last cigarette and tipping the ash into his empty crystal tumbler.

"We thought so at first," Nikita Sergeyevich said, stealing a glance at the file, "but that was before we received official confirmation that the last performance of the piece, the one that took place in...the Kiev Ballet Theater, had not only been recorded, but had since been picked up and transmitted by stations operating in Hungary, Poland, Czechoslovakia and Romania. According to the report, it was an amateur recording transmitted shortwave, which, judging from the distortion, originated from within the theater. This initial broadcast was followed for ten days in a row by another recording that showed signs of some slight editing, and at least half of these broadcasts were simultaneously emitted from stations operating in Moscow and Leningrad. I trust this is all news to you?" he said, his eyes once more boring into Alexei with distaste, his every blink a bitter denunciation. *Artist. Impotent wimp. Traitor.*

But these silent blows failed to reach Alexei in his state of utter stupefaction. The ash of his forgotten cigarette was growing like a fragile, yet confident penis. A live recording? Dozens of clandestine emissions, *Sixteen* broadcast all over the map, and he hadn't happened to catch a single one? Impossible. He just couldn't believe it. "Do you have an actual—" Khrushchev silenced him by rising with surprising sprightliness from his chair and motioning him to stand up as well.

"We most certainly do, so why don't you go ahead and take a look for yourself?" Crossing to the corner of the room, where the shrouded table stood, he grabbed the edge of the sheet and pulled it off with in one swift motion.

Alexei approached fearfully. The objects as revealed were still contained in distended envelopes bearing red CLASSIFIED stamps. In the midst of the semicircle formed by the envelopes stood a contraption which, although thoroughly familiar, caused Alexei the greatest amazement. It was the old RCA Victor recording and transmitting device bought by Uncle Petya during a trip to New York, which had been seized with a formal letter thanking him for the "loan," by the Moscow Conservatory. "I think you recognize the machine," said Khrushchev, who stood beside him, looking with malice at Alexei's expression of disbelief.

The Latin lettering on the device's faded gold stamp seemed, at that moment, like treason. *This American-made machine*, Khrushchev's tone implied.

"Of course, we were forced to take into consideration the evidence brought to our attention by our own trusted technicians and radio operators. And why shouldn't we? After all, the shortwave emission, even unauthorized, would come to light sooner or later and on its own wouldn't suffice to arouse suspicion; for why would anyone ever consider a simple music broadcasting suspicious? Nevertheless, since the growing number of defections was beginning to aggravate our good-for-nothing Politburo pencil-necks, an investigation into the matter was ordered. The entire affair had to be kept under wraps, of course. We couldn't allow the word to get out that the State was looking into something as preposterous as a musical conspiracy! We also gathered and cross-checked the reports received from police commissariats in Hungary and Poland. But once more it all came to nothing. Those who talked, and not a lot of them did, even under pressure, made no mention of the performance or the radio broadcasts. When further pressure was exerted, few of them confessed to having ever listened to the goddamn piece. Their statements amounted to no more than bitching and moaning about personal matters, though with a definite anti-Soviet twist. They all claimed to have parents, children, spouses and friends who had fallen victim to the Soviet state's brutality. This is a common enough slander among this sort of offenders. It's always the same bullshit over and over with them. The Gulags this, the secret police that. Some even went as far as openly denouncing Lenin himself! But still, we couldn't be certain that we were faced with a widespread conspiracy. Again we attributed these reactionary claims, despite their astonishing number and unusual vehemence, to the political instability of these past few months. So delay piled upon delay. It was barely three weeks ago that the idiots at the commissariats stumbled upon the fact that of the people actually associated with the performances, of the ensemble of toothless nobodies Rabinovich had employed in all three concerts, there was absolutely no trace. Four had been reported dead, two had been arrested when they were just about to kick the bucket, and of the remaining ten, we didn't have a bloody clue! A thousand years old combined, and they'd apparently crawled back into the holes where Rabinovich had found them! And, of course, since the 'true genius' couldn't be questioned, we had to make do with those two. And here is what was found on their persons at the time of their arrests."

Without further ceremony, the premier of the Soviet Union grabbed two of the bulging envelopes and tipped their contents onto the table. The first one spilled a bundle of sheet music. Alexei's trained eye noticed instantly that the part was written for a bass instrument. From the second, a spool of magnetic tape dropped with a bump onto the polished wooden surface, its glistening strip unwinding a bit before stopping.

Alexei stared at the two pieces of evidence while his mind played the few notes that could be glimpsed as the sheets unfolded. Then his eyes flitted to the unspooled tape, as if they could turn the strip of plastic into the music he still found it so hard to believe had been recorded unbeknownst to him. His gaze strayed to the RCA device, and he saw that there was an even wider spool of tape wound onto the reels. It had been right there in the Conservatory sitting under his nose this whole time! A fellow professor, a student, even a member of the secret police, could have grabbed it easily if, unlike him, they had known of the recording's existence. *Sixteen* had been there all along, free for the taking. Alexei reached out a shaking hand, fearful of its being struck, not by Khrushchev but by Rabinovich, whose presence suddenly seemed to permeate the room. He came closer on stiff, unfeeling legs and leaned over to examine the double bass score, piously urging the semitones and pauses, while mentally providing the sublime, higher-pitched bars that were missing. Why did it have to be the contrabass? And the tapes were lying so close. Did he dare stroke their shining lifelessness under the inscrutable gaze of Nikita Khrushchev?

"You claim you've never seen this music or these tapes before," the General Secretary said. It wasn't a question. Alexei's speechlessness couldn't have been rehearsed. He was so shocked he hadn't even registered Khrushchev's words, and the General Secretary was forced to repeat himself in a furiously commanding voice. No, Alexei assured the General Secretary, he had never seen a thing. No, he couldn't guess as to why the old woman had been carrying the spool of tape to the depths of Siberia, nor why the stricken nonagenarian would bring part of *Sixteen* to the site where, more than twelve years ago, all of his children had been slaughtered. "At a different time, we might have taken you at your word," Khrushchev said with an irritated sigh, "but you realize this claim of yours had to be authenticated."

Alexei's head jerked toward the General Secretary, his fascination shattered by the onrush of horror. Did this mean they'd searched his office, Uncle Petya's apartment, his own home? Was Faina at this very moment tied to the kitchen chair, gagged and terrified, while NKVD brutes tore the place apart? Khrushchev's disappointed look assured him that what breaking and entering was necessary had already been done. Yet the thought of agents skulking after him like vengeful shadows, violating every single place where he'd believed himself to be free, was too much. His hands itched to touch his breast, confirm that the photo and the book hadn't been snatched by those shadowy hands.

"We must assume, then, that all other trace of this accursed music is either ingeniously hidden, or else has been purposefully destroyed. The written pages are yours for the taking, although the recorded material has to remain in our custody until further analysis has been performed. The last piece of evidence belongs to you, too, so you might as well do the honors." He nodded at the smallest envelope.

It contained a gold ring with a cross pattern of encrusted rubies. Alexei studied it, looking for any inscription on the inside of the band. He made out two initials of the Latin alphabet, etched in a flowing calligraphy, and the moment he transliterated them his heart leaped. The photo, the bejeweled hand coquettishly hiding a grin.

"This ring you hold," Khrushchev said, his tone becoming pleased again, "was retrieved from the pocket of your friend, the so-called Pyotr Rabinovich, while his body was prepared for the autopsy."

Alexei looked up at the General Secretary with a frown, still holding the gold ring aloft like a man about to propose suddenly having second thoughts. So-called?

"And I'm afraid that, at long last, you must come to terms with the truth. While all these years you thought of yourself as a sort of secretary employed by a famous composer, you had in fact been collaborating, presumably without your knowledge, with an American spy."

The story was so outrageously romantic and Romanesque, Alexei listened to Khrushchev's embittered monotone as if he were being told a fairy tale. And what a tale it was! Yekaterina, the mother of Rabinovich, was born in 1885. She was the illegitimate fruit of the nephropathic yet still adventurous Alexander the Third's passion for a frisky Vlach chambermaid serving at His Imperial Majesty's pleasure.

The girl was hurriedly removed from the palace as soon as her condition became apparent. She was installed until her time of labor in a remote dacha located in some nameless hamlet just outside of St. Petersburg. One year shy of his coming of age, Nicholas II was so outspokenly unenthusiastic about his eventually becoming the Czar, that having a potential backup heir, albeit illegitimate, didn't seem like such a bad idea. Alas, the baby turned out to be female and was therefore raised in all the poverty of her caste. Her mother, loath to forget her daughter's illustrious bloodline, named her after the greatest Empress of all time. Being handsome and of a kind disposition, the fatherless girl could have had her pick among the bucolic crowd of suitors who'd begun to court her as soon as she grew breasts. But her poor mother, on the eve of Yekaterina's thirteenth birthday, fell deathly ill after being stung by a viper. On her deathbed, Yekaterina's mother had pressed a golden ring into her inconsolable daughter's hand, changing the young girl's destiny forever. It had been snatched by her mother before she'd been cast out from the palace. Stolen from the boudoir of the Empress, the ring was a masterpiece created by the famous Romanov jewelers Louis-

David and Jacob-David Duval. It bore the gem-encrusted Order of St. Anne cross and had Catherine the Great's royal initials etched on the inside.

At the time, Yekaterina knew nothing of the ring's glorious origins, and what few words passed her mother's lips about her daughter being an heiress to the throne of Russia, she'd quickly dismissed as the ramblings of a dying, feverish mind. Abandoned and alone, she forgot her mother's deathbed ranting altogether. Two days later, Yekaterina took off for St. Petersburg on foot, determined to sell the ring to the highest bidder.

Naturally, the first jeweler to gaze upon the priceless artifact, assumed correctly that the ring was the fruit of theft and alerted the *Militsiya*. Yekaterina was apprehended and dragged to the police headquarters, whereupon her mother's ridiculous confession came to her. Since it was the only thing that might possibly keep her out of prison, she howled that she was not a thief but the young Czarina. As luck would have it, a rabbi who noticed the young villager screaming her head off about being "Alexander's daughter" and a "Russian princess" instantly fell on his knees. Despite being three years younger, Yekaterina was the spitting image of Grand Duchess Olga Alexandrovna, and this was the name the rabbi cried out in a piercing shriek. Those were naïve times. Serfs weren't accustomed either to photography or to the art of royal portraiture. Seconds after the rabbi kissed the soggy rags on the girl's feet, everyone else fell to their knees as well, apologizing profusely to the Grand Duchess for their unforgivable mistake. But they were only human, her loyal and devoted servants! How could they grasp the imperial prank they had interrupted by dragging her away from her fairytale game of pretending to be a poor girl? They quickly summoned the Chief of Police's own chariot, and the highest-ranking officers drove a stunned Yekaterina off to the Winter Palace. The royal guards were too busy escorting her royal highness to her chambers to notice the details in face and form which should have alerted them to the unintentional impersonation. After being scrubbed, perfumed, coiffed and dressed in the Grand Duchess's most luxurious garments (they even placed the ring on Yekaterina's finger, although it was too big for her), the hapless pretender was visited by her mother, the Empress Marie of Hesse. The Empress was incensed by her daughter's insolence and the danger she had risked by the ridiculous masquerade. Why, the little demoness was supposed to be at her piano lesson and instead had been roaming the streets of St. Petersburg disguised as a filthy ragamuffin! The Empress burst into a torrent of furious French just as she was entering the miscreant's room only to find herself face-to-face with a stranger dressed in Olga Alexandrovna's loose-fitting clothes and smiling awkwardly. The Empress uttered a horrific scream, *"Ceci n'est pas ma fille!"* and fainted.

It was a scandal to surpass all scandals. An unsuspected bastard of Alexander's primped up in usurped finery, was brandishing Yekaterina Velikaya's own ring at the crinolined ladies chasing her! The maids and the cooks were in stitches! But as for the Crown—well, such a thing was simply unacceptable. The royal family had to rid itself of this screeching mistake at once. She must be tucked as far away as possible. The last thing the Crown needed was the serfs rioting and proclaiming this village idiot as their self-appointed princess! After some hasty deliberation, the members of the royal family agreed that the other side of the Atlantic Ocean was a safe bet. That same night they ordered the royal doctor to sedate the little half-breed then shipped her off, along with an escort of grumpy royal attendants and guardsmen.

After six weeks of regurgitating the finest broths and freshly baked brioches all over her gold-embroidered silken bedclothes, Yekaterina arrived in Boston, Massachusetts, where she was to remain cooped up in a remote mansion of British friends of the Romanovs, privately schooled and polished so as to resemble the royalty she nearly was. She had been given the alias "Rabinovich," chosen for the rabbi who had, by then, been exiled to the Siberian hinterland, as had the entire division of police officers (along with their families) who knew of the girl's existence. Within four months, the young Ekaterina, who had dropped the "Y" thinking it too Russian-sounding for her refined new home, became completely accustomed to her role as cruelly exiled princess and dismissed all notion of claiming her birthright in her frightfully uncouth motherland. People were so much friendlier here, and she lived in a palatial country estate where she had everything her heart desired. Why upset a life of such effortless splendor? The only trace of her true descendance that she was unwilling to relinquish was the ring bearing the *pierres d'achoppement*. This, she was determined to hold onto forever.

It might have ended at that, but on the fateful night of December 31, 1899, while floating about wrapped in a cloud of perfume and tulle at a feast thrown by the New England Conservatory, Ekaterina captured the gaze, heart and loins of a twenty-year-old man of Russo-Judaic extraction, the son of an eminent Bostonian textile Midas. The dashing youth had been as bored by the reception as he was of the prospect of a future in his father's textile company. He hated being the son of a Jewish magnate and longed for some adventure that would finally bring meaning to his languidly wasted life. A gifted pianist, he dreamed of giving concerts all over Europe and charming the hairpieces off music lovers. He couldn't be more pleased when his attempts to flirt with Ekaterina were rewarded with giggles. For all the acquired pomp, she had remained a country girl at heart and was prone to mirthful promiscuity. After she confided her fantastical story to him, they'd fled the party and hidden in an anteroom of the theater, which happened to be furnished with a grand piano. She later confessed that as soon as he'd played her the opening bars of the *Appassionata*, her heart became his forever. Her suitor was even more thrilled. Was this girl for real? She was so fetching, and the way she spoke! Well, her Russian was provincially flavored and her French left much to be desired, yet no one had ever made his heart beat such a blissful *presto*. The *coup de grâce* was delivered when Ekaterina finally revealed her assumed name. "Dear God!" the young courter exclaimed, for his surname, too, was Rabinovich.

It was the mother of all nights in which the couple's lucky stars aligned. The promise of a new life peeped at them like the yellow moon in the window. So, in the early days of March of 1900, after Ekaterina had stashed away as much jewelry and gold as she could get her hands on, and her daring paramour had managed to withdraw as much capital as possible without alarming the executor of his trust fund, the couple eloped on a luxurious cruiser. Their destination? Why, Ekaterina's homeland, the very hamlet she'd been born and raised in, which, beheld through the eyes of youthful infatuation, had redeemed its long-lost aura of innocent girlish delight. It was easy for Ekaterina to set her heart on this new dream. She was a rootless, restless soul, madly in love and pregnant. This last gift of the fates was more important than all of her American bounty. She cherished her life-creating tummy far more than she'd ever cared for the pleasant youth she'd been handed on a silver platter. To the shepherds and cheese-makers of the mountainous village were added a Russo-American Jew said to be made of money and his wife, Czar Nikolai's purported illegitimate sister. Then, in January 1901, came their baby boy.

For the next sixteen years, they were respectfully alienated from their fellow villagers in an enlarged, sumptuous version of the original dacha that had been Ekaterina's childhood home. It was all roses for the Rabinovich family. Even little Pyotr's American grandfather, after stewing in his own wrath for two years, was finally softened by the prospect of having a grandson. The old man couldn't die without seeing his namesake's face, of taking in his arms that part of himself, at once so tiny and huge. His grandfather's belated affection ultimately saved young Petya's life. At the outbreak of the October Revolution, while his birthplace, a festering hole of bluebloods and complicit villagers, was pillaged and burnt to the ground, while his parents' throats were slashed like those of the greater part of Russian nobility, Pyotr, or Peter, was a precocious freshman at the Yale Department of Musicology. With one swift stroke of the Russian people's justified fury, he'd been orphaned. His loving grandfather had died of a stroke upon learning that his only son had been massacred. Besides a considerable fortune, Pyotr Rabinovich had only two things to cling to—his mother's ring, given to him as a lucky charm before his first transatlantic voyage, and a burning desire for revenge. On the very day of the Revolution, while millions of his countrymen rejoiced in their deliverance from poverty and oppression, Rabinovich vowed that he would do whatever was needed to avenge his parents' unjustly shed blood and destroy the Revolutionary world imposed by the Bolsheviks.

This wasn't the story Nikita Sergeyevich recounted verbatim. Most of the embellishments came from Alexei's romantically inclined imagination. Despite his stern recitation, Khrushchev had indeed delivered the tallest of tales without digressing to tedious things such as proof, since he knew Alexei would not dare to ask for any. Presumably, no traces had been left, for the registry of the nameless hamlet had been reduced to ashes, as had the homes and all the witnesses. Since Pyotr Rabinovich was now gone, his ashes could be manipulated into those of a fabulous monster by the Party. Yet Alexei didn't care! Like a scorned lover who projects his unrequited passion onto a matter-of-fact breakup letter, he was absorbed by this delirious yarn. The mystery of Uncle Petya's past was woven into a story as heartbreaking as his mysterious final hours.

Alexei did not consider for even a second interrupting Khrushchev's implausible exhumation of early Rabinovich lore. When his host went on to unravel Petya's rise into Soviet and worldwide fame, Alexei kept on listening. His mind had become a voracious scavenger that couldn't stop feeding on this pile of garbage.

Not once did he question his eagerness to gobble up such a glaringly obvious fiction, for, as Rabinovich had written, "We crave the nourishment of lies like the necrophagous beasts we are not."

According to the next part of the apocryphal tale, it was only a matter of time before the adolescent Pyotr infiltrated the socio-intellectual milieu of the budding Soviet Union he was bent on annihilating. Like any true aristocrat, he possessed the means necessary to astonish the naïve Soviet intelligentsia of the twenties. A polyglot pianist, he was an alluring alloy of Russian highbrow breeding, East Coast sophistication and underplayed Jewishness, an educated and wealthy young man willing to bestow all the gifts of his bourgeois upbringing to the causes of the Revolution—or so he claimed. Lenin's mention in *Chto delat?* if authentic, had sealed the deal. The eighteen-year-old Rabinovich was a man to remember. During the early Stalinist years, some unsavory details of the young author's past might have come to light; suspicion and mistrust were the sustenance on which the soul of Comrade Dzhugashvili fed. However, Khrushchev hastened to assure Alexei that none of his minions would ever admit to this. Old Iossif was a deeply provincial man, as impressionable as any Tbilisian potato-farmer when dealing with people of better breeding than his own. Deep down, Dear Father possessed the famished peasant's fascination with everything American; his hatred of the United States stemmed not so much from a solid Communist ideology as from horrible feelings of inferiority. By the time Stalin realized what a potentially invincible foe he'd created with his championing of Rabinovich, it was too late. Uncle Petya had by then become an icon of brilliance and artistic integrity to the Russians and the "singing heart of the Soviet Union" to the socialist-leaning parts of the world, as well as a dignified representative of this vast yet claustrophobic nation. Rabinovich's overt contempt for the money earned by his musical labors was suspicious, but since his donations to the Party were often enough to cover the wages of entire departments of the Politburo, the Ministry of Culture and Pravada combined, neither his revenues nor the public stance could be condemned. In less than a decade, Rabinovich had successfully achieved the first important step toward his plan of subversion and destruction—he had made himself irreplaceable to the leader of the Communist Party and to the people of USSR.

It was then, Khrushchev went on, that the vital second part of Rabinovich's evil scheme began to unfold. If he had managed to keep up the deception for so long, if he'd survived unscathed the shameful purges of the Jews and if he had succeeded in emerging from those dark years even more venerated, then it was safe for him to proceed with his virulent anti-Communist plot. He knew, of course, that the NKVD's all-seeing eye was focused on him and that the Party's omniscience was a thousand times more accurate than any information the Western intelligence had. But his field of work was a carefully constructed protective shield. Who, after all, would suspect a composer, whose every piece of music seemed to exalt the haunting beauty of the Russian psyche? The kind of music Rabinovich churned out was the safest vocation. He'd survived the overseas fad from winning the Oscar and, as for the censors at home, he could fool them with both hands tied behind his back. Thus, he was free to pursue his plan of revenge.

The exact nature of these shady maneuvers accomplished by Rabinovich the Spy were unknown. Soviet Intelligence often wasted time and resources pursuing inane schemes as part of Stalin's paranoiac war against the fictitious enemy within. This meant that the U.S. Office of Strategic Services and its spawn, the deleterious CIA, were free to pursue an alliance with the untouchable Rabinovich, whose sole mission was the undoing of the Red Menace.

Of course, subliminal messaging, thought implantation and mind control had been the philosopher's stone for American and Soviet scientists for many years, especially since the global proliferation of telecommunications. Employed either as a weapon that presumably fortified national security or mere trickery, the concept of urging human beings *en masse* to act upon an exogenous command had grown. Unknowable sums had been steadily invested in meticulous studies and human experimentation. Besides driving hordes of American filmgoers berserk for popcorn and Coke during intermissions, human mind control had evolved on the sly. Its justification was the wish of powerful nations to guarantee that, when and if a global war broke out again, it would be conducted with much less bloodshed. Studies about trigger-words implanted during hypnosis that could provoke a specific behavior had become a secret so common that they made their way into popular fiction and movies. Even laymen, whose value as guinea pigs was no greater than that of a new laundry detergent, guarded themselves against this enemy who might assume the forms that were invisible, inaudible and imperceptible. It was the modern version of the evil eye. Music provided as good a medium for such deadly magic as any. Thus Rabinovich, taking advantage of the years he'd spent abroad, had been turned into a pawn of the American Intelligence Svengalis, who had devised an infallible aural device, which, upon being broadcast as a musical performance, would immediately inspire an acute loathing of socialism and the Soviet Union. And it might have been an even more intricate a procedure. Rabinovich could have been poisoning the minds of his fellow citizens with subconscious hatred for decades, and maybe that was why it had taken him so long to achieve his treacherous goal. *Sixteen* was merely the Pied Piper's final note.

His wish to be close to the helm and out of harm's way was the reason behind his kowtowing to Stalin. And the true motive for his suicide? Stalin was dead, his evil work was done.

Now there was no one to protect him from its consequences. That was why he had taken those last four trips abroad, pretending to be gathering material for an opera or whatnot, when he'd simply been putting the finishing touches on his master plan. He had been arranging smuggled copies of the musical score and the recording, so that the outbreak could spread as far as possible across the Eastern bloc. Ultimately, the proof lay in the incontestable fact that a ninety-year-old man and a frail old woman had perished from the cold while unconsciously following Uncle Petya's orders, to the point of carrying bits and pieces of their master's trigger-music. The performers had been selected because of their advanced age and had most likely been brainwashed even more thoroughly into complicity and secrecy.

"We even retrieved pieces of molten beeswax from the old geezer's pockets," Khrushchev scornfully remarked, "similar to the material used to make the candles those Orthodox reactionaries light before praying to their idols." After this sinister God had granted their prayers, Rabinovich also walked out barefoot in the snow to die a happy death, clutching in his hand the ring of his mother whose death he had finally avenged.

That Alexei had never caught the slightest drift of this plot had doubtless spared him and Faina their lives. Despite their personal relationship, Rabinovich had fooled his young friend the same way he had fooled millions of strangers. To prevent further damage, Alexei had to revisit this intimate partnership and use what knowledge he gathered about the "Sixteen master plan" in order to uncover any active co-conspirators and put an end to their ruinous enterprise.

Alexei was to leave at once and travel to all the destinations Rabinovich had visited before the premiere of Sixteen. Once there, he would meet the same people Uncle Petya had met on those occasions, or at least as many of them as the foreign Soviet agents had managed to keep track of. "It's a dirty shame what the decline of Stalin and this Korean business did to our European Counter-Intelligence resources. But now we're back in the game at full force," Khrushchev said.

Alexei's cover was to be a biography of Rabinovich, on which he'd been already working. Alexei didn't have the heart to wonder how this information, which only Faina had been privy to, had become available to the General Secretary. He would seek private meetings with famous men, former colleagues and close friends. As soon as he gained their trust, he would reveal his identity as a Soviet double agent and direct the conversation toward *Sixteen*, which was destabilizing the Soviet Union with a spreading wave of defections reaching beyond Russia and including East Germany, Yugoslavia, Bulgaria and even Albania. If these friends and contacts of Rabinovich's denied any knowledge of the musical conspiracy or refused to be helpful, the NKVD agents following Alexei would barge into the meetings, also posing as double agents. If this failed to bring results, the agents would resort to more immediately convincing methods. If all went well, Alexei's careful snooping would reveal the origins of the *Sixteen* music, so that it could be reproduced exactly as it was heard in the performances. This would allow the government to determine the mechanics of this musical manipulation. Perhaps seeing a question arising in Alexei's eyes, Khrushchev countered, "Yes, yes, we already thought of someone transcribing it from the recording! You think you're the only Russian with an ear for tunes? This has to be a precise re-creation."

If successful, Alexei's mission would reverse the frenzy of mass-flight. Provided there were any useful findings, "they would be applied for the benefit of the Soviet Union and the Russian people," the General Secretary said. Rising with a sigh from his armchair, Khrushchev added, "Naturally, all your expenses will be covered, so they must be documented in detail, but you should also cash that goddamn Oscar check. It would be best if your ties to American interests were made tangible through an account brimming with dollars." Alexei nodded, although he had no idea how he was to cash a million-dollar check. He just wanted to make sure Faina was okay, and right now he was praying that the frisking he'd been subjected to before entering the dacha wouldn't be repeated. What if they found the book and the photo? This was assuming they didn't already know about them, which they probably did.

Alexei lingered for a moment before the evidence lying on the table. Aching for the music on the tapes, he leafed hurriedly through the double bass score he was to pocket. Its counter-melody flowed before his eyes. Typical Uncle Petya, using supporting instruments as sparingly and awkwardly as he did his left hand when playing the piano. Though Khrushchev was audibly clearing his throat, Alexei's eyes welled with unrestrained tears. Savoring the moment he turned to the first movement's finale, Alexei realized that the last two pages were stuck together. He pulled and a piece of flattened white wax fell onto the table. Alexei turned to speak to the General Secretary. The sight of the security men, summoned by Khrushchev's throat clearing, silenced him at once.

"Ha!" said Nikita Sergeyevich, looking at the white morsel Alexei was nervously fingering. "Well, you can go ahead and keep that piece of filth, too. You're gonna need all the help you can get, so why not use a bit of Christian voodoo? Just make sure you remember your priorities here. Your loyalties, your life and the life of those you love belong to the Soviet Union. And don't worry too much about betraying your precious Rabinovich. You can't hurt the dead, now, can you?"

No, you can't, thought Alexei. But if you try to, they can hurt you back.

CHAPTER SIX

"**A**lyosha, my dearest, you're back! There goes the pride and joy of our neighborhood!" This inexplicable praise had been spoken by Irina Ivanovna Morensky, a widow living alone on the twelfth floor of their building, the moment Alexei had stepped into the hallway of his home.

That the two aging women, missing the company of their long-gone husbands and the balm of their children's presence, would meet up for a quiet night of small talk in each other's kitchen made sense. This assumed, however, that Irina Ivanovna was the sort of kind-hearted, helpful neighbor who would rush to her friend's side in times of need. As far as Alexei knew, the obese, white-haired woman and his mother had never been friends. Despite her kindness, his mother's social skills were hampered by a deep-seated wariness, stemming from having been wounded so badly in the past. The same was true of millions of Russians. Besides the actual losses they had suffered during the war and the various purges, the State-implanted thought of living surrounded by nameless enemies, a paranoiac uncertainty corroborated by the fact that neighbors, coworkers, friends and relatives could vanish forever without the least explanation, had turned countless otherwise good-natured men and women into cordial yet emotionally corseted beings. Alexei suspected that Faina's furtiveness was vicarious, becoming more pronounced by her sense of his increasing maladjustment and unutterable sexual misery. By loving him so greatly, she'd made his taciturn dysphoria her own. That was why it troubled him so that Irina Ivanovna was sitting in their living room, sipping the remains of Uncle Petya's tea and smoking. Underneath this woman's chummy manner was a soul that was petty and resentful. Her empty friendship with sweet old reticent Faina seemed a thinly disguised boast, a rubbing in of Faina's shortcomings through boasts of her family's accomplishments.

In the past, Alexei had endured the biting meanness that poured off the vile woman's thin false smile. Oh, it was such a pity that Faina's brother-in-law and his friends didn't drop by anymore but, ah, what can you do? Artists are artists, they always appear and disappear as they see fit! She would give anything to be able to travel to Paris and forget all about her miserable husband and ungrateful twins! On other occasions, such as during the aftermath of Alexei's father's death, even her condolences had turned themselves to her own advantage. "Ah, Faina, may your sainted husband rest in peace! He was terribly ill, but at least you were there by his side until the end. Sometimes I wonder if my poor Nikolai should drop dead in his office, will they even send word, or will they go ahead with their twelve hours of work?" This implied that Nikolai, a slothful bureaucrat at the Moscow Registry who probably spent his workdays inspecting the state of his fingernails and perfecting it with the blade of a letter opener, had a much more important job than Mikhail's at-home accounting. Irina Ivanovna's all-time favorite topic was Alexei and the prolonged postponement of his becoming a family man. Her two brats had been married for years now. Yelena's husband was a louse who'd often beat her black and blue. Andrey's wife had managed to produce nine children in almost as many years, which forced him and his spouse to work eighteen-hour days. But, "Oh, don't you worry, Faina!" Irina would say not even waiting for her neighbor's excuse-making. "At least your boy is doing something with his life, plus he's always there for you, night and day at your side. Hold on to him, that's what I say. After all, he's your only son, and he'll be such a comfort in your old age. You know what I would give to have them back just for a single day, like when they were little? Oh, it's so hard when they fly the coop to live their own lives."

All this meant that Faina had failed to produce a second, procreating child and that Alexei was as good as a corpse.

Despite all the flaws of their self-absorbed neighbor, Alexei had never truly resented her visits. Even spurious kindness was better than no kindness at all; a bragging voice preferable to silence. Though Faina never responded in kind to Irina Ivanovna's provocations, Alexei's professional relationship with Rabinovich conferred a vicarious glory on her that could not be denied. This made her resilient against the woman's ill-disguised jibes. Only one woman in the building had an offspring who had dined with Stalin, and who had traveled the world as an ambassador's cultural attaché. Faina, though not by nature inclined to *schadenfreude*, might still enjoy her own superiority over Irina, listening to her blow up her children's achievements and all the while thinking, Go ahead, you fat old fool! Spit out your venom. Do your worst! Deep down you know as well as I that you could never have raised a kid like mine. Not in a thousand years!

But the clock on the cabinet shelf said a quarter to two. It was late, extremely late for a casual visit, no matter who the visitor. While Faina was tactfully holding back successive yawns, Irina's alertness was abnormal, if not downright scary.

The moment she'd heard the sound of his keys outside the door, she'd stood up and turned to the entrance of the apartment, as if she'd been rehearsing her affectedly warm greeting.

As soon as she'd delivered her phony welcome, the corpulent visitor motioned Faina to sit still and began placing their tea things on the old copper tray and scurrying over to the kitchen, where she proceeded to wash the kettle, saucers and cups. The moment she'd passed by him, Alexei had noticed the twitching at the corners of her mouth, the telltale rigor of a forced smile. And that was the least of it. Irina Ivanovna's labored breath smelled not of tea, or even of nicotine, but of cheap vodka. Alexei frowned at his mother. Why is this woman washing our cups? And how come she knows where to put everything? But Faina smiled, rolling her eyes and enjoying a cavernous yawn. Then, she patted the arm of her chair, inviting Alexei to perch there for a moment. As he did so, he softly kissed the thinning white roots of her hair. Faina stroked her son's hand before looking up into his eyes with helpless devotion. Alexei was overcome by sadness.

Oh, mama. Whatever will become of you?

Five minutes later, the spying sow emerged from the kitchen, drying her hands on her frock and gesturing at them to stay put. "No reason to see me to the door. You've both had a terribly long day, I'm sure. Faina, my dear, thanks again for the wonderful tea. If I only I had a son like yours! That Andrey, bless his soul, spends his last kopek feeding that army of kids! No treats for his poor old mom. Alyosha, sweetheart, it was lovely seeing you. Keep up the good work; you're making us all incredibly proud!" And off she went in a reek of sweat.

They listened to her labored breathing on the stairs, and then, closing the living room door, Alexei whispered to his mother, "What was that woman doing here at two in the morning?"

Faina made an impatient gesture. "Ah, you know how Irina Ivanovna is. She just comes and goes as she likes; she practically invites herself. She's like the flu that way."

"But...?" But what, exactly? Did his trusting mother realize that her neighbor might be paying even more visits to their home while they were both away? That she might even have her own key? That while playing the meddlesome upstairs neighbor who "just drops by for a spell," she might have been going through their things, planting listening devices, sniffing out reactionary dirt? Yet, what if Irina Ivanovna did nothing of the sort? What if she simply was an overbearing but lonely old woman who picked at Faina's intimate wounds for pleasure? Did Alexei honestly want Faina to believe she was being spied upon? But then, his mother, forever intuitive of his least frustration and determined to remove it as tenderly as a piece of crust caught in his eye, took his hand in both of hers.

"Don't you worry about her, my angel. She's just a boastful, harmless old fool. I can handle Irina. You do what you must and don't concern yourself about me. I'll always be waiting for you to make me happy just by walking through the door. You know my heart opens only to you, my little bird. I don't need to show off to any silly old neighbor. I am your mother. Your secrets will always be safe with me, only for me to be proud of."

Alexei wondered when all was said and done about brain scientists and thought-implanting spies, if love wasn't in itself a form of mind-reading.

But love is kind. Love does not impose itself. It sits and waits. Love may even frighten you, but it will never put you in harm's way. So, reading the loved one's mind, yes. But to control someone? Love was sadly not enough. If it were, well, Alexei would have never let Uncle Petya...

Blinking away unwelcome thoughts, his eyes idly rested on a yellowed piece of framed embroidery hanging on the wall. Those dexterously stitched words in red silken threads represented the deepest connection that bound Faina to Uncle Petya. As in her relationship with her son, no small talk had ever been necessary between her and Rabinovich. She'd apprehended at once the riddle that Alexei had been struggling to unravel for years. She'd seen the core of the man that her son had merely glimpsed, and only now, after this baffling night of dubious revelations. It was the *Mat aforizm*.

Mother is root. Cut it and you wither. Ignore it and you know not yourself. Try to kill it and see how it does not die.

Though it was late, sleep was out of the question. Faina sensed her son's ponderous thoughts and had retreated silently to the kitchen. Alone, Alexei gravitated to the piano. Uncle Petya's musical farewell had been inside him all along, but somehow its memory had been blocked. Yet a glance at the double bass score had been enough to unlock the Rabinovich music box in Alexei's mind. Sitting at the living room's upright piano, pressing the silent pedal, he began.

It was simply a matter of going through the first dozen bars, and the theme of *Sixteen*'s first movement blossomed in all its beauty. Alexei had provided counter-themes and elaborated on the master's bare yet harrowing minor-key melodies. He didn't question himself for one moment. The first movement was written in A minor. A lilting, triple-time, songlike melody, *Tempo di valse*. No one but Uncle Petya would dare use such an unadorned waltz as the opening theme to a symphony. Only he possessed the brilliant ease of juxtaposing minor and major turns in the same phrase. His rare gift made his tunes as poignant and memorable as the finest penned by Mozart or Schubert. All the trademarks of Uncle Petya's genius were present in this short dazzling gem. It was such joy to listen to this music that Alexei made no attempt to discern any evidence of Krushchev's preposterous theory. He soon lost himself in the sheer pleasure of *Sixteen*. How could this glorious creation ever be construed as anti-Soviet? How could bliss so pure be evil? How could such transfixing beauty drive any listener to a self-inflicted death? Nonsense, Alexei thought, and proceeded *attacca* to the second movement.

A song again, an *andante* as mournfully *non troppo* as they come. Pacing along the opening bars, Alexei smiled at the memory of Uncle Petya's bafflement whenever a slow movement was called for. "For God's sake, if His Holiness Ludwig van Beethoven scarcely ever bothered with them, why should I?" He usually didn't. Afterwards, Alexei was often forced to draw out entire movements into a carefully balanced slowness, so as not to overwhelm the listener with a deluge of gorgeous tunes vying for first place. *Sixteen*'s middle movement was in truth a 6/8 *marche funèbre*, written once more in A minor. Playing it, Alexei could imagine a host of second-rate composers and critics tut-tutting while Uncle Petya grinned with satisfaction. "Oh, screw you and your rules of harmonic progression. Will you have left anything half as beautiful behind when your time comes?" But whose death had the Master been mourning? At the premiere, Alexei glanced at Uncle Petya's expression as the first violin picked up the movement's haunting theme and wondered whether this lament had anything to do with the Jewish genocide that still gaped like a fresh wound. The unprecedented massacres and death camps were things he'd rarely discussed with Rabinovich. Alexei had always sensed that the horror of the Shoah had shaken Uncle Petya terribly. In the past, he had composed several works influenced by the Yiddish musical idiom, among them a song-cycle with lyrics drawn from the *Bube Meyse*. Despite Rabinovich's friendship with Stalin, this was a daring act. This funeral march might be an expression of Rabinovich's guilt for being one of the Jews who had survived, a guilt that was said to be gnawing at the souls of many survivors. But now, Alexei's mind turned to a more profoundly personal loss. Could this have been a threnody in the memory of Uncle Petya's mother? The insinuations made by the General Secretary regarding the convoluted roots of the Rabinovich family tree had managed to overshadow temporarily the enormity of the loss itself. Now, as Alexei sat brooding at the piano, he imagined learning from a letter that both your parents have been butchered by a mob. The unavoidable projection onto his own life made him shudder. Nothing terrified him like the concept of Faina's death. He couldn't imagine life without her love, which was the only thing that kept him from breaking into a million pieces. Ever since he'd been a child, he'd been plagued by the fear of losing Mama. Imagine, then, how infinitely more horrible it would be to lose your mother not to disease, accident or even old age, but to a faceless horde. Imagine her body struck by axes, flayed by scythes, set fire while her heart was still beating and afterwards nothing—no grave or marker. Complete obliteration. Think of her death at almost the same age as Alexei was now. He couldn't say whether such anguish could transform the kind Uncle Petya into a vindictive soul, bent on the destruction of thousands of lives and the collapse of an entire country. Who knew what too much pain could drive you to? Alexei wasn't there when Uncle Petya was a youth of seventeen, alone in the world and faced with returning to his motherland as a prince without a throne. Alexei knew how mercilessly the Master would have teased him had he ever dared to suggest such a fabulist version of Rabinovich's younger self! Yet right now the conjuring of this fairy-tale scene helped carry Alexei along the second movement's closing *sostenuto* and deliver him upon the safer shore of the third and final movement of *Sixteen*.

A catchy, lilting waltz. A moving *adieu*. Midway through the eleventh bar, Alexei stopped playing, as if his right fingers had been stung by the chords they'd struck. The melody was damn familiar. He knew its winding path as thoroughly as a nursery song. He played it again, just the right-hand part with its A-minor theme, gripping like a bird's plaintive song in the deep of the night. Yes! It was a song he knew well, even though, incredibly, he'd failed to recognize it until this moment. With so many uncollected Rabinovich songs, it was only natural that Alexei had missed this particular one. The name of the song came to him—"Annabel Lee." It had been one of the earliest heart-wrenching Rabinovich sensations. The self-plagiarizing wasn't unusual. Besides using snatches or even entire phrases from composers he loved, like Schubert and Mahler, Uncle Petya had habitually pickpocketed his own youthful riches. "Well, if you have to steal, you've got to steal from the best, right?" At the time of its release, "Annabel Lee" had driven the twenties music crowds wild. Sung by Chaliapin in a surprisingly mellow baritone, "Annabel Lee" had quickly become so rabidly popular that even the most hardened Marxist critics had overlooked the fact that the song was a poem, written by a disgraceful, death-driven alcoholic American of the nineteenth century. Humming what he remembered of the lyrics, Alexei marveled once again at the song's raw emotive power. In this fairy tale, Annabel Lee is torn from the poet's loving arms by heavenly cherubs. Transported by the refrain, Alexei sang in earnest, and the sound of his own husky voice sent a shiver down his spine. The song elicited memories of Alexei's childhood when Faina had been little more than a maiden and, he'd imagine her as a fallen aristocrat, saved from the fire and brimstone of the Revolution by her son's heroic endeavors.

As both song and symphony drew to an end, Alexei marveled at the madness. How could violent chaos be attributed to music so stunningly pure in its wordless magnificence? He wasn't making a run for the borders now, was he? Nor was Faina, who had crept up behind him, wrapped her arms around his and pressed her lips to the crown of his head.

It was four in the morning. Faina had gone to bed. Alexei had toyed with telling her about his imminent travel abroad, explaining that he would be doing research for Uncle Petya's biography. Doing so would give her time to get used to the idea of her son's sudden departure. But in the end, he'd said nothing. Let the poor woman have a few hours' rest before she starts ironing, packing and worrying. As to his own chances of catching even a blink of sleep? Macbeth was more likely to doze off with dagger in hand right outside King Duncan's chamber. Excitement and dread kept him in a state of feverish wakefulness. The prospect of boarding an Aeroflot plane after so many years was heart-stopping. Just as the detailed account of a feast can make one suddenly famished, so had all this talk of defection awakened within him a ferocious desire to get away from Moscow's bubbling cauldron of trouble. Only now did he realize that since Uncle Petya's death, he hadn't left the Russian capital. Surely this added to his grief, sometimes to the point of making him feel like a prisoner who'd been denied even a brief walk. Now he'd been ordered to roam the European continent, on a possibly dangerous, yet alluring quest. Indeed, Alexei been given *carte blanche* for a journey to all the places Uncle Petya had visited without him. Of course, this unexpected boon came with stipulations, including a life-and-death vow of secrecy. The true purpose of his mission would be known only to a select few. The integrity of the Politburo couldn't be compromised by admitting to have authorized an intelligence assignment as ridiculous as the one Khrushchev laid out. Yet this only increased Alexei's dizzying excitement. He felt like a child who's been given an expensive chemistry set, itching to mix all the colorful powders into an alchemist's brew. Oh, to gaze once more at the wonders that lay beyond the grim periphery of the USSR! To handle foreign currency, to inhale the smooth tobacco of Western cigarettes and to drink real coffee and vodka! To shake off the tail and sneak into a movie theater showing one of the American films forbidden to Russian audiences. Above all, to be able to breathe the air of freedom that had been denied to Uncle Rodya and Vlad, those wonderful men who had drawn their last breath in the wilderness of some remote Siberian outpost just because they'd been in love with one another. To visit again places where, as Vittorio had many times assured him, men like them weren't exterminated for privately engaging in the passionate cavorting of which Alexei had only dreamt.

Taking a deep breath, Alexei lay back on his bed, still fully clothed, and opened the French copy of *The Aphorisms*. He had to process everything he'd heard and construct a coherent story out of the Secretary General's fabulation. Despite the aura of secrecy, which implied Khrushchev's wild allegations had been accepted by his cabinet and the NKVD, Alexei remained unconvinced. He couldn't reconcile the Rabinovich he'd known with this villainous Judeo-American double agent who threatened global Communism even from beyond the grave. Yet, in listening to all that hogwash, the seed of doubt had been planted, and Alexei knew that the suspicion he suddenly felt about Uncle Petya's past was the first step in the Party's plot. To allow anyone to instill the tiniest doubt into your mind is to pen yourself to being mentally manhandled. Khrushchev had certainly forced Alexei to question the little he knew by juxtaposing reality with a farcical scenario.

As if the events of the past few hours hadn't been confusing enough, there was all the tangible evidence. His thoughts touched the long-ago photograph that was still tucked away in his breast pocket; the double bass score, its paper creased and blotched by the snow that had soaked through the old man's clothes; the furtively made recording of *Sixteen*; and, more undeniable than anything, that magnificent ring belonging to Uncle Petya's mother and the incriminating initials etched on its inside: *E.R.*, meaning Ekaterina Rabinovich, or, worse, Ekaterina Regina. The tale of this mythical mother's adventurous life and untimely death became temptingly credible when set against facts about her son that Alexei could confirm. Rabinovich's extreme unsociability, his lifelong lack of close friends and the loving nature he shrouded in a façade of remoteness, suddenly made sense if he'd been truly raised as a covert aristocrat with a tortuous past. How can a child who knows himself to be the offspring of kings befriend other children? How can one open up when burdened by so many perilous secrets?

Who knew what prejudice or rancor his parents had filled his head with to make young Petya wary of people, rich and poor alike? Then, while still a youth of seventeen, he'd suddenly found himself alone, exiled from his own past, the blood of his mother and father smeared across everything that he'd held dear. No wonder he'd turned out to be a recluse. Even the American roots made sense for anyone who heard Rabinovich speak the language of Shakespeare; not the slightest Slavic heaviness affected his pronunciation. His English, French and German had been as fluent as only a mother tongue could ever be. His prodigious musical gift could also be explained if his father had been a talented pianist. Mendelssohn's rare precocity came to mind. Uncle Petya's singular relationship with Stalin was well-documented, in spite of the fact that he frequently went against the most powerful man in the world. It would be typical of one belonging to the elite to behave in a politically daredevil fashion. The bourgeois were notorious for considering themselves beyond the reaches of political power. Rabinovich, in many of his compositions and in his public stance, had often exhibited a scandalous disregard for hierarchy, Party decrees and all things Soviet. This indifference might have been Rabinovich's natural contempt for high-ranking bureaucrats stemming from an upper-class distaste for low-born power mongers. Khrushchev had even intimated that the mention of *The Aphorisms* in Lenin's writings, far from being an innocent display of praise for the book's literary worth, had been a gesture of reciprocation, a subtle way in which the leader of the nascent Communist Party could express gratitude for Rabinovich's secret financial aid to the Red Army. To Alexi, even more bizarre than the chance of such an apolitical book being hailed as a masterpiece by a firebrand like Lenin was the existence of *The*

Aphorisms in the first place. Its evident erudition aside, the simple fact that a seventeen-year-old boy could conceive such a cynical work of contemplation could only be justified if the author had suffered a devastating shock. It brought to mind an adolescent soldier climbing out of a trench only to stumble upon the mutilated corpses of his comrades. The slaying of his mother had aged Rabinovich almost overnight, forging his frail soul into a brutal maturity and finally eliciting a stream of bleak introspection reminiscent of those sages who wrote as if they'd witnessed life and death and found them meaningless.

Perhaps the missing pieces of the puzzle were contained within this slim volume lying upon his chest. Sitting up and lighting a cigarette, he turned to the last aphorism, that seeming afterthought published only in the French translation, to which Uncle Petya must have appointed a special significance.

So should the answer to my every mystery be sought out amid the unmelting snow I left behind.

Alexei stared at the words until the letters grew blurry. He must have wanted me to read this, he thought. That was why he'd kept this copy where only Alexei might find it, and why it was the French edition he had chosen. French, which was the stuttering bane of so many conversations with Uncle Petya.

How to interpret such a cryptic statement? What could the paradoxical "unmelting snow" refer to? What "mystery" was Rabinovich alluding to? Could it be taken literally? Suddenly, Sretensky's words came to him. He's not in that box of yours. Alexei shook his head at that morbid thought.

Suggestive of an agnostic's disinterest in the posthumous, Rabinovich had wished to be cremated and the ashes to be entrusted to his longtime associate, Alexei Samoilenko. Alexei recalled the mortifying meeting with the Politburo lackey who'd been assigned to deliver Uncle Petya's remains. The man

had come knocking at his Conservatory office, where Alexei
fled whenever grief overtook him. In a choked voice, he'd
cried at the man to wait, frantically rifling through his pockets
for a handkerchief. But the fool had barged in nonetheless,
dropped a large cardboard box on Alexei's desk and given him
a receipt to sign. The oaf looked bored, as if he'd just delivered
a box of paper clips. Once he was gone, Alexei had gingerly
removed the lid, but a single glance at the transparent plastic
bag of powder, white as unmelted snow, had set him wailing.
Finally, minutes before his next class, he'd grabbed a hand-
carved Khaya mahogany box from his desk, and exchanged
the office supplies it contained with Rabinovich's ashes. A
small flurry of soapy dust had escaped from the bag in the
process, and Alexei had accidentally inhaled a considerable
quantity of *poudre de Rabinovich* (as the Master used to refer
to his cremated body, back when the prospect seemed like a
ghoulish joke) and nearly choked. Ever since that dreadful
day, the wooden box lay hidden underneath his bed. "Not in
that box of yours." This box?

Alexei shivered. What he was about to do was so
unspeakable that he felt woozy. But before he could restrain
himself, the box was already lying on his bed, its heavy lid
opened and both his hands thrust wrist-deep into the powder.
Unconscious tears flowed from his eyes as he forced his hands
deeper into the ashes.

Was the powder warm to the touch? No, it was just his
imagination.

The fingers of his left hand touched upon something hard,
cool and metallic buried in the bottom corner of the box. An
inner hinge? No, it was loose. Its shape was somehow familiar.
A pin or screw? The lingering trace of some old fracture
never mentioned? Pinching his thumb and forefinger, Alexei

retrieved the foreign object, wiped it tenderly on his shirt and held it up to the bedside lamp. No surprise after all, but another mystery. A key.

PART TWO

My Heart Belongs to Stalin

CHAPTER SEVEN

What would Sherlock Holmes do? Alexei wondered, as the jam-packed Tupolev rose skywards with a shuddering roar. Or Commissaire Maigret, for that matter? First, they would light their thought-inducing pipes. In the case of Holmes, he would make fun of Watson, shoot up some morphine and play the violin, until inspiration flew through the window like a bumblebee. Maigret, on the other hand, would locate a dim *bistrot* and drink a glass (or twelve) of calvados until an epiphany presented itself, doffing its hat at whatever riddle he was dealing with. Alexei sighed. How come fictional snoops, faced with human malevolence, had it so easy? What efficient heroes they made compared to his antiheroic self! He'd give anything to possess the English genius's ironic suaveness or the Belgian *commissaire*'s dispassionate brilliance. But as to his real situation, neither detective offered any wisdom. Although they had confronted frustrating conundrums, Alexei doubted that either had ever faced a challenge with such painfully personal implications. After being introduced by Uncle Petya to whodunits, Alexei had quickly devoured one crime novel after the other. Rabinovich had been an ardent reader of detective fiction and his personal library included the complete works of Arthur Conan Doyle. The books, formerly banned in the Soviet Union and currently frowned upon as being immaterial to the

Revolution, stood prominently on one of the composer's bookcases, each bound in red leather and bearing, in a tongue-and-cheek display of recklessness, misleading titles from Lenin's bibliography. In order to read their thick printed pages, Alexei had to learn English. Fortunately, this language was easier for him to grasp than French. This was unexpected as Uncle Petya was an erratic tutor, expounding at length on rare words and idioms he found particularly fascinating, while leaving Alexei to learn grammar and syntax on his own. Rabinovich had been strict about correct pronunciation, so that whenever Alexei fumbled, Uncle Petya exploded into an exasperated fit. He had a metallic ruler which he'd suddenly bang against the edge of his desk, terrifying his stuttering pupil. Regardless of these obstacles, Alexei had soldiered on and eventually mastered the English language enough to enjoy its fiction. And he had been rewarded royally. How he'd adored the highbrow ease Sherlock exhibited in the face of adversity. Alexei identified with Watson for the doctor's manner and his endurance of mockery, which Alexei felt mirrored his own relationship with Uncle Petya. Alas, there was a limit to the powers of fiction, or of any art, when dealing with the oppressive urgency of crises like the one that had set Alexei on this unexpected journey. Conceivably he could have snuck one of the Sherlock volumes aboard in his suitcase. Even if discovered during the customs check, the officer would likely dismiss the leather-bound tome, believing it contained old Lenin's dull pearls of wisdom. But the volume including his all-time favorite, *The Sign of Four,* would be a papery suit of armor. Unlike Sherlock, he had no Dr. Watson nor any recreational drugs to illuminate the unholy *Sixteen* mess. If Alexei had packed alcohol in his suitcase, it would likely have been confiscated by a surly Bykovo guard. The young man might still possess the enviable green passport necessary for travelling abroad, but gone were the days of Uncle Petya's diplomatic pouch. Gone also were the days of flying first class, snugly ensconced in spaciously arranged seats, with hostesses rushing to freshen up his drink. The bloody Politburo tightwads had dumped him in the teeming economy class with its bawling babies, inconsiderate sprawlers and sleepers who'd conked out the second their behinds touched the seat. Funk quickly bred self-contempt. Not only was he incapable of any deductive reasoning that might explain away this mystery, but his participation in this spoof of hunting down some spectral criminal was morally repugnant. It was an admission of guilt and a condemnation of Uncle Petya's music as surely as if he'd signed a paper stating that *Sixteen* was indeed a source of evil. Wincing at a powerful nudge from his neighbor, Alexei rubbed his exiled elbow and thought how lucky his favorite detectives were in being motherless loners without deep personal ties. Inspector Alexei Samoilenko, on the other hand, had just suffered one of the most heartrending scenes in his adult life, even if it had all unfolded inwardly. He'd woken up to find a buoyant Faina bustling about the kitchen preparing him morning tea and a breakfast of ham and eggs. Although he had the appetite of a dying man, he'd forced himself to eat up and grin, while trying to find the appropriate moment to reveal his departure. Every moment felt worse than the one before, so finally he'd blurted out a ludicrous invention about traveling to Switzerland to retrieve personal documents Uncle Petya had left with a friend which Alexei needed for the biography he was supposedly writing. What had wrenched his guts like the blade of a knife wasn't the darkening of his mother's good spirits. Faina was intuitive enough to sense her son's gloominess and she put on a cheery face so convincing that Alexei wondered whether she really believed his sorry excuse. The sight of her imperturbable smile made him feel even more wretched. Leading such a celibate existence, one filled with shameful secrets, Alexei had learned to regard any prevarication as an insult. So, unlike a husband who has learned the harmless fictions that help sustain a marriage, he was devastated at lying so grossly to his mother. His devastation was so apparent that eventually the roles had been reversed, and it was Faina who sat next to him, holding his hand and telling him that she didn't mind, she'd have the chance to get on with her reading and knitting. But even this felt like a blow. The thought of Faina sitting in her armchair day in, day out, in the silent apartment, praying for his safe return while ignorant of the sword of Damocles hanging over them almost sent him over the edge. When Faina had suddenly struck her forehead and rushed to his room to pack his suitcase shouting, "Be sure to bring me back some of those famous chocolates of theirs!" Alexei could have wept. As it was, he'd barely managed to resist the urge until they'd hugged and kissed and said goodbye, and he was out on the street. But standing at the crowded bus station, he realized that it would be unwise to dissolve into sobs amid a bunch of groggy strangers. And now here he was, up above the clouds. Picking the wound, Alexei evoked her hushed steps falling into silence. He saw her straw knitting basket with its brightly colored balls of yarn lying next to her while the needles clicked. Mother and son hovered in a limbo as distance strained and frayed the invisible length of wool connecting their hearts. For several minutes, he'd been unwittingly staring at a plump Alpine-blonde *maman*, who, in turn, was beatifically gazing at the little boy sleeping in the next seat. Resisting a fresh wave of emotion, Alexei compelled his eyes to wander among the Helvetian-looking faces, conspicuous not so much because of some uniform trait of physiognomy, but for their lack of one. Their faces were seemingly smoothed over by the unfettered tranquility that comes with wealth, neutrality and healthy doses of chocolate. Alexei had been ogling his fellow passengers from the moment he stood in line with them at the airport's exchange counter where he'd swapped his faded rubles for the astonishingly velvety Swiss francs. The multicolored notes seemed nothing more than the make-believe currency of a board game. This must be what life felt like to these fortunate people—a lifelong pastime, enjoyed nonchalantly in their board-game country of affluence, security and sugar-coated mountains. Next to them, he was a poor specimen of humanity. Thoughts of defection flooded his mind. He imagined holing up in some uncharted Alpine retreat and spending his life in a cave fragrant with gentian and edelweiss. His companions would be the altruistic goats who'd feed with their milk, warm him with their wool and willingly submit to being slaughtered, impaled and roasted on a spit. That would be the life! Switzerland didn't extradite political refugees, right? Besides, the goats would never squeal on him. If only it weren't for Mama. A sudden turbulence rattled the plane, shaking people in their seats sending objects flying in all directions and eliciting invocations to God, largely in Russian. At ten kilometers above the earth, neither Marx, Lenin nor Stalin calls the shots. Alexei focused on remaining alive, preferably without wetting himself. The captain's voice came over the speakers, cheerfully assuring the passengers that the "minor bumpiness" had been caused by a pesky downward current, but they were looking at "smooth sailing ahead."

Alexei's fear of flying was a result of Uncle Petya's pathological aviophobia. Just as Rabinovich had made Alexei's air travel possible, he also bestowed the secondhand discomfort of flying with a man who was terrified of air travel. Back in the happy days, whenever an imperative trip came up, Rabinovich's first reaction was to do everything in his powers to postpone it. Should that fail, he self-medicated on alcohol and sedatives, a combination that sometimes knocked him out cold for the flight. When it didn't, Uncle Petya treated his terror as a sort of noxious digestive gas which, if released, might lessen his agony. In those times, he let it blast by sharing reassuring aviation facts that he didn't believe with co-passengers, strangers at the airport, taxi drivers and Alexei. Alexei was forced to breathe in Uncle Petya's fart-like fear until it permeated him. During the decade they'd spent on and off various aircrafts, Alexei had faithfully listened to interminable speeches on the relative safety of air travel as opposed to earthbound means of transport. He'd been told that it was safer to sit at the back of the plane. If some freak meteorological phenomenon ripped the plane in half like a can of sardines, the tail was most likely to remain intact. One should at all costs resist unfastening one's seat belt to use the restroom, stretch one's legs or retrieve something from the overhead compartments because at that precise moment some killer draft might strike down the plane like a gigantic fly swatter, so that you'd plummet thousands of feet within tenths of a second, during which your body, crushed against a series of unyielding surfaces, acquired the texture and vitality of mashed potatoes. In case of a nasty cold with severe catarrh one should never, ever set foot on a plane. The shift in the endocranial pressure resulting from the change of altitude would force thick clots of snot into the cavities surrounding

the brain and possibly even into the bloodstream, causing
fatal embolisms. Alexei also learned that to sleep on a flight
while Rabinovich sat next to you was the stuff of legends.
When intoxicated, his snore was so deafening that practically
no one on the plane could catch a wink of sleep, and, when
betrayed by his somniferous cocktails, he spent the entire trip
jabbering your ear off. These flight soliloquies often included
several pages of memorized details concerning the physics of
human aviation. But the recitation of hard facts could just as
easily deviate into the paranoid land of conspiracy theories.
"We've all been fooled by those Galilean myths," Uncle Petya
had whispered to him on one such occasion, his tone so
earnest that Alexei wondered whether the Master was having
a mental breakdown. "A spherical earth! Hah! That's pure
bullshit. Of course, the earth is flat. Flat like my ass on this
goddamn seat. If you're stupid enough to reach the edge of it,
whoosh. Down you go into the abyss. They just keep feeding
us this lie to keep us numb, to save face for having to admit to
the gravest scientific hoax in recorded history. I'll bet you that
none of the countries and oceans and all that crap they teach at
school actually exist. The moment you board a ship or a plane,
you're knocked unconscious. They probably gas everyone with
some sleeping vapor which makes you hallucinate, so that
you think you're flying or sailing or whatever. Controlled by
changing the scenery and moving stuff around, just like stage
props. There is no planet at all, globe-shaped or otherwise.
Everything's crowded together in a single spot where we're
all trapped for eternity. That's why people are stupid and
miserable wherever you go. I mean, think about the lie we're
being fed right now, boy. Is it even remotely possible that this
monster of steel that weighs a million tons can soar the skies
like a fucking wild goose? It's scientifically impossible, as

silly as believing in gold-guarding leprechauns and stardust-shitting fairies!"

It did feel like a bewildering, utterly convincing gimmick, being aloft as a bird in the belly of this artificial wonder, flying above the Urals. It boggled the mind to think that the dotted line on the map representing those same mountains that old Tisharenko, *Sixteen*'s contrabassist, had given his life to cross were those Alexei was crossing right now without the least effort. But then, what didn't feel like magic where Uncle Petya was concerned?

As per orders, Alexei had made a brief stop at the Conservatory before heading to the airport to catch his two o'clock flight. There, under the pretext of some administrative business, he had been exposed to the sophisticated wonders of the Soviet spying trade. These instruments, especially created for the purposes of his mission, had been presented to him by an unnamed, unsmiling technician. Each device was a costly prototype that had to be returned in pristine condition. The first item was a thick black volume with Капитал spelled out across the spine in gilt letters. Alexei was disappointed. However, as he discovered, the book replica didn't contain Marx's world-changing treatise on political economy. It was a state-of-the-art portable recording device with an approximate range of three meters and enough magnetic tape to last for two whole hours of auditory material. He itched to open his marvel of surveillance and take a peek at its mechanism, but the lid had been welded shut. Only authorized personnel could access the tapes. To operate the device, Alexei would press and release a switch hidden under the edge of the leather binding, and since there was no way to erase or overwrite on a previous recording, he had to be sparing with its use. He was strongly advised to save it only for conversations "pertinent to the case."

Then the man handed him a black pen. "Where do I sign?" Alexei asked. But since no paperwork was produced he realized he was meant to keep it. Some kind of secret-agent initiation gift, he thought. Uncle Petya, he recalled, had received fountain pens from Mao Zedong and Roosevelt, personally engraved with their signatures. "Why, thank you," he said with a smile and placed it prominently on his desk.

The agent blinked. "It is not a gift. You should carry it with you at all times, and you are expected to return it. In pristine condition."

"I shouldn't use it to write with?"

The man rolled his eyes. "Stick it in your breast pocket. It contains a transmitter. Keep it on your person at all times so that field agents present at the scene of your meetings are able to listen in on your... interviews."

Alexei dutifully tucked the pen in his inner coat pocket. "Is it on now?"

"We'll find out." The man opened his briefcase, which was a cleverly disguised listening apparatus, complete with buttons, dials and headphones. The man put on the headphones, then flipped a switch and told Alexei to say something. Alexei patted his left breast reflexively, as if afraid the pen had vanished. Head inclined to the left, he held out his lapel and spoke his name loudly into the pocket. The agent yelped, ripping the headphones off his head and sticking both index fingers in his ears.

"Don't shout into the goddamn thing! Just talk like a normal person having a discussion." Warily, he put the headphones on again and motioned at Alexei to speak. Suddenly, Alexei's mind became a complete blank. He couldn't think of a single thing to say. He grinned nervously, unconsciously patting his left breast.

The man winced. "Don't hit it. We know it's working. You just ruptured my bloody eardrums. Just speak." In a fit of despair, Alexei's mind leapt, inexplicably, to the *"Internationale,"* and he began to sing in a tremulous voice that grew impassioned with revolutionary zest.

The agent jumped back with a bark, removed the headphones and rubbed his ears. "Do you usually address people by singing the former national anthem?" he asked, glaring at him.

Embarrassed, Alexei shook his head. "Should I...what should I say?"

"You've said enough." The man explained that the pen also contained a tiny photographic device and microfilm with a capacity of 36 shots. Excited beyond measure by this miracle of technology, Alexei took out the pen and removed the cap as the agent yelled, *"Tvoyu mat!"* Apparently Alexei had exposed the film. Gritting his teeth to hold back more insults, the man said it sufficed to point the lower tip of the pen at something, then turn the cap and the photograph was taken. "I...I just wanted to see how it works..." Alexei stuttered apologetically, driving the cap back on forcefully, and causing the aural equivalent of a rifle shot to explode in the ears of the agent, who'd just put the headphones back on.

The final item was an envelope containing his international passport, plane tickets, vouchers to use at hotels and exchange offices and a sheet of instructions listing the destinations he must travel to, the persons he must interview and the people he must contact immediately, should anything go wrong.

"Like what?" Alexei asked, intimidated by the obvious over-planning.

"In case the project or you come into harm's way," the man told him, quickly gathering his equipment.

"But you said there will be agents present at the scene. Won't they be able to help, if anything goes wrong? And what kind of harm are we talking about? I'm supposed to be writing a book! I'm not trained in man-to-man combat. I'm just a musician!"

The agent massaged his forehead. "And I, Comrade Samoilenko, am just a miserable technician. I don't know the particulars of your mission, nor do I care. Just follow the instructions provided. And make sure to dispose of the list."

"What about the tickets? Do I throw them away too?"

"No," grumbled the agent. "Your expenses have to be accounted for. Only destroy the instruction sheet." Finally, the man produced a detailed acknowledgement of the items received, the confidentiality agreement Alexei had been expecting and a statement of intent which, in case of accidental disclosure of the mission or of transgressions of international law, absolved the Party, the Politburo and the NKVD of any knowledge and responsibility regarding Alexei Mikhailovich Samoilenko's deeds. Alexei felt like a condemned man.

"Is it okay if I read the instructions now?" he asked the man, who had pocketed the signed documents and was preparing to leave.

His face was stony. "If you wish."

"And then I just...throw them away in the trash?"

The man sighed, rolling his eyes again. "I suppose you could also have them mimeographed and paste the copies all over Red Square, or perhaps send them to *Pravda* to be published alongside our obituaries."

"You had best burn the thing once you've read it," said the agent as he left.

With the hectic preparations and the anxiety of getting to the airport on time, the dangerous piece of paper had slipped his mind completely, tucked away unread in his pocket. Now he was confined to his seat and surrounded by two hundred strangers who might all be American spies or secret police, except for the little boy and his mother, whose face was too kindly for a spy. What about the old man? Alexei eyed the passenger on his left, sleeping like a log. With every snore, his lips trembled and his dentures clicked softly. But he could be faking it. Joseph Tisharenko, too, had been older than the mountains, and he'd managed to get involved in the supposed conspiracy. Besides, even if it were relatively safe to read the damn thing, could he risk returning it to his pocket? What if he, too, dozed off or was somehow gassed, and his pocket was picked?

But it might get stolen anyway. Right this minute, before he'd even had a chance to take a look at the particulars of the mission on whose outcome his life depends! That seemingly angelic mother might bump into him across the aisle when he's disembarking and snatch it! The kid might be a front or a disguised midget! Panic tugged like a pulled muscle. Oh my God, where did I put the check? he thought. I forgot the check! I'm done for!

But Alexei had slipped it behind the tear in the lining of his suitcase. Anyhow, he should wait and read the instructions after they'd landed. His first destination he knew. He could do it in the taxi. And then burn it, or perhaps swallow it. Or he would go to the toilet and read it there, in the locked cubicle. It seemed a safe enough course of action, plus he badly needed to pee.

Maybe burn it while inside the cubicle? Too risky. Or shred it into tiny pieces and urinate on top of them and then flush them? What if they stick to the bowl and I'm forced to pry them loose with bare hands? Ugh!

But the terror Uncle Petya had instilled was too great to allow him to unfasten his seat belt while the plane was in flight. He didn't want to be puréed by some murderous turbulence. And then there was an ever greater fear to overcome. What if he forgot the instructions he'd just read when it was too late to salvage the paper from fire or gut?

To distract himself, Alexei slipped his hand in the left pocket of his trousers and palmed what felt like his most valuable asset in this mad whirlwind. This was his secret weapon, which neither the Russians nor the Americans knew about and one he had to be extremely careful in using. As Alexei followed the clues Uncle Petya had provided to discover the truth behind *Sixteen,* he was putting his and Faina's lives in danger. But he must know the truth, or else everything—the music, his life's work, Rabinovich's decades-long struggle—had been in vain.

And know he would, provided he could find a way to sneak into the notorious Katzenberg Vault without the NKVD skinning him like a rabbit.

Very early that morning, Alexei had taken the key he'd unearthed from Uncle Petya's ashes to his desk for a closer inspection with a magnifying glass. A number was etched on one side of the key, and on the other, in miniscule Gothic lettering, was a name that belonged in the realm of postwar myths and fables.

As he gazed at the name, the evening when he'd first heard it came back to him with crystalline clarity. Uncle Petya and he had been seated in the Versailles-like drawing room of the embassy, sharing a bottle of brut Grand Cru. Uncle Petya had drained his first glass and then pronounced, "Good Lord, these French secs! It's like drinking liquid chalk!" The champagne was accompanied by an even chalkier cheese, chunks of it broken off a gigantic twelve-kilo block that sat atop the ornate Louis XIV desk like an incongruous centerpiece. It was called Sabrina and was the most notoriously evasive of Swiss hard cheeses, although its few producers claimed it was the oldest European cheese in existence, first made before the birth of Christ. Alexei thought this last claim was disagreeably obvious, since the thing had the color and hardness of an old man's toenails. When sufficiently mashed and grinded by one's teeth, and after soaking up the saliva, it actually tasted like stale parmesan. Uncle Petya had assured him it was an exorbitantly expensive cheese, almost impossible to procure, then sat back and spoke of the tiny dairy farm which had produced that particular block and of its fabled catacombs.

At the top of Welpenstraße, a steep cobblestone road in the outskirts of Zürich, the adventurous tourist might come upon the Käserei Katzenberg, a small chalet of a cheese store with an adjoining cowshed owned by an elderly German-speaking couple, as plump and obliging as their meadow-grazing cows. Theirs was a humble family business, devoted to the manufacture of the intimidating Sbrinz, of which they produced no more than fifty heads per year. And yet, according to the rumors, the old cheesemakers were among the richest people in Switzerland, if not the world. The clandestine source of their mysterious wealth dwelled in their home's labyrinthine basement. This second place of business had also been a part of the family's estate for centuries. Inside approximately two hundred vaults were stored the most invaluable and morally questionable treasures known to humanity. Here were stored the clay prototypes of Da Vinci's Sforza monument, tomes containing lost Greek tragedies, works by Heraclitus and Diogenes rescued from the Library of Alexandria, the holy relics of Mary Magdalene and the elusive Philosopher's Stone. All these legendary works of art, considered lost, destroyed or stolen, were safe under tons of maturing cheese and scattered cow pies. As were the loads of Beninese blood diamonds and gold extracted from the mouths and anuses of Holocaust victims. And, allegedly, a vial cushioned inside a liquid nitrogen container filled with Adolf Hitler's sperm and destined to one day impregnate hundreds of Fourth Reich mommies. This storied vault was unassailable to rules of law and taxation. However, the fee for owning one of the coveted safe-boxes was surely hefty, given the value of the stored objects and the golden silence of the Katzenbergs, and was ensured in the most bizarre fashion. Customers were charged a small but daily fee for as long as they lived; the business operating like some subterranean leech that sucked away the clients' millions slowly and stealthily.

Alexei had found the Katzenberg story fascinating but improbable. So, when Uncle Petya had concluded his extravagant narrative, Alexei lit a Gitanes and said, "It all sounds riveting, although, for the money they charge, their cheese leaves something to be desired."

"Oh, definitely," Rabinovich had agreed, frowning at the mountain of cheese on the desk. "This thing is positively vile. It's just, I don't know, exciting in a way. You see, Alyosha my boy, you don't often get the chance to eat a dairy product that also happens to be a war criminal."

Now a key belonging to that Ali Baba's Cave was in his possession. Incredible. Of course, he knew that even if this place did exist it would be nearly impossible to venture there unnoticed, yet Alexei couldn't help a shiver of delight at the thought of the cryptic treasure. It must be something valuable since Uncle Petya had swallowed the key hours before his death. But what could it be? It must have been crucial to Uncle Petya, if he'd been willing to bleed financially for God knew how many years to keep it safe from prying hands. He was probably still disbursing the daily fee through some account that continued to operate from beyond the grave. Perhaps this accumulated expenditure had been the reason why he had never seemed entirely secure about his wealth despite all his fame and success, why he'd produced work after work with such maniacal frequency, why he had so meticulously avoided the merest political provocation and controversy. There must have been something so dear to him that had to be protected at all costs. The *Sixteen* manuscript was a potential candidate, though too obvious. It must have been something from his past. Perhaps another belonging of his lamented mother? A photograph, a letter, a lovingly preserved lock of hair?

Whatever it was, Alexei had decided he would move heaven and earth to reclaim it. In the ten hours since the key had become his, he had already placed his life in danger to keep its secret safe.

The first thing he'd done was slip on his coat and shoes and sneak out of the apartment at five in the morning in the glacial cold. He began walking to Uncle Petya's home with head lowered and chin tucked in his upturned collar. It was then that he noticed the gasping breath and hurried footsteps of a secret policeman running after him. The gigantic oaf with an oddly childlike face had evidently been assigned the graveyard shift in the rotation of goons guarding Alexei's apartment.

He must have fallen asleep at the wheel, as evinced by the dazed look of his tiny eyes. When he caught up with Alexei, the goon demanded that he give Comrade Samoilenko a lift to the Tverskoy place. Clearly the policeman was anxious not to shame himself further. Alexei accepted gratefully as he was freezing his nuts off. During the short drive, he worried whether the man would try to accompany him into Uncle Petya's apartment. However, as soon as the car stopped outside the building, his stalker/chauffeur gave him a serious look, and wagging a sausage-thick finger, said, "No funny business now. I'll be watching." Then, as if his job was finally over, he yawned and laid his head on the steering wheel, mumbling at Alexei to hurry up.

As soon as he was inside, Alexei rushed to the low shelf containing the huge volumes, each heavy as a Commandments Tablet, of the *Bolshaya sovetskaya entsiklopediya*. Though chastising himself for his ghoulish curiosity, he wanted to discover what metal could survive the destructive forces of gastric fluids and incineration. According to the entry devoted to the periodic table of elements, and the one describing the process of incineration, there were numerous candidates. Apparently human ashes must be brimming with bits of metal, for even tooth fillings survived intact. Then Alexei's mind, repulsed by the onrush of ghastly images, wandered predictably to those final moments of Uncle Petya's life. After replacing the dusty volumes, he spent a few fruitless minutes rifling through the random paperwork heaped all over the study's desk. Just as he was about to call it quits, he stumbled upon an unhoped-for piece of proof. His eyes fell upon a long receipt stamped with an old-fashioned seal that depicted a cow gazing mournfully at a block of cheese and an overflowing milk pail. At the bottom was a monetary figure, ostensibly for the purchase of *Milchprodukt*, that was so staggering it could keep a hundred Muscovite households well-stocked with Sbrinz for a long time. The NKVD must never know about this, Alexei thought, pocketing the paper. He retrieved the Oscar check from the drawer, which had been the alibi he'd concocted for the goon, and removed it from its frame. The agent had fallen into a deep sleep, and Alexei rapped his knuckles on the passenger window and shouted, "I'm leaving now! Good night," but in the end the icy cold defeated him and he let himself into the back seat. When the man's snore continued unabated, he sat back and lit a cigarette. Eventually the sloppy spy woke up and, barking that Alexei had taken his sweet time, began driving.

The worst part, however, had been the terror at the airport's customs check, when Alexei had realized he was attempting to smuggle an illegally obtained object out of the country. What if the security men, in their thorough search of his pockets, found the key and demanded to know its purpose? The first impulse was to swallow it, as Uncle Petya had. But what if the key hadn't been concealed orally? Had the fire cleansed it thoroughly enough? And what about retrieving it afterwards? Suppose it was too big to pass through his intestine and got stuck along the way, rusting inside his bowels? Uncle Petya didn't have to worry about such a possibility. So Alexei stuck it in his mouth and began to suck on it like on a chunky piece of candy. The bored-looking guard had been appalled by Alexei's slurred speech and, thinking the ashen-faced passenger suffered from some congenital abnormality, dismissed him at once. Alexei couldn't have been more grateful. The soap he'd used to clean the damn key had stuck in the grooves, and he'd begun frothing at the mouth.

* * *

Of course, this personal quest would have been impossible if the people handling his fate hadn't chosen Zürich as Alexei's initial destination. Despite the *passe-partout* of paperwork and money, no Soviet citizen, not even a spy with a task appointed by Khrushchev, would ever be allowed to simply hop on a plane for an unauthorized visit abroad, much less to Switzerland, a country known for its bizarre extradition policies. When Alexei had torn the envelope he'd received that morning with shaking fingers and extracted a ticket to Kloten, he nearly cried with joy. He actually turned his eyes naively to the sky, thanking Uncle Petya's spirit for watching over him, especially now that he most needed his protection. Then it hit him. This was no coincidence.

In fact, this was an ace in the hole deliciously typical of Rabinovich. It was a perfect example of the Master's playfulness, of his flaunting mortal danger as if it were nothing. Oh, Uncle Petya could outsmart the secret police with both hands tied, and by making sure Alexei would be sent to Zurich, he'd hidden the first clue right in plain sight. Alexei could almost see him smiling smugly on his way to a meeting with the infamous Thomas Mann in his magic mountainous lair, certain that the Party spies would be hot on his trail as he flaunted his deep ties to the morally corrupt aristocracy of the West by rubbing elbows with this personification of capitalist European decadence. The visit had been like wagging a juicy fat steak at the Communist bloodhounds. Run, boys! Grab the enemy of the people who dares mingle with a subhuman of his true class!

The thought that in a matter of hours he would be meeting the same man in the flesh was as exciting as the key to the Katzenberg vault. For who wouldn't blush at having been referred to, as Alexei had been, by such a genius in a letter to Uncle Petya, as "a most fetching specimen of Slavic loveliness"? Whose heart wouldn't quicken at the prospect of meeting with the single writer whose magnitude overcame the pettiness of politics, so that his work was celebrated in West and East Germany?

Oh, let the treasure hunt begin. The fiercely liberal literary giant, a self-exiled Goethe of his time, was as equally reviled by his Nazi compatriots as by the Soviet intelligentsia, and not even they had been powerful enough to keep his books banned. If the friendship of such a person is treason, Alexei thought, it is good to be a traitor!

CHAPTER EIGHT

"Ach, Alyosha, *mon bien-aimé,* please, do eat that Black Forest I ordered for you, because, so help me God, I will, and I can't. I simply mustn't. My doctors will skin me alive, the scoundrels. Old Faust had it right after all. To regain one's youth, now there's an idea! None of this aging business; one organ failing after the other until there's nothing left in one's decrepit carcass. To hand over one's soul to the Devil in return seems quite the bargain, I assure you. No wonder dearest Petya was so obsessed with the whole Faustian legend. He almost seemed to believe that it was possible to become a real-life Leverkühn, though I assured him he was nothing like that vile creature Adrian, and, of course, he was still terribly young, almost as young as you, my dear. So, I beg of you! Go ahead and eat that delectable-looking slice of Heaven before you wake up one day and find yourself in a Hell such as mine." Alexei blushed bashfully. He slid the gold-rimmed plate toward him, consumed the airy gateau in a few swift spoonfuls, then pursed his lips to lick them tactfully clean. It was exquisite, but nothing compared to the thrill of sitting in the Alden Hotel's glittering restaurant in the company of none other than Thomas Mann.

To follow the author's mellifluous French was almost as hard as reading Mann's dense, magnificent novels. It had taken him two years to struggle through the French translations of

The Magic Mountain and *Doctor Faustus,* which Uncle Petya had considered to be the Nobel laureate's best work, but it had been a transformative experience. Looking back, there was the old Alexei who had never heard of Hans Castorp and Serenus Zeitblom and the new, enlightened one who had. To share a table with the creator of those masterpieces felt as intoxicating as breathing the rarified air of that famous Davos sanatorium after months of constricted breathing.

The Russian genius' affinity with the German one had first manifested in the 1929 song cycle *Pesni Foma* (*Songs of Thomas*), scored for piano and countertenor, which Rabinovich had composed by setting to music passages from *Tristan, Mario and the Magician* and *Death in Venice.* The resulting work, a bleak collection of lovesick ballads, had soon been overshadowed by the composer's hugely popular film music. The contents of the songs had been frowned upon by the musical establishment as depraved and bourgeois. Most of the records had thus disappeared from circulation so that, by the Thirties, they were already a collector's item. It was even said that the name of the countertenor, who had never been photographed, had been an alias used by the young Rabinovich. No public performance had ever been given, and the youthful Rabinovich gem might have altogether vanished into obscurity. However, as luck would have it, Richard Tauber, a friend of the Mann family and at the height of his art back, had listened to a smuggled copy of the elusive record. To the Ministry of Culture's immense displeasure, he had performed a tenor version of *Songs of Thomas*, masterfully orchestrated by Maurice Ravel and attended by the lauded author shortly before his emigration. A profound friendship was established between Thomas Mann and Rabinovich. It was not until fairly recently, however, when Rabinovich had come seeking the mysterious inspiration that gave birth to *Sixteen*, that the two had met face-to-face.

If he were being honest with himself, it hadn't been literary merit alone that had drawn Alexei so inexorably to Thomas Mann. After he'd read the two behemoth novels, he had proceeded with *Death in Venice* and *Tonio Kröger*, luckily available in *samizdat*, and he'd been unbearably aroused by the protagonists' leanings, so tantalizingly identical to his own. His titillation had been so great that he'd asked Rabinovich whether the German writer was, in fact, similarly inclined as Aschenbach. To which Uncle Petya had replied with his customary frankness, "You bet your ass he's queer! He's just one of those buttoned-up, traditional ones, who marry respectably and raise a family."

This same man, impeccably dressed and as imposing as a Roman bust come to life, now sat smiling quizzically at him, so that Alexei didn't have the heart to lie about the Rabinovich biography he was supposedly writing, nor badger Mann with questions about *Sixteen*. The thought of the music's supernatural powers, which had twisted the Party's knickers, seemed too ludicrous to voice. No, what he wished to ask of Herr Mann was this: How does it feel to make love to a man? Describe, in your own inimitable way, what the flesh feels. Is it softness or hardness, is it pain and how much? There was also the favor he must ask no matter how intimidated he felt: the Katzenberg key he must at some point surreptitiously pass to the older man.

But just when the silence had become uncomfortable, the author leaned closer, and with a mischievous twinkle in his gaze, said, "Now, please tell me, since I've been dying to know what's going on ever since dear old Petya paid me his first and last visit. I had a million things to ask, but he'd been in such a terrible state he barely made sense. Apparently, he was convinced that the symphony he was composing at the time, the *Sixteenth*, I believe, could somehow be imbued with magical properties. That it might have a transfiguring effect on humanity, much like Leverkühn hoped of *Apocalypsis*. Naturally, I dismissed his ravings as some exotic creative fever, but a few weeks ago, a younger friend of mine from Poland, whose family immigrated to Paris in the Twenties, wrote a most baffling letter in which he claimed to be housing seven of his compatriots who had recently defected from Warsaw after listening to an illegal broadcast of Rabinovich's swan song. My young friend reported that the song is currently banned *chez vous* because it is considered dangerous. I admit his claims were so wild I had trouble believing him, but then my meeting with our late common friend came to mind, and I couldn't help wondering if the old rascal really didn't do it? Did he manage to raise some unearthly spirit by the striking of a celestial chord? Have I inadvertently created an actual musical magus?"

Alexei's arrival in Zürich had been jarringly dreamlike. There were only shards of sensations—the rough landing that woke him up, the dazzle of the immense airport, the silent taxi driver and the handsome bellhop who rushed to relieve him of his baggage the moment he stepped into the hotel's lobby. The bellhop informed him that Herr Mann was already expecting him at the restaurant and that Herr Samoilenko's friend—he had nodded toward a muscular, blond man who stood next to the elevators reading a paper—had insisted that Herr Samoilenko not forget his reading material before heading out to his interview with the author.

So, Alexei had sought out Uncle Petya's self-exiled friend and quickly matched the likeness of a dated black-and-white photo with the much older man who beckoned him with a warm smile. Cradling the glaringly bulky *Capital* under him arm, Alexei felt a complete fool. Yet, as soon as they greeted one another and Alexei had taken his seat, getting ready to start recording the conversation, Mann's cunning eyes pointed to the book. "Now, since I don't for a second believe that a student of Petya's would care to bore me stiff with edifying passages about the proletariat's destiny, and since I've known your teacher long enough to have gotten wind of your country's rather clumsy spying, I kindly ask you to refrain from operating that thoroughly unconvincing device and let us talk *entre nous,* like friends. I've already spotted that Slavic Argus over there. The poor man is louder than a priest breaking wind in the midst of the Eucharist. I'm sure he is more than capable of making sure the two of us behave."

When the old fox revealed that he already knew about the *Sixteen* debacle and was itching to share whatever gossip could untangle its mystery, Alexei felt it was pointless to try to outwit him. He spilled everything that had happened to him over the past week—from his summons to the Lubyanka right up to his perplexing meeting with Khrushchev and the dubious story about Rabinovich as a diehard enemy of the people bent on some quixotic revenge.

By the time he was finished, the novelist was staring at him in earnest fascination.

"What a staggering tale!" he finally said, hungrily ogling the cigarette Alexei had been unconsciously smoking. "Almost too good to be true. But the truth rarely makes for good storytelling; otherwise, we wouldn't need to invent so many stories of our own. The spying business. Music as a weapon of mind control. I must admit I have trouble accepting that part.

The human mind is too wayward an instrument to control. As for the Rabinovich demonology, I wouldn't exclude it outright from the realm of possibility. After all, dear old Petya certainly possessed a blue blood's unpredictable nature. It's also a fact that he was largely antipathetic toward the machinations inherent to Communism. He hated the way the State has the final say in everything and no matter what his enemies claimed, he was always vehement in his dislike of Stalin. And he was tight-lipped to the extreme when it came to his past; in over twenty years' worth of correspondence he never once mentioned his childhood. I never did press him on the subject. I know better than most that the past is a wound best left unpicked. I'm afraid your...handlers, or whatever it is they call themselves, have been far too hopeful in their estimation of my own contribution to Pyotr's ultimate composition. Though he did press me for details on *Doctor Faustus* and seemed eager to know whether I considered music to be anything other than an art that diverts us mortals from approaching death, I had little to offer in return. I'm going to tell you the same thing I told him, and feel free to report this to your intelligence agents: no, I don't believe there is an actual Devil to whom one could sell one's soul in order to achieve some superhuman feat."

So that was that. His mission had failed before it had even begun; Alexei had nothing to report to Sretensky and the rest of them, not even some convenient lie that would keep them occupied for a while, allowing him enough time to forestall the doom that threatened Uncle Petya's reputation.

But all was not lost, at least not yet. There was still something Herr Mann could do for him—if Alexei stopped fiddling with the damn key and rustled up the nerve to remove it from his pocket.

While he was desperately trying to find a way of phrasing his request, the old man exhibited once more an uncanny prescience, lowering his voice to say, "I'm sure that's not all you intended to share today, my dear Alyosha. In fact, I know there's something you've left unsaid, something to do with an utterly unpalatable local cheese called Sbrinz. Am I right?"

Alexei had to remind himself to shut his gaping mouth. So the old devil had known all along?

"I haven't read your mind, my boy, if that's what you're thinking. Not even Faust was granted such powers. I happen to possess a key identical to the one I'm positive you brought to our meeting. You see, it takes two keys to gain access to one of the famous Katzenberg vaults, and Petya had entrusted me with one saying that at some point a friend would approach me, and that I was to deliver to that friend the contents of the safe box. Which I'll gladly do, and I promise I won't take a single peek. I assume it's for your eyes only, and so it shall be."

"But...but how are we to...?" Alexei muttered, his eyes pointing at a nearby table, where his private goon had settled, lowering his paper every now and then to glance in their direction.

"Hush, there's no need to panic," the author whispered and leaned closer. "You simply remove the key from your pocket, slide it beneath your napkin and, while pretending to dab your mouth, slip the key inside the linen folds. Then I'll use it to wipe my own mouth, take the key and no one will be the wiser."

It turned out to be as simple as that. As soon as the novelist had slipped Alexei's key in his waistcoat pocket, he rose from his chair and held out his hand, which Alexei distractedly shook, rising to his feet wishing this meeting would go on, for what if their discussion took an intimate turn?

Herr Mann was already putting on his hat, so Alexei started to shower him with praise and gratitude, to which the old author nodded kindly. Just before he took his leave, however, he bent to Alexei's ear and said in a low voice, "My trusty bellhop will soon be delivering Petya's treasure to your room, and rest assured that he operates with the utmost discretion. Our paper-reading friend will never get a whiff of the boy's comings and goings. Which reminds me, as soon as the book I've been toying with comes out, I'll be sure to send you an inscribed copy. I do believe you will enjoy Felix Krull's escapades, and I daresay the little mischief-maker reminds me of you. After all, my dearest Alyosha, what description would suit you better if not that of a confidence man?"

CHAPTER NINE

Though the death-defying stunt that he'd just pulled off had left him highly agitated, as soon as Alexei was in the relative safety of his Alden suite, the extravagant creature comforts drove away the panic. One moment he was a failed spy harboring incriminating evidence on his person and the next a pampered traveler spending a short vacation in style. Alexei briefly wondered about the cost of this enterprise. What was the point of splendor when a much simpler room would have sufficed? Such a paradox, the Soviet state—a stingy mother, screeching at her kids, "Be frugal! We're dirt poor!" while hoarding untold riches.

A little later when Alexei's naked body was immersed in a fragrant bubble bath whose warmth eased the tension of his weary muscles, he recalled the Rabinovich truism on money.

Wealth, perhaps the most sentient of all man-made soulless creations, behaves very much like a lover. Treat it with miserly indifference, stashing it away where it cannot be appreciated, and it leaves you cold. Ravish it, and it repays you with delight.

The finishing touch came when Alexei was toweling dry. He drew the plush gold curtains apart and found himself gazing at a spectacular view of the city doused with thick, cotton-like flakes—a festive snow globe of a place. It didn't take much more than this to make one happy. His joy at the prospect of going for a stroll was such he wasn't dispirited by Sretensky's urgent phone call, which was put through as he dressed. The Colonel was livid and blind drunk. The NKVD was incensed by his failure to record his conversation with the author. What parts of his bourgeois filth they had managed to pick up on their devices had proven completely incomprehensible. Who was that bastard Adrian Leverkühn, and what was his precise connection to Rabinovich? The talking heads of the music department demanded Alexei obtain the original score of this *Apocalypsis* to study in detail whether it contained brainwashing mechanisms provided by American intelligence. The Colonel was even more imaginative. Judging from the closed-door rehearsals, illicit recordings of *Sixteen* and passing allusions the "disgusting German aristocrat" had made about Faust and the devil, Sretensky had deduced that Rabinovich had been involved in some kind of imperialist witches' coven that had manipulated unwitting audiences with black magic. That explained the gobs of beeswax that the old contrabassist had been carrying. The Colonel went on to accuse Alexei of squandering the workers' hard-earned money, overlooking that Alexei hadn't reserved the palatial suite and barked that if the "infernal bourgeois blizzard" continued, resulting in flight cancellations, Alexei would have to cough up the extra money himself.

These empty threats didn't shake Alexei. If anything, he was amused by the thought that the mighty NKVD was as befuddled as he. As he gazed at the quickening snowfall, feeling like a child on a snow-day, his thoughts turned once again to the phantom of Uncle Petya's mother. Some analogies could be drawn between the mysterious woman whose portrait Khrushchev had painted and the shady figure of Stalin's mother. Aside from sharing the name Ekaterina, both women had been born to lowly stock and risen to wealth. Moreover, like Ekaterina Rabinovich, Keke Geladze had been an extremely touchy subject with her fearsome son. Rumor had it that, upon her precious Soso's ascension to power, she believed herself invincible by proxy and had gone on to boast about a great number of infidelities she had committed in her youthful days as a charwoman. But even more important than the secrecy surrounding the two mothers was their determination to elevate their cherished only sons. This devotional fervor haunted Rabinovich and Stalin, so that neither ever seemed entirely satisfied with the glory he achieved. Both were constantly striving for more success, as if to please their Dear Mamas.

Alexei's mind strayed to the memory of a book by Sigmund Freud that Uncle Petya had translated from the German. It was a treatise on Leonardo da Vinci, based on a dream recorded by the painter in his journals. Freud made much of Leonardo's lifelong obsession with the mother he'd been brutally separated from. The book had a resounding impact on Alexei, robbing him of two nights' sleep.

That had been years ago, but now the remembrance of that treatise chased away the drowsiness induced by Alexei's bath. In the essay, Freud maintained that Leonardo's untimely separation from his mother at the age of five was the root of da Vinci's sexual frustration and his precocious, multifaceted genius. Freud's work vividly described this moment of separation during which the mother, yet another impoverished peasant, embraced her only son and pressed passionate kisses on this mouth as ferociously as a lover. It was this subconscious quest for his mother that Freud claimed had fueled the restless psyche of the Renaissance. Could it have been something equally painful that had endowed Rabinovich with his inexhaustible talent? Had Uncle Petya's wondrous gifts been merely the product of a child's violent separation from a loving mother? But even if every single word that Khrushchev had spoken about Ekaterina Rabinovich were the truth, no one is as vulnerable at age sixteen as he is at five. Alexei unthinkingly dialed the reception desk to place a long-distance call to Moscow.

Faina picked up on the first ring as if she'd been waiting by the phone, yet her voice didn't betray a hint of worry. Instead, she sounded overjoyed and made a terrible fuss over the cost of the call. After Alexei assured her it would all be taken care of by the State, he told Faina about his meeting with the Nobel laureate and how well the biography was turning out. He went on to describe the luxury of his suite's appointments, for knowing that her Alyosha was going places, meeting famous people and surrounding himself with riches was the greatest gift he could give to Faina.

After hanging up, Alexei stretched spread-eagled on the vast bed atop a cloud of silk, cotton and down in a moment of self-admiration. But since he wasn't by nature a self-important person, he felt the tug of guilt. Not only had he lied to Faina about writing Uncle Petya's biography but he had long ago abandoned the task of actually writing the book. This sting of conscience sent Alexei to his suitcase, from which he withdrew the thin sheaf of his neglected manuscript before settling back in bed.

His initial perusal was disappointing. He was not a gifted writer, and there were far too many direct quotes from *The Aphorisms*. It read like a compilation of the book's strongest passages. There were some keepers, especially in the passages devoted to Rabinovich's music. Could Freud's theory on Leonardo be applied to Uncle Petya as well? Could it be said that all of his music had been an attempt to grasp at the ghost of his lost mother?

"In music, one can find an abstract yet thorough account of the stunning tale that is humanity, which no other medium can offer. There's nothing in Goethe or in the historical texts relating Napoleon's rise and fall that can't be found intact, palpating and alive, in Beethoven's musical corpus. No scientist or scholar can recreate with such baffling mastery the promise and despair that humankind was faced with at the dawn of the twentieth century as Gustav Mahler does. Music is not merely a crumb of the eternal in the groaning belly of us mortals. It is, above all else, a synopsis of all things human."

One could argue that it's normal, or at least expected, for an artist to be obsessed by his work. In the case of Rabinovich, obsession was an understatement. Having lived by his side, Alexei thought it safe to say that music had been the only reality extant for Uncle Petya.

This musical monomania, which at times could reach a madman's intensity, was evident in Uncle Petya's indifference toward any aspect of life not related to music. He barely scanned the supplements devoted to the arts in *Pravda* and the foreign press; the rest of the news—politics, war, the economy, scientific matters—left him unmoved. "The world is a profoundly boring place," Alexei recalled him saying once. "Life is boring, death is boring, and war and hunger are colossally boring. There's no point in reading about any of it. It's all happened before and will happen again. The mere thought of the past, or the future, for that matter, is enough to deaden one's soul."

As a result of this disinterest, Uncle Petya had never heard of penicillin until 1949, when tonsillitis left him voiceless and hysterical. After treatment, he considered his speedy recovery nothing short of miraculous, describing his physician as a wonder-working saint. Unless it concerned music, nothing was worth his time. Where contemporary composers were concerned, however, he absorbed every detail with greed, engrossed by the changes music underwent in the early Fifties. In musical matters, Uncle Petya was not only extremely knowledgeable, but also a voracious gossip. He wanted to know everything about the work of his peers around the world, although most of the time he was annoyed by the twentieth century musical trends. "This Brazilian fellow, Villa-what's-his-name? He seems to have robbed Bach blind in a cute way. Find me some of his stuff." Or, "Is this John Cage for real? I mean, four-and-a-half minutes of fucking silence, filled ad-lib by the audience talking and farting, and he calls it 'chance music' and 'aleatoric art'?' Hush! Don't speak, boy. Just gobble up your beans and blast out a good loud one! There: *Fiat ars!*" On the other hand, when he received a telegram from David Ben-Gurion, the Prime Minister of Israel, inviting him to a banquet in Tel Aviv in honor of Rabinovich's long support of the Jewish cause, Uncle Petya had handed the telegram to Alexei, perplexed. "Hold on, so Israel is a state now? We're sure this Ben-Gurion guy is not some Manhattan Jew pulling our leg?"

Here the would-be Rabinovich biographer was confronted by a seemingly insurmountable problem. How is one to make sense of a world-renowned musician, a cosmopolitan artist and diplomat, who at the same time treated the constant evolution of humanity with the hostility of a burrow-dwelling gnome? Could this obsessive focus on music alone be viewed as proof of a lifelong endeavor to wreak havoc on the world by musical means? Alexei still did not believe that Uncle Petya was capable of such a supernatural influence on his audience. As for the lost-mother scenario feeding his mania, it might be intriguing enough for a novel. But life was rarely novelistic, because, after all, no single person was controlling it.

He'd have to dig deeper if he hoped to achieve a publishable judgment of Uncle Petya. He still hoped that some pertinent fact would be unearthed from the vault's contents. Maybe he should approach the maternal specter haunting Uncle Petya's oeuvre in psychoanalytical terms, as Freud would. But how was he to do that? Should he count the number of times the word "mother" appeared in *The Aphorisms?* Or in the self-penned lyrics of his songs and libretti, perhaps? In what context should he then interpret this profusion of mothers?

Mother, Alexei thought, as he lay back on the fluffy pillow, and slept like the dead.

Overnight the blizzard ran out of breath and the whiteness settled.

When Alexei took to the streets at ten in the morning, he was surrounded by a spectacle whose magnificence almost hurt the eyes.

Suddenly it was obvious why anyone would defy the law in order to cross the borders into the West. The proof was right here. He was breathing it in along with the crisp air that descended from the Albis hills. He was looking right at it in the jolly-red faces of the Germans crowding the streets in anticipation of the Silvester festivities. No one would ever attempt such a feat just because they'd been driven by some musical hocus-pocus. The throngs reportedly defecting from Communist countries were obeying a base yet all-too-human instinct—they were running away from poverty and ugliness and toward affluence and beauty.

It wasn't that Alexei loathed his life in Moscow or that he felt particularly tempted by the song of the capitalist sirens beckoning through the lushly decorated windows. If anything, having had the chance to assess life inside and outside of Russia, he'd concluded that if an earthly Heaven or Hell truly existed, he hadn't yet seen either. People in different parts of the world enjoyed different pleasures and suffered a different brand of misery. He was neither a dyed-in-the-wool Communist nor a xenophile with bourgeois inclinations.

Abroad, the olfactory sense was the first to come wildly alive. In this case, it was the sweet harshness of the Alpine air. There were the mouthwatering smell of baked pastry dough, the perfumes emanating from women's bosoms, the coffee, the chocolate, the tobacco—each dizzying enough to sell one's soul for a single inhalation. The absence of certain smells was also welcomed. Alexei appreciated that the collective exhalations of the passersby weren't infected, as they were in the Soviet, with the fumes of cheap alcohol.

Leaving the city streets behind, he climbed the Lindenhof hill for a view of the lake. When he reached the peak, he lit a cigarette and let his eyes roam the sights. Soon he was back at his morbid game of pointless melodrama counting the things upon which Uncle Petya would never again gaze.

For God's sake, lighten up! If anything, you should be grateful that Uncle Petya lived at all—it's thanks to him that you, right now, can enjoy all this!

If Alexei couldn't feel truly happy, he ought at least to feel grateful, he thought. Happiness is fleeting; it has wings. This is why you need other people: they help you pin it down.

* * *

After a bit of shopping, Alexei returned to the Alden, where he was met by an ominous surprise. While handing him the key, the concierge said that a voluminous package containing some sort of cheese had arrived for Herr Samoilenko. Shortly thereafter the package had been collected by a gentleman from the Soviet Consulate, the concierge reported. Alexei's disappointment turned to panic. It seemed that Herr Mann had kept his end of the deal, but thanks to Alexei's stupidity, the block of Sbrinz, along with whatever else was in the vault, had been intercepted by the KGB.

I should've stayed put! Alexei thought. I'm the greatest idiot ever born! There's no point in beating myself up. What's done cannot be undone.

The phone was ringing rabidly from beyond the bedroom door, now ajar, when Alexei entered the suite. He froze in terror, imaging that an assassin with a length of rope stretched between black-gloved hands waited for him by the phone.

Alexei staggered into the blessedly empty bedroom and picked up the receiver. Blame the package on Thomas Mann, a voice shrieked in his head. Yet that wouldn't only be dishonorable, but also ineffective. Why should the elderly author conspire against the Soviet Union? Sretensky once more barked what barely sounded like Russian.

It took Alexei a couple of minutes before he realized that, owing to some inexplicable miracle, his life had been spared. The Colonel was shouting, "What the fuck are we supposed to do with a ton of cheese that is stinking up the place? Is this that old faggot's idea of a joke?" When it finally dawned on Alexei that the package mentioned by the concierge had only contained a block of Sbrinz, Alexei felt such immense relief that he nearly burst out laughing. At the same time his heart sank. If nothing accompanied what the Colonel was describing as a "petrified turd that needed a fucking chainsaw to cut," it probably meant that the vault had already been emptied by Uncle Petya. "Wait for further instructions," Sretensky ordered before hanging up with a deafening bang. Alexei rushed to the sideboard where he poured a huge glass of whisky. As he tossed it back, someone softly rapped at the door.

The rather furtive knock seized Alexei with a fresh wave of terror. "Who's there?" he tried calling out but his voice had evaporated. The knock was repeated and this time a low, German-inflected voice said, "Special delivery from Herr Mann."

Alexei approached the door and held his breath. Before him stood the same handsome bellhop who had relieved him of his luggage; seeing Alexei's deathly pallor, he winked. He held a long white envelope with the monogram of Thomas and Katia Mann. The young man whispered, "It's okay. You see, most people confuse our country's famous neutrality with apathy. Let's just say that Herr Mann enjoys the friendship and respect of our preventive *Polizei*. Have a nice day, sir." And with that, the lovely youth departed.

The oddly religious thought that the Virgin Mary, too, had rejoiced in the arrival of a messenger crossed Alexei's mind as he tore open the envelope. Inside was a photograph, turned the other way around, so that Alexei first gazed at the inscription on its back.

The handwriting was unmistakably Uncle Petya's, its blue ink faded to a pale indigo. It seemed to be a fragment of Latin text:

Inflammatus et accensus Obstupescit omnis sensus

The couplet was at once obscure and familiar. Trying to remember where he'd encountered it, Alexei flipped the photograph over.

The face staring at him, although he'd never seen it before at so young an age, was instantly recognizable as Uncle Petya's mother. Ekaterina looked to be in mid-adolescence and, judging from the luxury of her surroundings, it must have been taken shortly after her rapid ascension from humility to princedom. Her dress, blooming with ripples of fine silk and lace, had likely been forced on her by watchdog maids. She was half-seated on a swing, probably her sole entertainment in the cloistered prison of the remote dacha. Her girlish face glared at the photographer, her upper lip curled slightly with a hint of malice, her entire awkward posture saying, "Let's get this nonsense over with."

These details aside, it was a beautiful picture of a beautiful girl. Uncle Petya had been right in cherishing it and in keeping it safe from prying eyes. But how had this memento survived the fire of the Revolution? What did the Latin inscription on the back mean?

Then it came to him, along with the music to which it had been set. It was an excerpt from *Stabat Mater Speciosa*, a Catholic nativity hymn evoking the Virgin at the manger, beaming with happiness just after she gave birth to Jesus. "Thus the beauteous mother stood." Alexei hurried to the suite's grand piano and played the music that accompanied the Latin text. It was such a simple tune, yet so achingly gorgeous. In its soft lilt tinged with melancholy, Alexei heard a recollection of this lost beauty, this youthful grace gone to waste as the mocking girlish grin turned into a charred skull, the ivy-woven ropes of the swing burned to ashes. "Thus, with the fire of love aflame, all other feelings silent, tame," Alexei hummed to the music, his eyes fixed on the photo.

The phone's brutal ringing interrupted him, but Alexei did not pick up. He knew it would be Sretensky and he knew what his orders would be. He was to depart at once for his next destination, which he also knew. The photo, this invaluable treasure of Uncle Petya's waiting in the Katzenberg vaults, had been a dead giveaway. The ringing became so annoying that he had no choice but to answer. The second that the Colonel furiously pronounced "Florentsiya," Alexei felt those four syllables race down his body like lightning, cutting him in half and leaving him numb. He could even tell whence this bolt of pleasure exited his flesh, almost burning the skin with the intensity of its desire. It was right there, in the center of his loins.

CHAPTER TEN

What rare gems were the dark eyes of Vittorio Amedeo Alessandrini! Like pools in a starless night they reflected what was before them—the ruby-red of a glass of Chianti, the shimmer of a dancing candle flame and the darkness stirred by the lithe beast of desire. At times, Alexei had thought that he could spend an eternity simply gazing at those eyes. He could forego food and water, the air he breathed, if allowed to look at what was clearly the work of a deity.

The rest of Signor Alessandrini was equally perfect, as if crafted by a host of gifted masters. He had the chiseled face of Botticellian splendor with a high brow, aquiline nose, full lips and a sinewy body reminiscent of Bellini's *Perseus*. His baritone voice was as mellow as the greatest of Vivaldi's solo cello passages.

Vittorio had been born exactly a year after Alexei and the two had met in Paris where the twenty-two-year-old Florentine had been stationed. At that time, the timid cultural attaché to the Soviet Embassy spoke a broken, Slavic-heavy French. The young Italian, on the other hand, was fluent; his singsong pronunciation added an enchanting sauciness to the snobbish French vowels and tricky nasal consonants. The result was that Vittorio usually did the talking and Alexei did the listening. This disparity ran deeper than mere linguistic ease. For although a year his junior, Signor Alessandrini was far more well-read, worldly and sociable than his awkward Soviet friend. Captivated, Comrade Samoilenko would listen for hours as Vittorio recounted stories from his motherland, each revealing a world unknown to Alexei. He had been rendered ignorant on hundreds of subjects by the Soviet education system, whose sole purpose was to wipe out all knowledge unrelated to Marx, Engels, Lenin and the victorious Bolshevik *Revolutsiya*. Alexei knew nothing about art, history or religion. Thanks to Vittorio's patient narratives, he first heard of Caravaggio, Oscar Wilde and Federico García Lorca, who bore an unnerving resemblance to Vittorio. Thanks to Vittorio, Alexei first heard Leon Trotsky described as an altogether different person than the vermin he'd learned to despise since childhood. Thanks to Vittorio, Alexei learned that not all Americans endeavored night and day to bring about the destruction of Communism. Alexei also came to understand that *bourgeois* didn't necessarily mean someone who would gladly step on the necks of the destitute; all sorts of artists and scientists and politicians had been bona fide bourgeois. Vittorio also introduced his Soviet friend to the concept that God was not the illnesses of a pagan intellect. Descartes, Voltaire, Liszt and Einstein, brilliant thinkers and benefactors of humanity, had been devoutly religious. Even Bach, the cornerstone of modern music, had been a pious employee of the St. Thomas Church, dutifully composing hundreds of Christian hymns, cantatas and oratorios that glorified God.

But it was neither through his diverse knowledge nor spiritual nature that Vittorio had reach into the deepest recesses of the young Russian's soul. It was the Florentine nuncio's conquest of Alexei's heart, for he had revealed to Alexei the self-evident truth about his body's long-suppressed need for love and comfort. Vittorio shared the same proclivities.

It had been an epiphany for Alexei to hear Vittorio utter for the first time the scalding word, its guilty syllables stretching out like a snake's limber body. A storm was breaking when Vittorio confirmed what he had long suspected as the cause of poor Uncle Rodya's undoing. And it was an outright shock when Vittorio went on to imply that Rabinovich might also be similarly inclined. Before meeting Vittorio, Alexei had often wondered whether his aberration was somehow unique and so all the more damning and unspeakable. He had regarded his excruciating adolescent urges and the wraith-like images of male schoolmates as the symptoms of some cruel disease. Now, from the mouth of the most unlikely tutor, he was discovering that the same affliction had ravaged millions of men since time immemorial. Not to mention the times when such abnormal practices were deemed honorable and indulged in freely and proudly! It baffled the mind that so many immortals could have been homosexuals. Could they be true, the things Vittorio claimed of Plato and Sappho, of countless Ancient Greeks of all social ranks, from the lowest of the low to Alexander the Great? Had this Catullus, whom Vittorio quoted often, have actually existed or was he a mischievous invention of his friend intended to taunt and excite Alexei to the point of shameful physical reactions from the waist down? And on and on the list went—Roman emperors, philosophers and painters, men of science and the cloth. It seemed that craving your own sex was a passion that knew no boundaries, social or otherwise. There were stories which, though they made his cheeks burn with lust, Alexei refused to believe thinking them tall tales designed to ridicule him. It couldn't be true that Michelangelo and Shakespeare had written sonnets inspired by their male lovers. Nor that Tchaikovsky, a figure widely venerated in his motherland, had been driven to suicide by a clandestine court of honor of his peers in order to save himself from being found out as a sodomite.

Alexei had little to offer in return for this torrent of illumination. He believed that Vittorio, though pretending to be fascinated by stories of Soviet daily life, secretly pitied him for the meagerness of the socialist creeds he'd been brought up on and for the mundane reality he had inhabited prior to meeting Uncle Petya. Since their mutual attraction, for all its flagrance, never crossed the line of the accidental grazing of knees under the table, Comrade Samoilenko spent most of their meetings simply listening.

But there was one more area of common ground and here Alexei was the expert—the private life and the music of Pyotr Rabinovich.

Vittorio had been an avid admirer of Uncle Petya's music since his early years in Catholic school, when, as a soprano in the boys' choir, he'd sung several of Rabinovich's popular choral works. Their soaring melodies belied the fact that they were mostly settings of dull proletarian poetry exalting the heroic struggle of the working class. Being as musical as Alexei, Vittorio had spent many years studying Rabinovich's music. He had eventually developed such an obsession with the Russian composer that he had arranged his transfer to the Parisian Nunciature in the hope of meeting the great man. So, there was nothing he liked better than to sit back and relish the stories Alexei told concerning Vittorio's favorite genius. These images of the composer's daily life engrossed the young nuncio like fragments of some lost masterpiece finally coming to light.

During his first visits to the *Ambassade,* whenever Rabinovich happened to come upon the two of them chatting, Vittorio had been awestruck to the point of muteness. He stared at his idol, also tongue-tied by such reverence. Even when Vittorio managed to overcome his initial bewilderment, the two of them had nothing to say. Worse than that, *il Maestro* had taken an instant dislike to this goggle-eyed visitor who interrupted his daily routine and distracted Alexei from his secretarial duties. "Does that swarthy friend of yours actually live here?" he would ask in a sudden burst of anger. "Because I'm constantly bumping into him sneaking along the hallways like a burglar. Is he casing the joint? Is the Vatican planning to invade us? And what is so amusing, all cooped up in the library, that you're both constantly screeching like a pair of hyenas?"

Almost a decade had passed since those carefree days, and during all this time Alexei had neither seen nor heard Vittorio. The two of them exchanged the occasional letter, which had to be meticulously chaste lest their correspondence be intercepted by a censor. But not a day passed that Alexei hadn't thought of those lustrous eyes catching the light, of those perfect lips curved in a smile, of Vittorio's hands cradling his own in an achingly prolonged handshake. Whenever assailed by insomnia, his favorite fantasy never failed to bring the most delicious sleep. It was based on Vittorio's talk about Plato and that ethereal realm where things and people had first come to exist in their pure form. In that place, Vittorio and he were not separate entities but a single being who never knew longing or the misery of solitary nights. Nowhere was Alexei happier than in that make-believe land of dreams.

Yet tonight, despite the ampleness of his hotel bed, Alexei couldn't rely on the lulling effect of that fantasy. He tossed and turned, his mind flickering like a lamp unable to bear the wattage of desire. Part of him couldn't wait to take in Vittorio's feline smile, those coy eyes but another part of him was terrified. Would things go back to the way they were, with their comfortable companionship, or had something changed in the meantime? After all, Vittorio was a nuncio and had likely moved on from the simple innocence of those days. What if he'd crossed the threshold Alexei was still too cowardly to consider and put his fancy talk about male Eros into action? How childish his old Russian friend would seem to him. A man almost thirty years old and still a virgin!

There was another question that kept Alexei in a state of restless fervor, this one tinged by jealousy. Why had Uncle Petya visited Vittorio in secret almost a year ago? What could Vittorio have contributed in the creation of *Sixteen* that Alexei couldn't provide? Rabinovich hadn't even liked the high-and-mighty Signor Alessandrini, yet he had sought him out in the final months leading to his death.

The thought of the two men meeting in secret behind closed doors incensed Alexei until he had to bite the pillow so as to not cry out.

The following morning Comrade Samoilenko was little more than a staggering husk, stumbling from his room to down a cup of coffee in the hotel restaurant before shuffling outside to a taxi. He conked out in the back seat, and the driver had to shake him awake when they arrived at the airport. If it hadn't been for a secret agent who materialized out of the airport crowd to lead him to the correct departure gate, he'd have certainly missed his flight. But when he sank back in his seat, hoping for a couple of hours of rest before the plane landed in Florence, Alexei once again found himself too agitated to sleep.

Alexei was afflicted by a severe case of Imminent
Happiness Psychosis. The term, which he had coined, was
inspired by Rabinovich, who all too frequently had been
stricken with the same nonsensical illness. The malady
usually occurred whenever the composer had been anxiously
awaiting some happy occasion such as the performance of
a much-loved work. The condition was similar to hysteria.
Just when everything looked like smooth sailing ahead, he
would call Alexei on the phone or start yelling from the next
room to demand an ambulance to rush him to the hospital to
be treated for palpitations, a lethal bout of asthma, incipient
anaphylactic shock, spontaneous metastatic cancer or some
other life-threatening illness he'd run across in a medical
book. There was no talking him out of it, since the panic
transformed him into the picture of sickness. He would be
soaked with sweat, his heart racing like a bird's, his mouth dry
and his voice issuing a veritable death rattle.

He soon transmitted his terror to Alexei, who would rush
to call for a doctor, while Rabinovich, usually exhausted by
this time, lay on the sofa with his hands crossed on his chest
like a dead Pope and entirely out of danger.

As the plane soared across the beryl skies, Alexei
unconsciously mirrored Uncle Petya's neurotic behavior
and became convinced that his approaching meeting with
Vittorio would never come to pass. The plane would fall prey
to the dozens of misfortunes Rabinovich always claimed
were lurking to exterminate you the moment you boarded
an aircraft. A fatal downward draft would hurl the aircraft
down in a tenth of a second reducing him to a fine paste;
the engines or the wings (or possibly both) would catch fire
or fall off; the plane would collide with another airplane or

with an unseen mountain; a flock of suicidal birds would hurl themselves against the cockpit's windscreen, blinding the pilot; a comet would strike the earth, dragging the plane into the gravitational field of its apocalyptic descent; they'd run out of fuel and go down like a colossal turd of steel, and the shot of cognac he'd just knocked back to fortify himself would be regurgitated in his sleep, causing him to choke on his own vomit. Or, in a more realistic approach to insanity, the plane would land safely, but Alexei would be detained by the airport authorities, kidnapped by American spies or assassinated by an inexplicably vengeful NKVD. Whatever the tragedy, he'd never see Vittorio again. After resigning himself to an untimely death, Alexei went so far as to fantasize about Vittorio's reaction when he learned the news and was brought to the morgue to identify the remains. What a scene he would make! The gorgeous priest falling to his knees, wailing, rending his garments and tearing at his hair, turned white overnight from sheer anguish, like a Sicilian widow.

However, when the cheerful voice of the stewardess informed the passengers that they would soon be landing at the Portola Airport, the intoxication of fear began to diminish, turning into maddening, childish impatience. When he gazed from the window and saw the glistening ribbon of the Arno bathed in sunlight, serenity overtook him, like a voice whispering a tender *Benevento* to his heart.

What a beauty Florence was, and how he had missed it, even though he had visited the birthplace of the Renaissance only once. With its trove of masterworks so abundantly displayed, its glorious architecture and the splendor of the Tuscan countryside surrounding it, the ancient city seemed the ideal setting for a creature as beguiling as Vittorio.

As the plane landed, Alexei wondered about the reason behind all those defections Uncle Petya and *Sixteen* were accused of having provoked. From what Khrushchev had revealed, the two old musicians had both been raving about people lost to the cruelty of the regime, claiming that they simply wanted to be reunited with loved ones who had died. Perhaps music had nothing at all to do with their mad determination, and all that was driving them was love. Even if *Sixteen* had somehow caused this death-defying need to seek out the final resting place of their loved ones, what was so wrong with that?

As Alexei gathered his luggage to disembark, his mind went to the photo of Ekaterina Rabinovich as a young girl, utterly unaware of the love that would enfold her on the other side of the Atlantic and the brutal death she and the father of her child would suffer. If all that had been true, what would Alexei have done in Uncle Petya's place? If someone had murdered Faina or even Vittorio, what would he do in return? Though he couldn't speak for Rabinovich, Alexei knew that he would make it his purpose in life to find the evil entity and destroy it.

Alexei's only visit to Florence in the spring of 1951 had been threatened early on with catastrophe. Rabinovich had had some pressing diplomatic business to attend to and thought that they could prolong their stay, so that he'd have the time to show Alexei the city's spectacular sights and flavors. Alexei had been overjoyed and had even done some reading on the masters of the Renaissance he'd soon be feasting his eyes on. He'd even gone ahead and bought a Russian-to-Italian book of basic phrases.

Then, just as they'd arrived, things had gone horribly wrong. Although Uncle Petya had assured Alexei that he'd booked a regal suite at the Villa Lucrezia, the magnificent hotel in question happened to be situated not in Florence but in Venice. Moreover, that weekend Florence had been overflowing with tourists, and everything short of a stable had long been booked. Alexei couldn't find a single room. By the time he'd gotten back to the taxi, Uncle Petya was by turns livid and devastated, shouting that unless the situation was resolved at once, he'd throw himself into the Arno. On the verge of tears, Alexei turned to the taxi driver for help. Luckily the man was more than accommodating. After a few minutes of haggling, Alexei managed to secure a room in what the driver assured him was a luxurious hotel that had once been a duke's palazzo.

However, this was not the case. Sure, the building was grand with dozens of rooms facing an inner courtyard, but the old palazzo was dilapidated, had no electricity and had only one bathroom per floor. As for their room, it had likely been the servants' quarters. The long, gloomy bedroom had a view of a brick wall, twelve single beds, a huge fireplace and little else in way of furniture. When Alexei had shoved the stuck door open, laden with their combined luggage, Rabinovich threw a fit. He cursed everything and everyone who had ever lived, Alexei included, for what was clearly the result of his own mistake. "If I spot a single one of those beastly Mediterranean roaches this place is surely infested with, I swear I'll strangle you with my own two hands! Do something immediately and get us out of this shithole!"

Alexei had burst into tears. Uncle Petya, overcome with guilt at having ruined his secretary's first visit to Florence, contacted the Soviet consul, demanding that they be put up at the consulate for the duration of their visit. Terrified at the thought of provoking the wrath of Stalin's pet composer, the man assured Rabinovich he was willing to give up his own bedroom to make up for the trial they'd been through. Presently a limousine rumbled down the *stradone,* and a panicked chauffeur, bowing incessantly to them, loaded their luggage in the trunk and told them to make themselves comfortable for the short ride.

The two of them had spent a marvelous week strolling the city's meandering streets and sweeping hillsides, visiting museums and churches and gorging on the local cuisine in cheap yet astonishingly good *trattorias.* Alexei's heart sank at the prospect of returning to dreary and inhospitable Moscow. Compared to the hastily consumed alcohol of Russian pubs, which could cause blindness, delicious house wine was available for a few hundred *lire* even in the humblest *osteria.* And it could be drunk while gazing across piazzas teeming with dark, attractive youths in tight white pants who lounged and smoked on their *Vespas.* The place was heaven on earth. How unfair life had been to exile him in the freezing northern reaches of the world, when he could have been born right here, with music-like Italian as his mother tongue. How different things might have turned out with Vittorio! Ah, but dreams were dreams.

As he plodded out of the airport and into the glaring sun of Florence still woolly-headed, a word suddenly shone in his mind. *Animula.* Alexei cherished the memory of the word, repeating it under his breath like a charm, a prayer of the faithless.

In his final hours, the Emperor Hadrian famously composed a poem, addressing the opening verse to *Animula, vagula, blandula,* a "tender, roaming little soul." Many had since viewed this poem as a dying man's farewell to life itself, but the truth may have been far more intimate. As Vittorio had told him, the little soul in question had in all likelihood been a Greek youth by the name of Antinous, who had been Hadrian's lover, and whose untimely death at the age of nineteen the Emperor had mourned. Such had been the greatness of his devotion that he'd named an entire city after Antinous and ensured that his lost lover would be revered and glorified as a god. Ever after, in their gradually dwindling correspondence, the young priest always greeted him in his letters with "My dear *animula,*" confident that the private reference would be too vague to attract the potential censor's attention.

The Apostolic Nunciature to Florence had ceased to operate back in the 1860s, yet the Holy See still retained a consul in that city. For the last two years, Monsignor Vittorio Amedeo Alessandrini had been installed in a villa on the Oltrarno hill, an elegant seventeenth century building surrounded by cypress trees and graced with a stunning view of Florence. And now a long black vehicle with Vatican plates, chauffeured by an exceedingly polite, red-haired priest waited to transport Alexei to the nuncio's abode as per His Eminence's orders.

Alexei spent the short drive with his face glued to the window. When the car crossed the Arno and climbed the sparsely wooded hill, his excitement escalated. He might have been a dog whipping his tail with joy.

At the entrance of the villa, Vittorio was waiting for him in his new finery. The purple *ferraiolo* was parted to expose a thick golden cross perched on the swell of his brawny chest. Alexei was barely out of the car when Vittorio enveloped him in a tight embrace. Alexei felt the tautness of Vittorio's body pressed against his own limp flesh. Terrified that his groin would reveal the fact that his penis had risen to participate in the hug, Alexei thought to pull back. No, nothing had changed.

He could feel it in the tingling pleasure of their joined bodies even when he finally stepped back, with his hands instantly dropping to his crotch. There was the old spark—a flame, really, a wild, untamable conflagration— still raging. He was finally, blessedly, home.

Love will do you a world of evil before it does you any good, Rabinovich seemed to whisper. A few years ago, Uncle Petya'd come upon Alexei re-reading a creased letter from Vittorio. Alexei had hurriedly thrust the letter in his pocket, face aflame with embarrassment. The older man was gazing forlornly from the doorway. And then, as he turned, Uncle Petya had delivered that oddly hurtful pronouncement.

Perhaps what had brought that awkward moment back was the solemn look that now crossed Vittorio's face. In a serious tone, he asked Alexei to hand over any recording equipment he might be harboring. "I'm sorry for this intrusion, *carissimo,* but my hands are tied. I'm sure your visit is of the purest intention, but His Holiness views this house as sovereign Vatican soil and is very strict about the presence of devices used for espionage."

Alexei had quickly removed the Capital recording contraption and the camera-pen from his suitcase. It hurt to be treated like a spy, especially since Father Alessandrini was something of a double agent. According to allusions made in his last letter, Vittorio had been involved in an intricate Vatican conspiracy during the last two years. On the one hand, he had confessed in his letter, Vittorio appeared to enjoy close ties to Cardinal Roncalli, his old boss at the Parisian Nunciature, and had taken active part in the cardinal's discreet campaign for the papal throne. On the other hand, he was a sworn *in pectore*, a confessor secretly appointed by Pius XII, who, though gravely ill, was loath to surrender the papacy to the one-time farmer from Bergamo.

Vittorio led Alexei to a ground-floor study, closing the door behind them. There must have been furniture in that room—books, a desk, a chair into which he felt his weary body sink, an open window that gave onto the garden—but Alexei barely noticed them as his entire being was trained on Vittorio's face. It was as though a hypnotic, mesmerizing halo emanated from the sun-kissed features and the shock of black hair.

"First, allow me to offer my profound condolences on the passing of Signor Rabinovich. At times, it still seems unreal that he's no longer among us. And second, please accept my apologies for keeping from you the visit he paid me almost a year ago. I wanted so much to tell you about it, *carissimo*, because the poor Maestro seemed so overwrought with anguish, but he swore me not to breathe a word to anyone. He actually demanded my confessional confidence, which, of course, I granted him."

Alexei had minded at the time and had been terribly angry with Vittorio, but now he couldn't bring himself to resent his old friend for complying with the rules of his profession. He was curious what it had all been about. Why had Uncle Petya chosen to confide in the young priest who he never seemed to like?

"Did his visit have anything to do with the composition of *Sixteen?*" Alexei asked.

Vittorio shook his head. "Nothing of the sort; he never even mentioned the piece, though I supposed it had something to do with the Maestro's most peculiar question. It took me by surprise so that, at first, I thought Signor Rabinovich was joking. But no, his query seemed to be in earnest. The fact is the Maestro wanted to know if I had positive proof that God existed, and if He did, whether He might be bent to someone's will."

The ties of Pyotr Rabinovich to the Roman Catholic Church had been perhaps the most irritating thorn the Party had had to suffer in its godless paw. By the late Twenties, with Christianity all but eradicated in the Soviet Union, the Pope had naturally become one of the most fiercely reviled figures. He was branded a typical aristocratic power monger, an enslaver of the ignorant masses and the last in a long procession of brutal oppressors who obfuscated the proletariat with the opium of religion. However, at around the same time, Rabinovich had made the acquaintance of Cardinal Valeri, a much more moderate prelate, and during the composer's first appointment to the Paris Embassy, the bond between the two had become even stronger. Alexei knew that this friendship hadn't been of a religious nature but more a sort of a musical affinity. Valeri loved the music and songs of his Russian friend, and Rabinovich was a man incapable of not loving anyone who loved his music. Thus, the first colossal scandal had ensued—an unannounced Rabinovich premiere of *Ave Maria* at Notre Dame de Paris, dedicated to his Catholic friend. The Politburo had been apoplectic with rage yet unable to correct the offense without further advertising the scandalous event. Also, the fact that the concert had been sold out and was followed by a month of weekly performances in churches and music halls, with all the revenue handed over to the State by Rabinovich, was enough to dismiss the whole thing. The Vatican's considerable wealth was its one asset that was acceptable to the Soviet Union. And so, another, unusual manifestation of the composer blossomed.

Within the next year, Rabinovich had produced a steady flow of religious music that became instant hits, gripping worldwide Catholic audiences like an exotic Russian virus. The foreign press had a field day. *The Times* and others called him an atheist Bach. The composer never spoke publicly on the subject, as though it was indeed through divine inspiration that the hymns, cantatas and Masses came to him. During that period, Rabinovich poured out some of his finest music for the benefit of churchgoers and the national Soviet budget. Then, in 1944, when Valeri's nunciature in Paris ended, Rabinovich abruptly ended his religious music career.

But his preoccupation with religious music didn't extend to metaphysical need. Uncle Petya had been as unmoved by the greater mysteries of life and death as any faithless contemporary. Alexei still recalled Uncle Petya dismissing the whole question of God's existence as a matter of no personal importance. "I mean, could a tiny cell in my gut, whose sole purpose in life and subsequent conception of the universe is the breaking-up of the food I eat into nutrients and shit, ever grasp the things that go on in my mind? Of course not! Well, neither do I presume to understand how the cosmos was created, or by whom, and what that Creator might be like. It simply doesn't concern me."

However, that was not the man who had suddenly barged into Father Alessandrini's study.

At first, Vittorio told Alexei, he had hardly recognized the disheveled man with nicotine-stained fingers darting nervously through untidy hair, red eyes gleaming with a barely contained madness. How could the poised and cool Maestro be the same person as this wreck teetering before him, his breath sharp with gin? "Signor Rabinovich! It's a pleasure and an honor to welcome you to my humble abode, though I wish you'd informed me of your visit so I could have made the necessary arrangements. Please, sit. Is everything okay at home? There's nothing wrong, I hope."

"Alyosha is fine," Rabinovich had said curtly, sinking into a chair. "But he doesn't know I'm here, nor must he ever know. It may be dangerous for him and that cannot happen at any cost. In fact, consider this a confession, if that'll make you keep quiet. I mean it, Padre. You mustn't breathe a word, because this might turn out to be dangerous for you."

Letting out a pained sigh, the Maestro coughed, took a cigarette out of a crumpled pack and lit it with trembling hands. As he exhaled a thick tendril of smoke, Rabinovich surprised Monsignor Alessandrini with a question no one had ever uttered to the priest.

"Don't give me any of your official bullshit. I didn't come all this way to be jerked about like the idiots you preach to. Answer me truthfully, as if you're unbiased in the matter. Does God exist, and if he does, what is he made of?"

It took Vittorio a while to come up with a reply he hoped didn't sound too stolidly pedantic. "God is timeless, ageless, and—at least according to Saint Thomas Aquinas—He is incorporeal. He is not made of anything, rather He resides in every single part of His creation, be it animate or not, in spirit. He is present in the air we breathe, in the food and water that sustain us, in our thoughts and dreams."

"You're just serving me the same warmed-up dogma. I'm asking you to give me an honest, impersonal reply. So, let's try again. Does God exist, yes or no?"

"Signor Rabinovich, I can hardly be impersonal in my reply to such a question. I wouldn't be worthy of the position I hold or of the trust God has put in me if I answered that question in the negative. Yes, God does exist. I'm as positive of that as I've ever been."

"Doesn't it bother you that you have absolutely zero proof? That you have nothing to hold onto, really, other than your own conviction?"

"But that is precisely what faith is. The Lord requires that we believe in Him, in His Mercy and His benevolence, even though we don't have a shred of proof."

"That sounds a lot like self-suggestion. But let's say that you're right in your conviction, and that your God does indeed exist. The question remains: what comprises this omnipresent, omnipotent Supreme Being? Is he ghost-like, composed of nothing but thin air? What if he's not immaterial as you claim, but actually made of something? And could that something be, oh, I don't know...let's say, music?"

Vittorio had smiled and crossed his hands on top of his desk. "It's certainly quite poetic, this musical God you propose, but I'm afraid the answer is once again, no. Music is a human creation. It is one of the most transcendent, to be sure, and one often put in the service of the Lord. Yet it couldn't begin to encompass the incomprehensible miracle, much less the nature of God."

"But let's say it does encompass Him, and that what to us seems like our own creation is actually the incorporeal substance of a Supreme Being who thinks, speaks and even creates using what we perceive as notes and melodies. All this in the same way we feel our lives belong to us, while your Church holds them to be a gift from God who made us in His own image and likeness." Rabinovich leaned closer. "Bear with me. It would be like speaking a foreign language without being aware of doing so, without even knowing what the words mean, but simply enjoying the way they sound to us.

Yet all the while, unbeknownst to us, we may be addressing God in the very medium of which he is composed. And what if, somehow, by speaking to him in his own tongue, one could compel God to do one's bidding?"

Vittorio said, "Again—a charming theory, but no more than that. This whole fiction you're proposing is frankly childish in its concept of God. It's just a pretty tale I would never for a second seriously condone. I wish it were as simple as that, but trust me, God is not made of music, nor does He do anyone's bidding. The Lord's voice is the all-powerful Logos, which we humans could never hope of using to converse."

With a growl of disgust, Rabinovich ground his cigarette in the ashtray and rose to his feet. "Then neither you nor your God is of any use to me. All you do is parrot the theology you were taught at the seminary."

As Rabinovich walked toward the door, Vittorio observed the old man's slumped shoulders and wobbly legs. He was desperate to make the Maestro stay. He needed to protect the old man who stood before him as a broken soul which only the love of God could mend. Yet as he reached the door, the Maestro turned, his eyes glaring.

"You never fucked, did you? The two of you?" he'd said.

Monsignor Alessandrini's protean eyes had grown wide as saucers. "How did you..." he muttered. "Has Alexei...?"

"Oh no," Rabinovich had said with a smile. "Our dear Alyosha would rather die than speak to me about what's eating him up. He's been in such agony all these years apart from you that longing is visibly corroding him like acid. In front of me, of course, he behaves as if he took an oath of celibacy similar to yours, but anyone could see right through that. And to me it had been obvious ever since you two first met, back when you were practically joined at the hip. I'm sure you thought you had everyone fooled, but it was clear as day how painfully in love you were. And I do wish you'd gone ahead and broken your respective vows, because, let me tell you, life is fleeting, and no one, when lying on one's deathbed, ever regretted having granted himself just a little bit more of that oh-so-elusive happiness, even if it was a matter of a single night's indulgence of the flesh."

Then he approached Vittorio's desk and sat down again, his smile now one of mischief.

"This Logos you speak of," he said. "Tell me, is it actual speech, some sort of immortal breath reciting words that animate us the same way Adam rose from clay? Couldn't it, oh, I don't know, be composed of notes instead?"

Jumping at the chance to evade the humiliating excursion into his private life, Vittorio tried to humor his agitated visitor. Besides, it was his priestly duty to comfort this haunted man, who'd turned to him in his hour of need. If he had to lie to achieve this (well, not quite lie, just stretch the truth a tiny bit thin), so be it.

"You raise an interesting question, Signor Rabinovich," he said, trying to sound malleable. "But no one really knows just what the Logos is. We don't even know how to pronounce the Lord's true name, hence the indecipherability of the Tetragrammaton. Why, it could well be music-like in nature. After all, the Lord moves in mysterious ways, and nothing is beyond His infinite power. Still, I'm afraid I'm hardly equipped to tackle such weighty matters. I am no more than a simple servant groping blindly through the wonder that is God's love and armed solely with my own unshakable faith. Not even His Holiness, may the Lord preserve him, would be capable of offering a definitive answer to your question, for he, too, is only human."

"His Holiness, you say..." Rabinovich said, fingers stroking his chin as his smile widened into a grin. "One last thing and I'll be out of your hair. Is it true that some of the Vatican's collection of ancient manuscripts have never been seen since the destruction of the Library of Alexandria? And that the whole of them are kept from public knowledge because the wisdom they contain might prove a threat to religion's grip on humankind?"

Vittorio tried to deflect. "I'm afraid you have been carried away by baseless gossip. The Holy See does indeed possess certain rare documents and artifacts of antiquity but nothing of the sort you suggest."

"Could one visit this collection and peruse these documents?"

Vittorio bit his lower lip. "I'm afraid that would be a severe breach of the Vatican's sovereign right to safeguard its properties from intrusion. Maybe a private visit could be arranged, but it would have to be a clandestine one." Then he fell silent, considering whether he could reveal more. He found himself unable to lie to Rabinovich in the same way he wouldn't bear to lie to his beloved Alyosha, the dear *animula* he hadn't seen for so very long.

"This must never be repeated to a soul," he'd said, lowering his voice, "because the thing I'm about to reveal to you constitutes grave heresy. There is indeed a collection of ancient texts which the Vatican would never share with the world at large. It is not out of the question that you, thanks to your diplomatic status, could visit the place where the said documents are stored, but you would have to do it on your own. I could conceivably receive permission for an unofficial, unprecedented exception to this strict rule of secrecy, but thereafter you'd have to proceed on your own. I would advise you to do so with extreme caution. No servant of the Lord is allowed to even glimpse these texts, so I can't join you in your search nor do I wish to. I may be repeating baseless gossip, but it's been said of this collection that people who have attempted to read the texts it contains have been driven mad." Rabinovich had let out a long sigh and sat back, looking content for the first time since he'd burst into the priest's study. "I wouldn't worry too much about that, your eminence. I assure you I'm in no danger whatsoever of going mad—because, you see, I am already quite insane."

Now it was Alexei's turn to interrupt Vittorio's narrative with an urgent question. "You mean that in all that vague talk about music's divine nature, Uncle Petya never once made mention of *Sixteen*?"

"None whatsoever, *carissimo*. In fact, the first I ever heard of *Sixteen* was that it had been banned in the Soviet Union and across most of the Eastern bloc. I nearly dismissed this as rumor-mongering, but then suddenly, here you are, and I suppose your visit isn't a spur-of-the-moment thing. So, no, the Maestro never mentioned *Sixteen,* and I've been itching to hear the thing. I even went so far as to try to procure an illegally made recording, but to no avail. Would you be so kind, later on, to play it for me?"

"Gladly. But, wait, he never mentioned his mother? A woman by the name of Ekaterina Rabinovich, killed during the outbreak of the Revolution?"

"What curious questions you ask! And the answer is no." Vittorio lay back in his ample chair and lit a cigarette, enjoying a deep drag. Alexei would readily give up his life if he could become that filtered cigarette, if only to feel the moistness of those full lips, the grazing of that tongue. But then the implication of what Vittorio had recounted struck him with the force of a slap across the face. *People have been driven mad...by the things they discovered.* Anger spilled into his chest. "And did you secure that permission for him? Did the two of you go to Rome behind my back? Did he visit that infamous collection? Is that why he killed himself, because of the goddamn things you allowed him to read?"

Vittorio hung his head, his voice on the verge of tears. "Believe me, *carissimo*, I have lain awake many nights asking myself that same question. I don't know. I have no idea why Signor Rabinovich, so blessed by God, would throw away the gift of life so inconsiderately. I can only pray his death was not the result of my own doing, for if it was, God help me. And yes, we did go to Rome together, drove all the way into the Vatican, and I'm willing to tell you all about it, even if these are things you'd be wise not to repeat, no matter how your handlers back in Russia pressure you. But I can't do that right now: the memory of the dear Maestro looking so lost breaks my heart. I need some time to think things over, and I'm sure you need to rest after your trip. Shall we meet for a late lunch or an early dinner? I promise I'll tell you everything I know."

Alexei found that he couldn't stay mad at Vittorio nor blame him for something as horrible as a man's suicide. Even if he had definitive proof that Father Alessandrini was responsible for what drove Uncle Petya over the edge, Alexei still couldn't manage to hate him—he loved him too much. Whatever Vittorio suggested, his answer would always be an eager, desperate "Yes."

Sretensky's explosive phone call—occurring just as Alexei was getting settled in his spacious bedroom overlooking the garden—barely registered. He stood next to the nightstand, listening without listening, offering the occasional apology as Sretensky unleashed a hailstorm of abuse. The Colonel accused him of incompetence, insubordination, treason and, mortifyingly, of sodomy. Alexei realized that it would be unwise to take Sretensky's threats lightly. He also recognized that he'd put himself at risk by surrendering his spying equipment to the red-haired priest. But he was too elated to care.

Not that Vittorio opened the door to hope. Deep down Alexei was resigned to the fact that their friendship would never advance to the vague cavorting of his fantasies. However, the thought that the two of them were sharing the same roof, that Monsignor Alessandrini was probably in his own bedroom, possibly in a state of partial undress with his muscled chest exposed to the caresses of a breeze, afforded Alexei almost unbearable delight. It was as if the conjuring of Vittorio's naked torso allowed Alexei's eyes to linger upon him, so that his fingers could almost touch the priest's smooth skin.

So, instead of fretting about his mission or Uncle Petya's reputation, he lay back on the cool bedspread, closed his eyes and let his hand wander toward his aroused loins.

Oh, what a tangle life was. What a foul and beautiful mess.

CHAPTER ELEVEN

Dinner went by in an awkward silence. The two of them ate their pasta and sipped their wine with barely a sound as if the coziness that had always extended between them had suddenly evaporated, leaving the proximity of two strangers seated at the same table of a train's restaurant. The gloomy dining room and the city spreading below were steeped in stillness as if they were the sole creatures awake in an enchanted world.

Mostly to swallow his lump of discomfort, Alexei suggested they refill their glasses and retire to the drawing room where the grand piano he'd glimpsed earlier stood shining like a centerpiece. He didn't feel a particular desire to play for Vittorio, but music had always saved them from the dark, unspoken things that lurked even in the briefest silence.

Like Rabinovich, whom he so ardently idolized, Vittorio was a self-taught musician relying on his innately perfect pitch to guide him through the jungle of notes he couldn't read. His mellow baritone voice was ideally suited for French arias and Alexei had once—just once, alas—listened as the love of his life sang the single most heartrending execution of "Je crois entendre encore" in living memory. However, like a bird that spreads its gorgeous plumage only in solitude, Vittorio exhibited his musical gifts only when no one was listening. Unlike Uncle Petya, who'd never seen a piano whose keys he didn't wish to tame into some improvised beauty, Vittorio seemed wary of the instrument, as though his inability to read music rendered him unworthy to stir the imposing beast from its slumber. Pleading was pointless; Alexei had once gone as far as to offer a mauve silk kerchief Rabinovich had given him, and which he knew Vittorio positively coveted, if he would only play. Sometimes this blunt refusal so vexed Alexei that he played at being difficult too, claiming that he couldn't remember this or that piece Vittorio was asking for or that he simply couldn't be bothered with tiring out his wrists thumping out that monstrous *Hammerklavier* finale.

Now, Vittorio jumped at his suggestion and practically shoved him to the drawing room, clamoring to get his first listen of this infamous *Sixteen* that had gotten *"your Marxist dolts in such a tizzy."*

Alexei would rather play something other than that—for reasons he couldn't explain, tackling Uncle Petya's swan song on the piano for company like some corny popular encore seemed irreverent, if not downright offensive—and preferably something by a different composer altogether, since playing the Master's music lately put him in a dour mood, as if the favorites that had once offered such refuge had been soured by the death of the man who had delivered them to the world, and who had taken with him some vital part of them back into the original darkness.

It was with a heavy heart that he raised the creaky cover. Despite the green felt band stretching across them, the keys were thick with dust; really, this poor piano had been terribly neglected, starved for the touch of fingers. He'd be surprised if it hadn't gone out of tune.

Vittorio carried the overflowing glasses of Valpolicella and placed them atop the piano's lid. He leaned on his elbows, eyes trained with a naughty glint on Alexei and his posterior suggestively protruding. At some point, he'd exchanged his cassock for a short-sleeved black shirt and a pair of tight-fitting black pants. In the dimness of the drawing room, it almost seemed as if he wore nothing at all, having transformed into some black-skinned, strapping demon with a shiny grinning mouth. "You know, for all I know, this may well be *Sixteen*'s first performance in this country!" he said in a husky voice. "Oh, this is so thrilling!"

Alexei, feeling the opposite of thrilled, poised his hands over the keys—and then the oddest thing happened: suddenly there was an unprecedented lacuna, and he was unable to summon the opening theme that, just now, had seemed at his fingertips. Startled by this failure, he glanced up at Vittorio's face, and before he knew it, he was waltzing his way through *Sixteen*'s first bars.

So great was the force of the music that Alexei was instantly carried away, his entire being contained in ten incandescent fingertips. What had Uncle Petya been if not the music he'd created? Alexei still remembered their first delicate conversation. Back when he was still a seventeen-year-old student at the Conservatory, and, lost for words in the presence of Russia's most famous composer, he'd stammered inanely, "I want to know so *much* about you, Comrade, sir! It's like I know everything about you, and yet, at the same time, nothing at all! Who is the man behind Rabinovich?" Uncle Petya (who hadn't yet earned this nickname) had frowned at the effusiveness (or possibly the imbecility) of the question, and simply replied, "I am my songs."

And so it was! This, the first movement of *Sixteen,* was no untimely end, *but the man himself.* Uncle Petya was in every note, urging him to live, to love, to make more music! Songs like this—oh, they never died. They lived on and on as long as there were people to sing them. Could one ever listen to the muted, heavenly *Kyrie* from Schubert's E-flat Mass and actually believe that its composer had died an ignoble death of sickness and poverty, without ever having attained the glory he deserved? Well, no more could one hear this music and accept that the man who'd written it was no more. The living heart of Rabinovich was still beating every time his melodies were summoned.

By the dirge-like second movement, Vittorio was in tears—yet he never raised a hand to blot them out. He just let them spill down his cheeks. One even dropped from the tip of his softly trembling chin into Alexei's wine, so that when he took the next sip it would be like drinking the swelling of his beloved's heart, the tear becoming part of him.

When at last he proceeded in an unbroken flourish of notes to the third movement's opening bars, a miracle happened: Vittorio's eyes grew childlike in amazement. His prodigious musical memory had identified the lilting tune in its original form as the introductory theme of a song, and closing his eyes, he began, for the first time in Alexei's presence, to sing the Italian version, one of the numerous translations Rabinovich's youthful hit had engendered.

Molti e molti anni or sono, in un regno vicino al mare, vivena una fanciulla che potete chiamare col nome di Annabel Lee...

If only it weren't over so quickly! No more than two minutes remained until the closing bars' dwindling arpeggios. If only there was some way to preserve this magical moment— Vittorio's voice as it soared along the chorus. *La luna che non mi porti sogni della bella Annabel Lee...* For a second, Alexei wished, absurdly, that he'd been allowed to keep his recording equipment and that he'd somehow managed to sneak the bulky *Capital* volume and conceal it somewhere close to the piano so that he could at least have a recording of this dazzling phenomenon—a shooting star trapped in a room during its fiery descent, a storm exploding inside the empty skies of his chest—but no, he'd never be able to hold on to the invaluable tape. The idiots over at Lubyanka would stash it in some airless basement room to gather dust. They might even question him about why exactly he had recorded the priest's singing instead of some remarks pertinent to his mission. No, the holiness of this moment lay in its fleetingness, in the fact that he was never meant to possess it but simply to bathe in its solace for the little time that was afforded him; the same way that his desire for Vittorio was never meant to be fulfilled, but merely to ignite him, to course through him on solitary nights, and slip away like a breath of air. Oh, how it hurt to force a muzzle on your love. A maliciously subtle pain like cutting your finger on a shard of broken glass and though it looks like nothing at all, it is only a matter of time before the shallow graze starts bleeding profusely, stabbing into the wound.

His fingers lingered on the keys even after he'd finished, seemingly held there of their own volition, as if reluctant to let go of the final chords that echoed in the stillness.

Vittorio's riotous clapping startled him back to reality. His friend was smiling at him with a pure, adoring smile. "Bravo, *carissimo!* Magnificent!" Then he sniffled his nose, wiping away the tears as though suddenly ashamed of all this emotion. He let out a nervous bark of a laugh. "Oh, the Maestro would be furious at me if he could see me right now, making a spectacle of myself! I can almost hear him, delivering a stern lecture, lovable old cynic that he was!"

Alexei smiled, although his friend couldn't be more wrong. Uncle Petya had loved nothing more than to make people cry with his music.

"And now I want the story you promised me."

They'd moved on to the far end of the drawing room. It was nearly ten and they were on their second bottle of wine. A strong fire crackled in the marble hearth, dispelling the December chill. Alexei was sitting cross-legged in an old leather chair while Vittorio lounged on a matching couch across from him.

Upon hearing Alexei's request, his friend glanced left and right, as if he'd sensed some unseen presence. He raised a finger to his lips and produced from his pocket a notebook and a small gold pencil. Finally, he leaned onto the low coffee table that stood between them and began to scribble furiously on a blank page, and when it was filled, he tore it off the notebook and continued writing on its back.

Alexei stared at Vittorio in bewilderment. What had gotten into him? Had he remembered something all of a sudden and felt he must take it down this instant? But then, when the second page was also filled with his tiny handwriting, his friend slid the piece of paper noiselessly toward him.

It took a moment to decipher Vittorio's hurried scrawling, which, moreover, was in French; but even when he did, Alexei had to read it over again, because he couldn't quite believe that what he'd just read was meant in earnest, wasn't some weird joke on him.

Don't speak another word about this, Vittorio urged him at the top of page one. *It's too dangerous. Roberto the carrot top is devoted, but I can't even trust him about this, for all I know he's had the whole place bugged. I'm not kidding, Alyosha. People have died over this, over less than this. Priests have been excommunicated, nosy intruders have been killed under mysterious circumstances or inexplicably taken their own lives. I repeat: this is really, REALLY DANGEROUS territory we're straying into here. Now please, please, do exactly as I say: the second you've read this, stand up, go over to the fireplace and toss the paper in. Then you must say, loud enough, but so that it sounds natural: "I'm suddenly homesick for some Russian music. Would you, by any chance, have a record handy?"*

Alexei could laugh out loud, though part of him also felt a little piqued; was this whole charade necessary? What was the point? Yet, when he looked up, Vittorio startled him by glaring furiously.

Alexei rose to his feet, walked over to the hearth and fed the paper to the flames just as the note instructed. Then, ridiculous though it felt, he performed the last bit as well, and nearly shouted that he'd love to listen to some Russian music.

"Marvelous idea!" Vittorio leapt to his feet. "And I think I've got just the thing!" Off he scurried to a sideboard where the record player stood, and a few moments later, the room was filled with the plaintive chords of a group of balalaikas and with the booming, rolling voice of Alla Bayanova—the volume turned up so high the coffee table shivered.

Alexei stared at his friend and pointed at his own ear— as if saying, *Does it have to be so loud?*—but Vittorio's look stopped him cold. The priest, who'd always seemed to him so unshakable, looked truly afraid; Vittorio looked downright terrified, and Alexei also felt the icy hand of fear down his spine.

Before he knew what was happening, Vittorio had rushed over, grabbed him by the elbow and dragged him over to the couch, where he sat him down before taking a seat so close that their hips and shoulders were touching. His tanned face was still a mask of fear, and by now, Alexei was really worried. Should they be talking about this after all if it was clearly something dangerous?

Vittorio scooched closer, wrapped an arm around his shoulder and whispered in Alexei's ear over the racket of the balalaikas, a wild, incredible story. Alexei was tempted to dismiss what his friend was telling him but somehow the story was too gripping to resist—and besides, anything that involved being hugged by Vittorio, having his warm, winey breath blow on his cheek, he'd never dream of interrupting. For all he knew, this was the closest he would ever get to feeling the touch of that body he so madly desired; and so, he listened.

"The Maestro and I did travel to Rome, yes," Vittorio was saying. "I had to improvise some last-minute business at the French Embassy, and even so I had to get permission from the Pope himself; luckily, the Holy Father is a huge Rabinovich fan, and so he indulged me, though he did give me an earful warning me that I'd have to repent for the rest of my days for polluting my soul, mind and lips with *this vile devilry.* So, you see how serious a transgression this was, just to get Rabinovich through the door. From thereon after, I'm afraid he was on his own."

The door in question lay in the bowels of the ancient city, in one of the Vatican's meandering catacombs. The exact location was known only to a handful of people—the Guardians of the Filth, a select group who served for life; they were orphans who'd been born blind and raised in secret, taking a vow of silence as soon as they could utter their first words and training in the martial arts so that they'd be able to neutralize any potential intruder within seconds.

As to the nature of this "filth" they were guarding, no one knew exactly what it was. Everything concerning it had circulated for centuries as gossip: tales shared to scare novices, but also to keep them safe from danger. Vittorio had been told all about it during a cardinal's deathbed confession, which he'd been privileged to give His Eminence, along with the last rites. The unspeakable secret behind the door those mute, muscled moles guarded day and night consisted of documents, incunabula, most likely, collectively known as the *Doppio Vi* (from the words *Venenum Viscerum*, meaning, *poison of the entrails*). No one knew a thing about their provenance, nor when and why the Holy See had acquired them, only to keep them hidden and forbidden under penalty of excommunication. Unfortunately, those who'd been reckless enough to visit the *Doppio Vi*—supposing they had actually managed to pull that off, for only the Pope could grant access to the venomous collection—had left no record of what they'd discovered, and not a single one of them was still around to tell the tale. Sooner or later, they had all disappeared.

"Some claim," Vittorio went on, "that all the documents were in fact *acheiropoeita,* of a miraculous origin, or that the Lord Himself wrote them down. Others say it's the exact opposite, that the scrolls, parchments and tablets date from before the birth of man and are thus the work of primordial demons or a cunning trickery perpetrated by the Father of Lies to lure innocent souls into taking his own foul words for holy script." Alexei nodded eagerly, half intrigued and half in resilient disbelief. Mostly, he was trying to determine whether Uncle Petya had been malignantly influenced by the things he'd seen in that library of accursed knowledge and whether the *Doppio Vi*'s purported noxiousness had been what finally drove him to kill himself. There remained a final question he refused at the moment to consider: could *Sixteen*, just as Sretensky and a host of panicked Communist figureheads were claiming, have also been instilled with something dark and arcane, potentially harmful to the unsuspecting listener? This, he squarely refused to accept the music was too beautiful, and besides, it would mean that he, too, had already unknowingly imbibed this notorious poison of the soul.

Once more, Vittorio was swearing him to secrecy, insisting that Alexei mustn't speak a word about this to a soul, not even to Faina. Unless the NKVD were actually ripping out his fingernails, he must promise to take this secret to the grave. With his dying breath, the cardinal who had revealed the whole story to Vittorio had begged him to steer clear of the *Doppio Vi*, which he claimed had almost been his ruination and had condemned many a worthy but curious soul before him to an ugly death and eternal damnation.

Suddenly Vittorio's grip around his right shoulder tightened, and his friend leaned so close that his lips grazed Alexei's ear as they formed the nearly soundless words—an unanticipated move, a dream almost come true. (For wasn't this how lovers confessed their undying love to one another, right before sticking their tongue in the beloved's ear?) This provoked an instantaneous standing ovation from his crotch, which his hands were unable to conceal: like a horny, helpless twelve-year-old, he was pitching a bloody tent, which Vittorio couldn't have failed to notice. Alexei caught his friend's eyes darting furtively over to his legs and back, before he resumed his unendurable monologue.

"I still can't promise," Vittorio whispered, "that the Holy Father will indulge me twice in such a request—the *Doppio Vi* is truly abhorrent to him. He was one of those originally in favor of destroying the whole thing back in the 1920s—and even if he will, I might end up losing my position or get sent to some godforsaken Catholic province, and, moreover, *mio caro,* I'd be remiss in my duty as a friend if I didn't implore you to reconsider ever setting foot in that damned place—for I do believe it's evil or something worse than evil for which there is no human word. *Don't do it, please.* I'd kill myself if anything happened to you because of me. But if you're positive, if you really, *really* want to do this, I swear I'll do anything in my power to help. We can leave first thing in the morning. I'll simply tell Roberto some fib and off we go. Again, I fervently advise you against it, and I'd be sticking my neck out for you, risking everything I've worked so hard to get. Yet, if there's anyone in the whole wide world I'd do this for, then it's you, Alyosha."

Alexei was so astonished by Vittorio's final words that he froze, could neither nod nor speak; even the *Doppio Vi* seemed to wane like a distant tale. He had to keep still, control his breathing, (by this time, he'd even forgotten about his hard-on, which stood prouder than ever) because if he broke his concentration even for a second, he'd give in to the impulse to grab Vittorio and kiss him harder and longer than he'd ever done in dreams.

Then, Alexei was granted the most unlikely salvation—the needle skipped to the next track, and the air was filled with a jazzy tune familiarly enhanced by a bouncy balalaika. Alexei's eyes, as he recognized the song that was about to begin, grew wide with horror.

He drew back from the crook of Vittorio's arm and shouted above the music: "Oh, God, Vittorio, *no!* Make that awful thing stop, make it stop *at once!*" Since his friend just looked at him with a faintly amused smile, Alexei attempted to rise from the couch yelling, "Uncle Petya would be rolling over in his grave if he knew I was listening to this monstrosity!"

Vittorio shot out a powerful arm and restrained him, nailed him to the back of the couch, and his smile widened into a wicked grin. "Firstly, I do believe the poor Maestro was cremated, so I wouldn't worry too much about the rolling-over bit. And secondly, you're being quite silly—I happen to love this song. It's bloody *genius!*"

A whirlwind caught Alexei up before he could blink an eye, much less put up any actual resistance. Vittorio's lean body concealed great power. He was strong and agile like a panther, and seconds later Alexei found himself pulled to his feet and then dragged to an uncluttered part of the drawing room. Vittorio's placed his hands in a steel-like grip on his right hip and left shoulder, as if he intended—"No! No! Let me go! Vittorio, I'm not kidding around now! *Let. Me. GO!*"

Yet deep down, he knew he was too weak to get away from Vittorio's clutch. The priest could toss him about like a puppet if he wanted to, and even deeper down, he *craved* to be tossed about. *God,* how he'd *longed* for this to happen, even if it had to be a parody of the desirous thrusting and heaving he had dreamed of, even if it meant allowing Vittorio to lead him around as they danced to the song Rabinovich had hated more than anything in the world. "An inexcusable mistake that will haunt me to my last breath," he used to call it, "it makes me want to puke the milk my mother fed me." Alexei still recalled that mortifying soiree in Leningrad to which Uncle Petya had dragged him. One guest had the brilliant idea to put "the Stalin song" on the turntable. He could almost see Uncle Petya's hand freeze as it raised a glass of champagne to his lips, then he'd turned around, hurried over to the gramophone, snatched the rotating record with a hair-raising scratch of the needle, threw it to the ground and stamped it into shards while the guests looked on, appalled and thrilled by Rabinovich's public tantrum.

It had all begun with little Svetlana Alliluyeva, apple of Stalin's eye and thorn in his backside.

Alexei even remembered the occasion which had led to Uncle Petya's lifetime musical embarrassment and he smiled at the memory as Vittorio led him around the impromptu dance floor.

In the winter of 1942, he'd been in the Master's employment for three months. It was a grim time for those on the blood-drenched fronts of the war that had been raging for more than three years. That privileged occasion to observe the General Secretary's family life up close had been the product of Svetlana's passion for Uncle Petya, who was more than her favorite composer of all time: the girl clearly nursed a secret crush for the forty-ish Rabinovich—as Alexei had ample chance to observe on that unforgettable evening. This crush was indicative of Svetlana's fondness for older, paternal men which would plague Stalin in the years to come. Despite indulging her fawning over him with saint-like endurance, Rabinovich didn't in the least appear to reciprocate her attentions, treating her instead with an avuncular tenderness.

Upon first meeting the sixteen-year-old girl, Alexei had thought how greatly she resembled her father. It was as if her father's reputedly blind love for Svetlana had transformed her into a much prettier version of himself. Theirs had not been an easy relationship. Perhaps it couldn't be, given her father's status. Moreover, the shadow of a terrible loss still cast a pall over the family: the girl's mother Nadezhda was an unstable, difficult woman. She'd died when Svetlana was six— and though she'd been officially pronounced a victim of acute appendicitis, rumors said she had committed suicide.

On the evening in question, Uncle Petya and Alexei had been fetched by Stalin's private limousine for dinner, an invitation undoubtedly occasioned by Svetlana's pleas to spend time with her idol. The General Secretary had barely ventured from his study, where, behind closed doors, he was holding crucial discussions on the phone. He had a war to win and Operation *Uranus* had just been a resounding success so that victory in the brutal Battle of Stalingrad finally seemed close at hand.

Their young hostess had spent the dinner bombarding Uncle Petya with questions about famous people he'd met and faraway places he'd been to, which Rabinovich answered with an unusual kindness, giving the girl the juicy tidbits she was clearly after. After the maid had cleared away the table, and the three of them had settled in the dacha's rustic living-room, Svetlana had jumped to the turntable and put on a record so scratchy she'd obviously been listening to it incessantly. The song had been her latest craze: Mary Martin singing Cole Porter's "My Heart Belongs to Daddy."

Alexei found the jazzy little number pleasing enough but Svetlana was enraptured, dancing in the middle of the woolly carpet, swinging her hips in what she thought was a provocative fashion and crooning the mangled lyrics with closed eyes. The study's double doors swiftly drew apart and Stalin barged out in a fury.

"Not that goddamn song again, Lana! If I have to listen to it one more time, I swear I'll lose it!"

Alexei had cowered in terror. The glaring, maroon-faced man who stood in the doorway seemed to have lost it *already* but when Stalin turned to Rabinovich, his frown somewhat relaxed.

"Would you look at that, Petya? Stalin's own daughter going about like some dirty little minx and all because of this stupid American song!"

Despite his disparaging comments, Svetlana rushed over and wrapped her arms around him. It was a sight to remember: the man who, seconds ago, looked as fearsome as rough-hewn stone at once melted like butter.

"But, Papa," she mewled in complaint, "that's not fair! It's a beautiful song, the most beautiful song ever written, and it tells the story of this young lady who is constantly urged to stray into temptation by several men, but she never does, because above all men she loves her Daddy!"

That seemed to give the General Secretary a boost of prideful pleasure. "Well then, that girl has a brain in her head. No one will ever love a girl more than her Papa. But I still find the song a silly nuisance. Plenty of Russian songs are infinitely superior to this imperialist rubbish."

At that moment, Rabinovich—who also happened to love the song—was inspired. He and Cole Porter had been close, if long-distance, friends for years. Their friendship, forged by mutual admiration, led to the liberal appropriation of each other's material for their own songs. So, he booked a studio, hired a small jazz orchestra (sufficiently de-Americanized by adding four balalaikas), transcribed the lyrics into Russian, giving them a slight twist so as not to arouse the censors' suspicions with anything too flagrantly provocative, then had Alla Bayanova, back then at the peak of her fame, sing the song to cut a solitary ten-inch record intended as gift to Svetlana for her upcoming birthday.

Little did he know of the consequences of his generosity. Svetlana had loved her specially made gift, and after listening nonstop to the single record for three whole days (on her brand-new headphones recently acquired by direct order of the General Secretary), she played it for him. Stalin greatly approved of the Russian lyrics that spoke of a young proletarian girl who is constantly propositioned by rich foreigners but never betrays her virtue or her country, because, as she sang in the chorus, "her true love was her Papa"—a declaration of filial devotion that, in his opinion, clearly referred to him, the Father and Teacher of all Russians. When Svetlana begged him to have the record properly released, so that everyone could enjoy a song that had been written for her and her alone, Stalin thought nothing of it and made sure that several thousand records were produced within a matter of days.

And so it happened that, one fine morning, Rabinovich had turned the radio on, only to be assaulted by his own jocular creation, which he'd never intended to publish. Nonetheless, it had swiftly become a smashing hit, selling countless singles and becoming a staple in the dance halls. People everywhere were singing at their top of their voices of their devotion to Leader and country, for the majority of them took it to be a war song, strictly composed to boost their valiant warriors' morale. Forever after, the song would be referred to by the nickname "My Heart Belongs to Stalin." End of story and beginning of Uncle Petya's grief.

But now the song was over, their playful dancing embrace had broken up and once more they sat across each other in awkward silence, as if the intimacy they'd shared a few moments ago had never been.

After another pause, Vittorio asked, again in a low, conspiratorial voice, "Do you truly believe that *Sixteen* is causing the defections like they're saying?"

There were many doubts in Alexei's mind, but none whatsoever about this. "Of course not," he said firmly. "Not for a second."

"I mean, you played it to me and I didn't move an inch, did I? There's nowhere I would rather be."

"Me either."

"And you're still determined to get to the bottom of this, right? Find out what the Maestro discovered in the *Doppio Vi*?"

Alexei nodded.

"Then it's settled," Vittorio said. "As soon as you're up, we're leaving for Rome."

It was a night of mysteries and miracles. Stirring from his sleep a little after three due to an urge to pee, Alexei was astonished to find that he was no longer the single occupant nestled in the cocoon of the double bed's warm covers. A naked body was snuggled against him, head resting on his shoulder, a limp hand placed upon his chest. Despite the near-total darkness, there was no doubt as to the nocturnal visitor's identity. Alexei instantly recognized Vittorio's masculine perfume and the barbershop smell of the pomade in his hair; he felt his friend's naked, muscled limbs clinging to him as the slumberer breathed softly, lost in sleep. There was also a telltale stickiness in the hair of his groin and upper thighs that Alexei was all too well familiar with, even if, till now, it had always been the result of the strenuous efforts of self-pleasure.

That had to be it—a vivid, lifelike dream, for Alexei remembered neither the creaking of the opening door nor the intruder's footsteps as he padded over, undressed and slipped into the bed. He felt neither pain nor muscular exertion, only this incredible, indescribable warmth. This feeling of his body, after a lifetime of incompleteness—an absent limb, some vital organ missing—becoming finally complete.

Then, lest he disturb this wondrous dream, he closed his

eyes and slowed his breathing to match his fellow sleeper's. Soon he was out like a light.

When he woke up again, this time for good, it was still dark though the night had faded somewhat to the indigo haze of the small hours—and now he was indeed alone. The bed was empty, the warmth was gone. It had been a dream after all.

But his pubic hair was stiff with the dried remnants of lust. And the pillow next to his own looked slept-in, creased in the middle by the weight of a head, and the linen still retained the faintest redolence of pomade and musk. He might have forgotten all about it, missed out completely on the pleasure of which he had dreamt for so long, but even if he'd been half-asleep while it had happened, he was *there*—for once in his life, he hadn't slept alone.

He pulled the bedside lamp's frail chain and a yellow pool of light bathed the room. His suitcase, which he'd rested, gaping, on a chair, stood by the door upright with both clasps fastened. A clean suit and shirt hung on the wardrobe's knob; they both looked freshly pressed.

Alexei's heart sank and swelled all at once.

Vittorio was waiting for him at the bottom of the stairs, smiling up at Alexei's sleep-rumpled face. He was impeccable in his long, black coat. One could hardly imagine the man who stood there sneaking, naked, into another man's bed to stave off his loneliness. Something possessive was in his gaze as he looked at Alexei, something that until last night had been kept in check (a hungry beast caged for long, long years) and there was no mistaking the shine of pleasure on his face.

The landing smelled of coffee and bread rolls. Alexei was starved. Resting his coat on the crook of his elbow (the stairway was cold so early in the morning), he said, "Someone packed my suitcase while I slept—and ironed a fresh set of clothes, it seems. Is our trip meant to be one-way for me?"

Vittorio's smile faltered, and he lowered his eyes. "Ah, yes that was Roberto. He's extremely efficient. I trust he didn't disturb you, did he?"

"No, not at all. I was just surprised." His mind was still too foggy, too caught up in the question he daren't ask Vittorio: *Did last night really happen?* Deep down he knew the meaning of the packing and was resigned to it.

"I'm afraid a Colonel friend of yours got himself into quite a state overnight," Vittorio explained. "He called at some ungodly hour—four in the morning, it must have been—and luckily Roberto was up and took the call. The name eludes me just now—Slavenski, Slonimsky?"

"Sretensky."

"That's it. Well, the man was quite frantic. He was shouting so loud Roberto had to hold the receiver at arm's length and the trouble was he understood neither English nor French—nor Italian. So, in the end he hung up, and some poor interpreter was roused and called again on his behalf, stating in a fearful voice—the old man was dictating the orders to him, his shouts could still be heard over the phone—that your business here is finished, and that you are expected at the Ciampino Airport of Rome at exactly two in the afternoon. A ticket in your name will be waiting for you at the Aeroflot counter. And since it's roughly a two-hour drive to Rome and another half hour to get to the airport, I'm afraid we were rather pressed for time. Hence the preparations."

Alexei felt a surge of bitterness rising in his throat. He had to leave already? He wasn't even allowed a measly couple of days to give at least a pretense of a thorough investigation? What sort of spy darts from one place to the next like that?

Was there even a point in pretending that this charade was getting the results the NKVD demanded? Though what hurt the most was the prospect of the lonely hotel room he'd be whisked away to, his one day in Florence a fleeting dream. "The man is vile," he said, "and I'm sorry he disturbed you in the dead of night. I'm sure he was rude as always and drunk to boot, though I hope some of the worse stuff got lost in translation."

"Don't even mention it—I slept right through it. I'm sorry to see you go so soon. I thought..." and his voice trailed off. Roberto was quickly advancing from the kitchen with a steaming cup of coffee, which Alexei received with grateful thanks. He took a sip, placed the mug on the wide newel of the staircase and put on his own overcoat. The question neither dared to ask lingered between them.

To make sure the photo of Ekaterina Rabinovich was still safe in his inner pocket, Alexei slipped his hand in and was horrified to find the pocket empty. Had someone taken it while he slept? Roberto, who had handled his things? Surely not Vittorio. Or had some third party intruded in the black of night...

"Looking for something?" Vittorio asked.

"I could swear it was there, I even checked last night before going..."

Then he felt something slip against his leg and fall with a dry leaf's faint flutter to the floor, next to his foot. Alexei, mortified, realized what had just happened: a tear in the lining of his worn coat's inner pocket had allowed the photo to slip through, fall through the rest of the lining and out through a tear in the hem.

Burning with shame at the shabbiness of his clothes, Alexei stooped and picked up the photo, but not before Vittorio had cast a curious glimpse.

"Someone I ought to know?" he asked, after briefly examining the photo and the inscription on its back. "Your mother?"

Alexei smiled as he placed the photo in his other pocket, which was luckily undamaged. "Rabinovich's mother, actually Ekaterina, back when she was very young."

"Ah, I see," Vittorio said. "Well, I failed to notice the resemblance."

"Really? I thought she looked like him a lot."

"No, I believe the Maestro had a leaner, more angular face, and his eyes were bigger, and set farther apart...but anyhow, I gather it has something to do with your sudden trip, this photo?"

"Yes and no," said Alexei. "It has something to do with a long story I was told, which I have to corroborate, though it might not even be true to begin with. I'm not supposed to have the photo; I only do because I was the first to unearth it. It's all too complicated to explain right now. I must have some more coffee before we go, it's really delicious."

"A long story, you say," Vittorio repeated with a naughty grin. "I love long stories, especially if they have to do with the Maestro. Perhaps you'd care to tell me about it on our drive to Rome—though, of course, I wouldn't want you to compromise state secrets."

Alexei smiled dismissively. "It's a whole lot of nonsense, really; you'll say so yourself when I tell you about it. It's a typical example of Politburo madness: everything has to agree with what they already believe. So off I fly to wherever they're sending me now, to make sure I find whatever it is that pleases those idiotic bureaucrats."

"Well, I'm sure everything will turn out for the best," Vittorio said. "They'll get over this invisible culprit of theirs, realize how ridiculous it is to blame music—especially music as beautiful as the Maestro's—and move on to the next scapegoat, the new enemy of the people. They're quite childlike that way." The priest glanced at his wristwatch. "It's not six yet, but I'm afraid we must be on our way; we mustn't keep his Holiness waiting, now."

Alexei's eyes grew wide with astonishment. "We're really going to meet the Pope?"

"Not you, *carissimo*—and trust me, you're better off not meeting him when he has to wake up before nine. You'll have to wait for me in the car while I do my pleading for you."

"Thank you so much for doing this," Alexei said. "I hate to put you in an awkward position."

"Ah, I could never deny you anything, Alyosha. I hope you know that. Now, have some coffee and a bite of brioche Roberto is quite the baker—and off we go!" Vittorio's smile looked forced as he patted Alexei's arm. Then, he leaned closer, lightning-quick, and gave him a peck on the lips, like the aftermath of proper, passionate kisses already exchanged, or the promise of yet more to come. "And cheer up, for God's sake! The sky is clear, and it looks like we'll have the most wonderful road trip. *Andiamo a la Città Eterna!*"

CHAPTER TWELVE

Coat collars raised against the wind, they drove into the predawn darkness, both of them trailing tendrils of smoke.

The car wasn't the luxurious vehicle one would expect of a diplomat. Vittorio drove a humble VW Beetle refitted with the engine of a much stronger car. It growled like a huge beast trapped inside a smaller one. Alexei could relate to the feeling.

For the first time, the silence between them didn't feel strained; it was a cozy, intimate wordlessness shared by people who know that everything worth saying has already been said and everything worth doing has been done.

The proof Alexei had craved when he'd awakened in that tousled bed was abundantly in evidence, for every now and then, Vittorio's right hand would stray from the steering wheel to stroke Alexei's knee, often climbing as far up as his crotch, where the bulging stiffness proved, in turn, how much he was excited by these caresses. Again, there was something deliciously possessive about Vittorio's casual touch, about the playful glances he threw at him whenever the road ahead was long and straight enough to take his eyes off it for a moment. *You're mine,* said that look.

The drive was so smooth that Alexei often slipped into a state of semi-drowsiness, but even when fully alert, there was no denying the dream-like feeling of these past few days. Days before, he was conversing with a Nobel laureate, and just as suddenly, after years of pathetic, forcible celibacy, he was a virgin no more—and now he was being driven by his friend— no, his *lover*—to the Vatican to delve into an arcane collection of forbidden documents.

Honestly, what was the point anymore? What clues were there for him to go on? Some tall tale probably cooked up by the Politburo to rationalize this wild goose chase? Some old photo stashed away for unknown reasons? Alexei thought about the photo once again and of Vittorio's comments. His lover (oh, how he *adored* the sound of this!) had thought that the woman didn't resemble Uncle Petya at all. And really, did he have undeniable proof that she had been in fact the infamous Ekaterina Rabinovich, slain by a horde of bloodthirsty Bolsheviks? Aside from the *Stabat Mater* couplet scrawled on the back, there was no way to positively identify the woman as the mother whose murder had haunted the son to the point of making him forge a secret weapon that could reverse the October Revolution.

Sheer insanity. *Sixteen* was no more than a beautiful piece of music—certainly no devious mechanism of mind-control. Alexei recalled Vittorio's words after he'd finished playing the third movement. *There's nowhere I would rather be but here.* It had been the same for him. If it weren't for Faina, he would gladly defect to Italy, though it wasn't Italy, or Florence, or Rome he truly wished to live in—it was the warm bed with the slept-in pillow. Vittorio was the country he wanted to defect to; his body ached to abscond straight into the priest's embrace.

As for the *Venenum Viscerum*, its plausibility decreased as they got closer to its legendary crypt, as did the latest scenario cooked up on the alcoholic fumes of Sretensky's rage. Uncle Petya delving into the dark arts of the Ancients, dredging up some ruinous wisdom and then incorporating it into music? It was as preposterous as the prospect of him visiting the damn place.

Why, for all he knew, despite his facility for languages, (he was one of those people who, if dropped in Warsaw on a Monday, by Friday would have picked up a fair command of Polish) Rabinovich had known no classical ones. Alexei could remember him saying so.

It was late in the evening, and for hours they'd been struggling with a difficult piano sonata. It was an unusual work for Rabinovich, heavily chromatic; at the time, Alexei had thought that Uncle Petya seemed to be growing envious of Shostakovich, the strides the fellow composer seemed to make with every new work—it was almost as if Rabinovich was afraid that his more traditional idiom lagged behind the tides sweeping through contemporary music.

Then, apropos of nothing, the Master had looked up from his notes, frowning as if he'd just lost a train of thought, and said, "Sometimes I truly pity those dead-language scholars."

Alexei had looked up, startled by Uncle Petya's declarative tone. Was he supposed to say something? The mind of Rabinovich was an odd creation, often sprouting unexpected tails he then set about chasing like a mad dog until he tired himself out. Perhaps if he said nothing, this odd deviation from the hard work at hand would outlast the Master's short attention span.

"I mean," he'd said, hunting in his pack for a cigarette, "they must feel so bloody *lonely*, with everyone who ever spoke the languages they study long dead. It's not like you can find someone fluent in Linear B and chat him up, is it?"

Alexei had cleared his throat. Should he offer an opinion on the matter after all? "Perhaps that's not the reason they study a dead language. Maybe they merely wish to be able to enjoy an ancient text in the original."

"But *why?*" Rabinovich had said, almost growing desperate about the vainness of it all. "There's a million translations lying about, so why should anyone bust their heads learning Latin, or Etruscan, or whatnot?"

"I believe Etruscan hasn't been deciphered yet."

"Don't be a contentious prick, Alyosha. You know I prefer it when you blindly agree with everything I say."

Alexei fell dutifully silent. It was true, Rabinovich didn't like naysayers. It was an uncomfortably Stalin-like trait of his otherwise lovable behavior.

"Suppose they love the language itself, then, its beauty and conciseness. I mean, why do people learn *any* language?"

"No, I don't think that's the real reason. I think they like feeling lonely, without anyone to talk to. Loners, that's what they are."

Alexei nodded, hoping that Uncle Petya would move on to the sonata's finale. He was tired, he had a headache, he didn't want an argument about something he'd never felt passionately for either way.

"I'm not making this up," Rabinovich continued, "I'm talking from experience here. You see, I have actually met a man like the ones I'm describing. He was a mousy sort of person. Around my age, actually, which means this happened way back in the Pleistocene. It was some state dinner, I don't remember, and I was off-my-ass drunk. So this guy was going on *interminably* about some Roman fool he'd been translating—

Tacitus, Ovid, one of those fuckers, and apparently he'd been at it for, like, ten years, a decade of his life thrown away, and *still* he wasn't finished, and I was so tempted to tell him to put a sock in it, he'd bored me to tears with his bloody translation, but no, this fella wanted to tell me everything. He was fascinated about a two-thousand-year-old legal text, can you believe it? Suddenly he burst into tears and confessed that his wife had just left him, gone off with his best friend, because she couldn't stand his obsession about fucking Seneca anymore..."

Had any of this actually happened, Alexei had briefly wondered? Was Uncle Petya making it up as he went, for some unfathomable reason?

"By that time, I was so sick and tired of this colossally important translation of his he wouldn't shut up talking about, that I said to his face, 'She did the right thing, deserting you. You're insufferable.'"

"No, you didn't!" Alexei said, really shocked. "That wasn't nice at all."

"I know. I felt guilty afterwards. But it goes to prove my point, wouldn't you say so? I mean, if his own wife was willing to destroy her marriage and elope with another man, imagine how bored the poor woman was by this Antiquity pervert."

"I still believe that wasn't a very nice thing to say to a recently abandoned man, especially if he was in tears. Unless you didn't, and you're just making this whole story up just to prove a point."

"You're calling me a liar, now? I should fire you on the spot, but I'm too fond of you. You really break my heart, Alyosha. You know I'd never lie about a single thing. I'm a naturally sincere person, innately averse to prevarication."

None of this was absolutely true, but Alexei opted once more for silence.

"Anyhow, none of it matters anymore, because a few months later, the fella offed himself. Shot himself in the head, I believe. He missed, but the bullet still blew half his face off, and though he survived, he was in atrocious pain and his life was ruined. No one can survive with half his face gone. I mean, imagine trying to have a social life looking like that, people will run off shrieking, so eventually he attempted suicide again by jumping out the window of his hospital room, and second time was the charm. The room happened to be on the thirtieth floor, so there was nothing left of him. *Splat,* bloody human soup on the pavement."

"Oh my God, that's *horrible!* What's the point of telling me such a ghastly story?"

"The point is, promise me you'll never study Ancient Greek, or anything like that. I don't want to end up picking you up off the pavement with a spoon."

Returning to the present, after having—even briefly—dwelled in his treasure trove of Rabinovich memories was always hard; at such moments, to be alive and draw breath while Uncle Petya had been left forever in the past felt like a betrayal. It pained Alexei absurdly that he'd never have a 1954 memory of the Master, that he couldn't share new songs, new sights, new experiences. But right now, the pain was dulled—was almost rendered sweet—by Vittorio's presence.

His friend, thoughtful as ever, had rummaged through the nunciature's vast library and managed to find a few dictionaries—so that, if he did receive permission from the Pope and visit the accursed collection, Alexei (who knew no ancient language other than that of love) could hope to find his way through the formidable documents. There was a bagful of them perched on his knees: Latin to Russian, Koine

Greek to French, Sanskrit to English. Though the lot of them might be useless in the event—for he still hadn't made up his mind as to whether he really did wish to cross the threshold of the *Doppio Vi,* to visit a place whence, purportedly few, if anyone, had ever returned.

Now Vittorio was humming a song in his velvety baritone: *Gretchen am Spinnrade.* Listening to his voice as the car ate up the distance had a hypnotic effect on Alexei. *My peace is gone / My heart is heavy...* Soon he felt his eyes grow heavy, and before he knew it, he'd fallen into a deep sleep.

Dreams are but instants; they never portray more than a fragment of time. A fleeting memory, the fragment of a face one's loved and lost, a fantasy that seems as concrete as reality: a brief flight from the constraints of reality. But there is no place for "*always*" in a dream, no place for "*never.*" Perhaps this is the unconscious work of the mind itself, which, knowing that these images aren't meant to last, wishes to protect the sleeper and itself discovering, on waking up, that the sweet eternity of which one dreamt isn't true.

Yet, as Alexei slept, head leaning on the passenger seat's window like a child's, he did dream of such a magnificent endlessness. In his sleep, this drive never ended; he was always with Vittorio sitting next to him, his breath as one with his heartbeat.

They arrived at Rome at the crack of dawn. Alexei had just stirred from his slumber, and the sights of the sprawling city were too much to absorb just yet: it was all one glorious blur. Vittorio took a long sip from a thermos, then passed it on to him; it contained strong coffee, though Alexei would happily drink chlorine if his lips would touch the same place which Vittorio's lips had graced.

"We're almost there, *caro*," Vittorio said, squeezing Alexei's left hand, as one would do an impatient boy's. He went on humming—another song this time; "Scarlet Rain," a Rabinovich favorite.

> *All is as promised, Gentle Lady, upon*
> *your long-awaited, tear-fogged coming.*
> *Air was my sustenance—and this, silently drawn*
> *not to disturb my grief's unceasing drumming*
>
> *on my poor soul; it drank from this, like rain,*
> *my weak devoted heart which lies in tatters,*
> *praying for your return, my Lady. Again*
> *my breath is heard now, grateful as it stutters.*

A legion of fountain pens had been emptied in attempts to guess at the identity of the mysterious *"Gentle Lady"*—for Rabinovich had never offered the slightest clue. Since it had been written as the fearsome Russian climate was annihilating the Germans, many had ventured that the song was an elegy to Mother Russia.

Alexei knew such suggestions to be nonsense. Even if there still hovered a thick fog of mysteries to be solved, until Ekaterina's spirit and *Sixteen* could finally rest in peace, one thing was certain: for this Gentle Lady, Rabinovich had literally gone to the corners of the earth.

They approached the Vatican City proper through a back entryway, guarded by a Swiss Guard in his colorful, slightly ludicrous, uniform. Before he raised the bar to let them through, Alexei caught a brief exchange of a wink and a smile between Vittorio and the young soldier. It might have denoted nothing more than normal familiarity, yet Alexei felt a jab of infernal jealousy—he hated that smile, that wink. He'd like to pluck that impertinent clown's eye out with his own thumb.

Vittorio parked the car among a throng of behemoths with diplomatic plates and squeezed his hand once more.

"You should wait inside the car," he said. "If anyone asks about the nature of your business here, tell them you're here with the explicit permission of Nuncio Alessandrini—and if, by any chance, they ask you what the password of the day is, tell them 'macchiato,' and they'll leave you alone. Okay, my love?"

Then, looking left and right, he lunged to give Alexei yet another kiss—a momentary grazing of the lips, the faintest promise of a real kiss—and he was off, hurrying into the most imposing of the surrounding buildings, where, presumably, the Holy Father resided.

No one came to ask questions or make trouble. But Alexei couldn't stop thinking of the password: *macchiato, macchiato.* And not the coffee named after the word, but its literal meaning: tainted.

This was what they were, Vittorio and he: a pair of male lovers, a pair of *queers,* a taint on the face of the Church, if not of the world itself. Yet Alexei felt anything but dirty; since last night he felt purer than ever, cleansed like a newborn baby from the original sin of celibacy. He was so clean he shone.

Vittorio was back in a surprisingly short time—no more than ten minutes—and when he sat down in the driver's seat, he looked stunned.

"Well, that was odd," he said.

"What happened? Tell me. Oh, please tell me I didn't get you in trouble. Did I, now?"

"What? No, *caro*. Far from it. In fact, the second I mentioned the Maestro's name, the Holy Father was so overjoyed, he granted you permission without even mentioning what I'd have to do in order to repent for my second association with the forbidden collection. It was as if I didn't exist, as if I weren't present in the room at all. The only thing he asked for was, if you'd be so kind, the briefest sketch of *Sixteen*—apparently, he's heard all the rumors circulating about it, and he's dying to have a listen—even a few bars will do. And that was it; he just sent me on my way, he actually said to me, '*Now, shoo, don't let your friend wait,*' as if I were your errand boy or something."

"Oh. I hope you don't mind too much—being my errand boy, I mean."

Vittorio turned and fixed him with those astonishing eyes of his, a smirk on his lips.

"I'd rather be your boy, plain and simple, *carissimo*."

After he'd handed him a tarnished key, Vittorio led Alexei into a tall building through a pair of equally tall doors, through a much smaller door and down four steep flights of stairs until they'd reached a subterranean space of ill-lit, meandering corridors dug so deep into the ground that the air was perceptibly colder. It was hard to imagine the pathologically claustrophobic Rabinovich treading these sepulchral tunnels, yet, apparently, he had—so great had his determination been to delve into the mysteries of the *Doppio Vi*.

Suddenly Vittorio stopped, showed him a corner turning sharply to the right. "I'm not allowed to proceed any further," he said. "You just go that way until you come upon a door on which you'll knock thirty-three times—then you unlock it, and in you go."

Feeling even warier now and wondering how Vittorio

knew so much about this place, Alexei followed his instructions, found the door and knocked until his knuckles felt sore. Then, his heartbeat almost audible in the tomblike stillness, he unlocked the old, worn wooden door and crossed the dreaded threshold.

Having been exposed to such a fantastical buildup, Alexei didn't quite know what he'd been expecting: skulls buried deep inside cobwebby niches, perhaps? Thick curtains, swords hanging on the walls, some sort of Masonic vault? The blind monk, the Guardian of the Filth, pouncing on him and knocking him out with a karate chop? Whatever it was, it certainly looked nothing like the cozy sitting room he found himself in: two old, comfy-looking leather chairs, a tiny fireplace blazing, end tables—one of them taken up by tea things, as if placed by an accommodating host expecting company—and lastly, the venomous collection itself: an innocuous-looking bookcase that took up one wall, crammed full of nearly disintegrating volumes, their cloth and leather spines in tatters. Sheaves of parchment and rolls of papyrus stuck out. *So, this is it.* Alexei felt at once thrilled and let down—as if he'd been promised Satan in the flesh, only to come upon a statuette of some ancient demon, all funny fangs and horns.

The host—the notorious Guardian of the Filth—emerging from a pokey bedroom to the left of the sitting room, proved to be equally a misnomer. For one thing, he was obese and smelled of soap; and for another, despite the vow of silence he'd supposedly taken back when he was still a child, the man spoke. In fact, he couldn't stop speaking, the poor fellow, and turned out to be hospitable to a fault—introducing himself with a warmly proffered hand as Fra Enzo, offering Alexei a cup of jasmine tea and a plate of shortbreads, and urging him to take a seat, relax, make himself at home.

Despite his milky, unseeing eyes (his only unnerving feature), he'd recognized Alexei at once—mortifyingly enough, from the residue of Vittorio's cologne on him—referred to him respectfully as "Comrade Samoilenko," and claimed to have been expecting him, "ever since Comrade Rabinovich graced us with his presence."

As to the *Doppio Vi*, he was extremely dismissive, describing it as "the Vatican's worst-kept secret" and insisting it was anything but dangerous, no more than a curiosity, really, which no one ever bothered with nowadays. "Feel free to peruse it, by all means—though I'm sure you'll come upon its infamous secret in no time, as Comrade Rabinovich, may God rest his soul, did."

Alexei wondered briefly about the lonely life the wretched fellow must lead, buried alive, receiving visitors so rarely he got overjoyed like a neglected puppy. The man couldn't sit still.

Then Alexei's gaze wandered above the bookcase, where, carved on a wall, was a word that Alexei took to be a misspelling. *SILANCA*, it read.

The blind monk seemed to have intuitively followed his glance, as if it were a warm ray he'd felt on his ruddy skin. "You must be wondering about the inscription, am I right?"

"Yes, as a matter of fact I was. Is it a...?"

"A misspelling? Oh, no. It's a cipher, made up of three Latin words: *Silentium, Angelus Canit.* 'Silence, the Angel Sings,' though no one knows what it truly means. Come, I'm sure you've pressing business to attend to, a man of the world like yourself, so, go ahead, rifle the old forbidden volumes. There's no danger to it, I assure you."

So, Alexei, after accepting a cookie from the plate constantly pressed on him, approached the bookcase and chose one volume at random: an ancient handwritten Bible, stunningly legible. It was an English translation.

As Fra Enzo had assured him, it took no more than an hour to come upon the secret of the *Doppio Vi,* so obvious it was. He barely had to take recourse to the dictionaries he'd brought along.

It was all about one small yet vastly important discrepancy and, unsurprisingly, it had to do with music.

In these volumes (a great number of them French and English translations of the original texts), God, or *the* Gods, never spoke: instead, they sang. *In principio, Deus cantavit... In the beginning, God sang...* He didn't create rather, *He sang into creation.* The same went for the sacred texts of all major religions: Brahma chanted, Allah intoned, Nyx and Erebus *"hummed the world into existence."* Hades, the Underworld, wasn't described as the abode of the souls of the dead: it was *"the Vault of Lost Songs."* Satan, the Devil, Shiva—any incarnation of evil, of destruction—was depicted in words as *"the perverter of melody," "the off-key cantor," "the negator of music."*

What was this obsession with music really about? Some melomaniac heresy? Or were *these* the original texts, distorted thereafter in the official versions of the Vedas, Hesiod, the Sefer Yetzirah, the Bible and the Holy Quran, so that speech and Logos had eventually replaced music and song?

Dizzy and dazed after an hour of page- turning, Alexei sunk into a chair right across from Fra Enzo who was humming something familiar... Could it really be...? Yes, it *was!* The first movement of *Sixteen,* which, apparently, had been conceived by Uncle Petya's prodigious mind before he'd even set foot in this eerie place to search for God knows what wisdom in those same volumes Alexei had just leafed through.

But how did it all fit in with the wave of disruption *Sixteen* was supposedly provoking? If God was music, and souls were song, and everything really—Creation itself—was but one long, melodious chant, then...

Alexei's gaze once more rose up to the odd inscription on the wall.

Silence, the Angel Sings.

Could it be that *Sixteen wasn't* an instrument of vengeance, as Khrushchev seemed to think, but rather Uncle Petya's undying soul transformed into music, so that it could linger in this world to exact its unknowable revenge?

Alexei's farewell with Vittorio was a dismal affair.

They sat in the wasteful warmth of a mostly empty café in Piazza Navone, and even the view of the otherwise marvelous square had a depressing look.

They drank *caffè ristretto* that wouldn't sweeten no matter how much sugar they'd stir in and shared a tiramisu, acrid from the dusted coffee. Vittorio denied Alexei the full flame of his eyes, as though he were saving fuel for his soon-to-be-frozen heart.

He didn't ask him anything about his visit to the *Doppio Vi*, and Alexei made no comment. Alexei kept thinking of the inscription and of angels: fearsome, winged, sexless, immortal creatures. Oh, to be able to fly, to have no need of sex, to be alone and pure and indestructible.

Before escorting him to the airport, Vittorio made him a parting gift: a box of Romeo y Julieta cigarillos. Alexei insisted that they sit on a bench and smoke one together despite the cold. They didn't speak and Alexei kept glancing at the garish drawing on the cigarillo box, wondering at his friend's unfortunate choice of gift. Like that of the *"star-cross'd lovers,"* theirs was a love by definition doomed; to an outsider it might seem horribly romantic, but to them it was just plain horrible. He threw his cigarillo away half-unsmoked, thinking about Uncle Petya, frozen on a bench like this, an ice sculpture with a stopped heart. He thought of the Capulet crypt, of pointless love.

Love will do you a world of evil.

PART THREE

A Maiden There Lived

CHAPTER THIRTEEN

A child, Rabinovich wrote in his famous book, *is any and every human being, who is—only too humanly—afraid. But that does not mean that children are innocent (for no one is ever truly innocent). They are merely weak.*

Never before had Alexei felt the truth of this aphorism more penetratingly than now, crammed in the middle seat between two NKVD agents on a plane headed to Tel Aviv. Travelling in the company of these two grim watchdogs, combined with the worsening situation back home, made Alexei so rigid with fear that if he spoke or breathed too audibly, the air would solidify and stop his throat.

Judging from the apoplectic mood of Colonel Sretensky who had been awaiting him in a storage room at Ciampino Airport, and from what he could untangle from the Colonel's roars, he and Faina were, to use one of Uncle Petya's favorite expressions, "screwed as the sole sow in a pig gangbang."

Within weeks of realizing that there was a situation in the first place, the problem had gotten so completely out of hand that Khrushchev had placed the NKVD and all chief members of the *Cominform* in a state of Pan-Communist alert. It wasn't an interior problem that could be dealt by gagging all news outlets and eliminating a few scapegoats—but seemed rather like an emergency of pandemic proportions affecting only the subjects of socialist regimes.

Though its population of more than a hundred million people made the Soviet Bloc seem invincible, only last week there had been reported 28,310 cases of defection to the West, 11,507 suicides, some separate, others *en masse* and a number of incidents of civil disobedience involving a terrifying two-and-a-half million people. People all across the USSR and Eastern Europe were going berserk. One moment they were faithful comrades, and the next they'd become savage beasts, driven to treason and self-destruction. Those who survived and were apprehended exhibited a shocking disregard for their respective countries' authorities. They mostly babbled unintelligible nonsense concerning their personal sorrows about friends, lovers, parents, relatives and children lost during the war or in the carnage of political purges. "We've got our soldiers shooting fucking widows in the back!" Sretensky had groaned as if he were one such widow running across the border in her black stockings.

At the same time, an estimated five million four hundred thousand people in all Communist countries had erupted into an unprecedented orgy of adultery, spousal desertion, rape, incest, pedophilia, sodomy, the entire Apocalypse of unspeakable vices. Those arrested, prosecuted and imprisoned had no arguments to offer besides their own uncontrollable passion. Self-restraint seemed to have been rendered as obsolete as the year 1953. Now, it was mostly *baise qui peut*.

Meanwhile, the purveyors of imperialist propaganda were cracking open the champagne. Having ample proof of this outbreak, they were already publishing pieces declaring the Soviet Union (if not Communism itself) defunct, claiming that the balance of power was tipping in favor of the U.S. There was no official response to these allegations because Khrushchev had put a gag on his puppet premiers abroad under penalty of being torn apart by famished bears, and the Soviet-dominated press still treated the matter as non-existent. Nonetheless there followed a barrage of brutal investigations at universities and branches of the U.S. Embassies which produced no evidence. No criminal mastermind or common subversive agenda connected any case with another. It was all random chaos.

Of course, the *Sixteen* theory was still their most solid lead, even though the authorities' precursory numbers showed that none of the so-called perpetrators had actually confessed to having any knowledge of the symphony. Another seven members of the original string orchestra had been captured in the meantime and resisted arrest. In fact, three of the bedeviled old geezers, not even responding to police warnings, had been shot on the spot. It was clear as day, Sretensky claimed—those traitorous pieces of shit had been so deeply immersed in the conspiracy, they no longer cared to save their own necks. From one body a complete score had been retrieved, and the musicologists and cryptologists of the Seventh Directorate were in over their heads with possible clues and mind-control techniques which they were desperately trying to extract from the twelve-minute piece.

Meanwhile, efforts were being made to impose a discreet embargo on the entirety of Uncle Petya's musical output. The circulation of his music abroad was impossible to control, but they had confiscated all privately owned short-wave radios.

Confronted with Sretensky's threats, Alexei could not bring himself to report his obscure findings from the Vatican burrows. It was hard enough having to listen to Uncle Petya's name and musical legacy being dragged through the mire. Yet after the Colonel had threatened Faina and him with disembowelment, Alexei attempted a hesitant version of what he'd read in the *Venenum Viscerum*. It was in vain. Sretensky could bear no more than two minutes of Alexei's stuttering remarks about Genesis and the New Testament, turning from crimson to burgundy and, finally, to an almost royal purple, before he hollered, showering Alexei's face with vodka-smelling spit, "You think I care if the Jews' God sang, Samoilenko? You think I care if the fucking Christ danced and his bitch of a mother played the goddamn balalaika?"

To make matters worse, the NKVD and the Politburo hadn't been able track the pawn/spy Alexei Samoilenko across the global chessboard. Then, this morning, a Telex arrived at the NKVD headquarters in Moscow. A Jerusalem number had sent it and in it the anonymous sender stated three facts: first, he identified himself as a high-ranking member of the Mossad; second, he claimed to possess information on *Sixteen* received directly from the composer and third, he was willing to volunteer the information in question. However, he would only talk to Alexei Mikhailovich Samoilenko, and the meeting had to be private.

Of course, as soon as Sretensky mentioned these terms, Alexei realized that it would be a blazing hot day in Siberia before the NKVD allowed him to go to Jerusalem on his own to meet with an Israeli spy who claimed to have been friends with Uncle Petya. Not a man inclined to leave things hanging, the Colonel told him quite explicitly. "It's out of the question! I consider you perfectly capable of going native and holing up in some cave to wait for the Second Coming!" The two ogres who had led him to the Colonel would be accompanying him on this next part of the trip. "You'd better get it into your stupid head," Sretensky concluded, handing him the ticket, "that this isn't a joke anymore or some luxurious vacation in five-star hotels like those you and your mentor used to enjoy. This is life and death we're talking here. Your life and death."

As he watched Sretensky's tantrum, Alexei became alarmed that the balance of fear had somehow shifted. The fear that continued to leak out of Sretensky like waves of sweat seemed to be directed toward Alexei rather than Rabinovich.

If the NKVD and the Politburo were seriously considering Uncle Petya's swan song as the instrument that led to this baffling surge of social uproar and if Rabinovich had been such a harbinger of evil, what did that make of Comrade Alexei Samoilenko? What confessions had his evil Master made over the years to him that led to his receiving confidential treatment by a member of the mighty Mossad? Was it wise to let this inscrutable young man roam free, or should they perhaps simply throw him in a cell and beat the truth out of him?

Alexei felt the imaginary blows that Sretensky and his goons were itching to deliver, yet at the same time he'd chanced upon the age-old secret of all human desire for brutality: it was an animal instinct, rooted in deep, agonizing fear.

But what is it they think I can actually do? Alexei wondered. *Shoot communist-blasting music rays out my ass?* And the concept, ridiculous though it was, was like a fit of diarrhea—at once repulsive and cleansing; horrible and liberating.

This knowledge sustained his nerves even now, aboard a plane, recreating Uncle Petya's mysterious wanderings. This, and the thought that the intimidating giants escorting him might well be wishing they were seated anywhere else than next to him—Samoilenko, Fruit of the Poisonous Tree.

At some point his overwrought brain shut down, producing a curious half-slumber. He was dimly aware of his jailers' silent massiveness. He was also dazedly conscious of the danger lying in this new twist of fate. Who was this Jewish spy who wanted to meet him? What had been his relationship to Rabinovich, and how wise would it be to appear with a NKVD escort for a rendezvous with a Mossad agent who had specifically demanded a one-on-one meeting? But to know the answers he could only go on waiting. Even the most harmless inconvenience, such as the walk down the narrow aisle of the plane became an excruciating trial. What about the impossible wait at passport control, even though he was supposed to be a fucking diplomat? Exasperation boiled up into a sudden need to cause a horrible scene! Inevitably, it made him think of Uncle Petya. Had this been the reason for his violent mood swings? Had his life been one long, exasperating wait, made worse by fear and pain? But what had he been waiting for? What was the face of his pain? Could it all have been building up toward this disaster? Was it possible that his entire life and all his wonderful music had been a delay while he waited for this havoc to erupt, a prelude to *Sixteen*'s creation?

Alexei couldn't say. But as soon as they escaped the airport and stepped out into the stifling air of the Holy City, Uncle Petya popped up again, for Rabinovich could absolutely not abide heat.

If this Jewish spy was to be trusted, Uncle Petya had ventured to this blazing city, seeking knowledge whose exact meaning Alexei seriously doubted he could fathom. Once the Mercedes dropped Alexei and his two NKVD companions near the city center, the goons slowed a few steps behind him so as not to give away their presence.

Fat chance, Alexei thought. That pair of upright bulls couldn't fool a blind person. As the sun climbed, Alexei began sweating in his winter clothes even though it was January 1.

In a second Telex, the anonymous informer had appointed their rendezvous place as a Moroccan hookah café next to an old bookstore in the old Russian Compound. Alexei was to walk along the bustling Jaffa Road until he came upon a fishmonger at the corner of the Mahaneh Yehudah Market and there make a left turn, walk a distance of two blocks then take another left. After this part, Alexei forgot the remainder of the directions. He knew he was supposed to sit at one of the outdoor tables of the café and order a cup of extra sweet coffee and a peach-scented hookah. But the names of the streets and the café had slipped his mind. It wasn't getting lost that worried Alexei. He could always ask his bodyguards to procure the piece of paper. No, what worried him were the teeming throngs packed into the narrow streets. Alexei remembered reading about the Palestinians' violent hatred toward what they viewed as a criminal Israeli occupation of their land. He also knew about the suicidal attacks of self-detonation that often claimed the lives of dozens of passers-by.

As Alexei's eyes flitted among the veiled figures, a small, black-clad creature darted through the crowd and grabbed him in a powerful chokehold. Alexei tried to scream, but his mouth and nose were firmly pressed against a cloth drenched in some sweetish-smelling liquid—and that was the last thing he remembered. A few minutes later, he looked around woozily at a dim, cavernous room with stone walls. He was not in the company of the souls of the dead, as he'd expected, but of his grinning Israeli contact.

The wiry locks of the diminutive man sitting across from him were copper, his feline eyes restless. His most uncanny feature, however, was his agelessness. He was either an old-looking child or a dashingly youthful old man.

Alexei gazed at his captor in disbelief.

They were seated across from one another on creaky leather ottomans. On a low round table between them were two steaming mugs of coffee. Candles illuminated the room.

"Alexei...may I address you by your given name?" the man finally said, his voice hard to place, young and old at once. "I do apologize for chloroforming and kidnapping you, but I assure you that my hands were tied in the matter."

He raised his hands to show they'd been finally untied, and Alexei glimpsed a tattoo that might have been a number on the underside of one sinewy forearm.

"Because, as a little bird told me, the two gentlemen escorting you had no intention of leaving you alone with me and I couldn't afford that. This little tête-à-tête of ours is entirely unauthorized and must remain a secret which means I couldn't be seen with a pair of NKVD agents. The Mossad would have me skinned. Now, as to my name, seeing as I've barely grown an inch taller since birth, let's say I'm called... Nemo Klein? Will that do?"

Nemo Klein paused to light a thick, rolled cigarette, whose smoke smelled like burning dry grass. *Cannabis?* Alexei wondered.

"Now, then, before we begin, I'd like to know one thing. Please tell me, my dear Alexei, do you really think Rabinovich was capable of wreaking such a tuneful havoc?"

Reaching to take a sip of the coffee, Alexei muttered that no, he didn't believe it for one second. "After all, nothing's wrong with me, is there? I've been exposed to the music more than anyone."

"They say they fuck a lot and get killed a lot, these victims of this madness. Is that so?" Nemo Klein asked, his voice relishing the obscenities. "It's certainly a powerful piece of music. I've heard it myself. Got my hands on a smuggled recording and I must say I find it quite addictive, although it might be simple longing for Pyotr. The fucking bastard, offing himself like that. You miss him terribly, I imagine?"

Alexei couldn't answer this question without bursting into tears, so he kept silent, offering the briefest nod.

"Those fools get their knickers in a twist, usually over nothing. Too much oppression can make you paranoid. But this thing could be different. This could be the real *Geist*, you know? After all, surely you know how single-minded old Pyotr could be. If he'd set his mind on destroying Russia, I'd say he might just be able to pull it off!"

Alexei was losing patience. Was there a point to this meeting other than his host getting stoned?

"What was it you wanted to talk about that was so important you had to gas me?" he asked.

Taking another luxurious drag and grinning at Alexei, Nemo Klein finally came out with it. "Do you believe in angels, dear boy?"

It was all he could do not to laugh. "Of course not."

"I knew you wouldn't, ignorant old Bolshevik that you are, just like Pyotr. But I can tell you they're right here, boy, right now, as we speak. They're all over this place and in the air we breathe and they're interwoven into the stones of the walls and lying inside your body and mind, listening to your every single thought, on everyone's every single fuckin' hint of a thought! *Oy vey*, my boy! They're fuckin' everywhere!

"First of all," Nemo Klein said, once he'd recovered from a long coughing-and-laughing fit, "you must try to rid your mind of all the theological crap that has been passed down to you. Drugs may help, by the way, though they, too, are parts of the physical world as we perceive it, as is the cock-eyed, drug-induced vision that may appear as a higher state of consciousness, but that they can as easily distort to their own unfathomable will. You must realize, boy, that we're not talking winged fairies here. They are entities, as real as you and me, though infinitely more evolved and unimaginably powerful.

"For all we know, they've been here forever. They may or may not be of extraterrestrial origin. They may have created the earth and the universe or they may be particular to our own solar system, and simply be our planet's first inhabitants. What we know for certain is that they exist, and yet their existence can't be proven through any faculty of our intellect. They aren't God. However, they seem to possess all three of His major traits: omnipresence, omniscience and omnipotence. This does not mean they are of Godly status; they're simply made of energy able to shape, direct and transport itself. Their mass is smaller than the smallest particle imaginable. This is not to say that they're dimensionless. Yes, they can all fit on the head of a pin. And they can move so quickly and so freely between planes of existence that the entire cosmos could shoot in and out of their asses like a fart (presuming they have asses, which they don't).

"You would be right to wonder how humans could ever become aware of such otherworldly beings. And the answer is so simple, no one would ever think of it: because we speak their language! It is the language of their own thoughts, which they convey to one another instantaneously. I'm sure from the expression on your face and from that wicked shine in your eyes that you've already guessed what this language is because, like dear old Pyotr, you, too, have been to the *Venenum Viscerum*. Am I right?"

A shiver ran down Alexei's spine. *SILANCA: Silence, the Angel Sings.* It was music, the language of the angels. The answer to everything was music! Or, his struggling voice of reason uttered, it's possible that right now you're high from this second-hand smoke.

"That's right, it's music," Nemo Klein went on. "Music, which has been part of us forever, although no one knows its use, its precise nature, the manner or the cause of its value to our race. Evidence of its power abounds in all cultures, including those who feared and persecuted it, as some Christian and Islamic sects have done, and in others who exalted in its ability to invoke fairy-tale divinities through the throats of choir boys and the pipes of church organs. Granted, the combination of certain sounds, harmonic or dissonant, may qualify as an aural stimulus triggering a neurochemical reaction that takes the guise of emotions. But this has never been proved. The astounding fact is that music requires no preconditioned or trained faculty. The ability to hear suffices. And the same musical piece can evoke a million different reactions in a million different people. Music is crude and incredibly elaborate. It doesn't need an alphabet. Moreover, music, more than any other human creation, is purely related to time. Think about it. The words of poems and novels, the images of pictures moving and static, the elation of prayer and that of science—they are all inseparable from the interpretation, recreation and emotional connotations of our three-dimensional existence. On the other hand, what makes music musical is the separation of sounds by specific moments of silence; time interwoven with yet more time, waves of acoustic energy meted out in snatches of audible or silent temporal distance. Thus music is perfectly abstract, even when it mimics natural sounds or accompanies words. Melody is as elusive and unattainable as absolute zero. However, the entities have a knack for what is beyond our grasp. Nowhere else is this more evident than in their favored language, the only one we can perceive and simulate.

"The saddest part is that the most profoundly moving music ever written might sound to the angels as foolish and pathetic as a dog seated at a table fumbling with the plates and the cutlery. Or maybe they appreciate the effort. In fact, although it feels as though we enjoy music, when it comes to the essence of this enjoyment we shall never know whether we are the ones drinking the inebriating wine or the unwitting vessels carrying woozy clarity to the lips of those other, vastly superior, sommeliers.

"Apart from being their fleshy music boxes, we can't claim to be of any significant worth to these ethereal beings. I say this because they seem to leave us wandering in the dark, occasionally throwing us a pittance of second-rate genius by possessing the minds of certain unfortunate luminaries and ersatz immortals. We can surmise that the loftiness of thought and the incorporeal turbulence of our emotions draw them. They flock to those persons and places that are most fraught with human feeling. They favor mothers and their offspring, maybe because they are impressed by the process of this inner mental growth and by the vanity of the reproductive instinct, so utterly brutalized by time and yet intent on fighting it. For the same reason, they rush to sites of death and mass extinction. Quicker than vultures, they arrive at any battleground to devour the throngs of dying thoughts and spasms of wasted neuroelectricity flowing with the blood. Try not to judge them too harshly because of their apathy to the human condition. They should be exonerated on the same grounds that would hold no human accountable for crimes committed against a spore or an inert virus.

"Lastly, based on my extensive ethnomusicological research, I am convinced that these sublimely indifferent deities are attracted by music written in triple time. Please don't laugh. Hear me out. I've discovered that, besides the vast variety of folk music and dances that are strictly three-beat, such as the waltz, the tango and the *çiftetelli*, most can be broken down to a three-quarter tempo. I can't for the life of me guess why the fuckers who can fly across the universe in less time than it takes an electron to complete its orbit should get so stark raving mad over a musical idiom perfected by musical idiots, but there you are.

"Now, I'm sure you're bursting with questions. I've only got the shittiest answers. The really interesting question now is whether your mentor was brilliant or lucky enough to have come upon a way to focus the activity of these buggers. It's funny to think that dear old Pyotr instinctively knew that he should use a triple-time beat to this purpose! I mean, if there ever was a way to unleash legions of celestial fuckers on humanity, why, I'd say our friend quite nailed it, don't you think? It's as though he already knew the pieces of the puzzle, since, as you no doubt know yourself, music doesn't really raise any questions, because it doesn't need to. Be it a means to get laid or an elaborate scheme to bring about a Communist Armageddon! My boy, music is an answer in itself."

CHAPTER FOURTEEN

The sky was a mournful gray and the air as cold as icy water on the morning of January the second as Alexei trudged along the crushed stone, trying to block his mind against the soot-stained buildings looming ahead. It was early and very still. Alexei knew that he was succumbing to a massive force of suggestion.

Snap out of it! he reproached himself, fighting off the jitters. Death is intimate and you have no involvement in this place: no personal loss connects you to its horrors. Not even Uncle Petya's ethnic origins, whatever they were, could justify the bleakness that filled Alexei. Alexei's mind retreated to the events of the last twenty-four hours.

As Nemo Klein assured, from the moment he'd fled from that subterranean hideout, Alexei had refused to accept that the fantastic angelic cosmology was credible. Musically inclined angels addicted to death and waltzing? Really, now! Even if it weren't for the accumulated wisdom of centuries old philosophizing, Alexei had ample cause to suspect the Mossad agent of either purposefully misguiding him or of suffering the same logorrheic insanity of chronic cannabis abusers. After all, the man had smoked four or five joints! When Alexei rose to leave, he'd found his own lower limbs weak from narcosis, whereas Klein looked the picture of drug-induced stupor. The man couldn't stop giggling, every other word was "fuck," and his eyes were more bloodshot than those Latin American statues of the Madonna who shed tears of blood. Adding to this was the outrageous image of Uncle Petya conducting a swarm of invisible demons in order to plague the Soviet bloc. The entire visit had been a colossal waste of time.

There was a single fact that gave Klein's argument an authority Alexei could not deny. Clearly, Uncle Petya had trusted this man, made some sense out of his ramblings, and these notions had helped shape *Sixteen*. Calling Nemo Klein a madman was akin to suggesting that Rabinovich was roaming the globe in search of a miraculous musical balm to restore what? His dead mother? It was too painful. Alexei instead considered ways to approach Klein's supernatural scenario.

First, there had to be some truth to the mystical aspect of music as a supreme form of spiritual communion. A profound connection between music and political power was evident throughout history. Alexei didn't know much about Christianity, but he knew that following the schism, the Russian Orthodox Church had been quick to banish musical instruments from all liturgies. Certain Islamic fundamentalists were wholly and violently opposed to any musical performance. Catholics and Protestants, on the other hand, had given themselves over full-blast to the ecstasy of sacred music. However, music was often harshly persecuted, as any musician who had lived under Zhdanov's reign of terror knew firsthand. Uncle Petya, along with a number of composers who knew of Victor Fleishmann's work, passionately mourned the man's untimely death. One of Russia's finest composers, Fleishmann had perished in the whirlwind of anti-Semitic and anti-formalist purges. Even if, taking a fervent socialist stance, one argued that novels, poems, plays, pictures and films might harm the People's cause if used as imperialist propaganda, in what way could a symphony or a sonata endanger the purity of the listeners' minds?

The same thing was happening now with *Sixteen*. It was as if the Party was hoping to catch one of these immortal destroyers by the wing. Could Alexei blame them? How would he react if he were in their shoes, trying to find a reason for this chaos? He sympathized with their paranoia as he walked across this devastated land, shivering as much from the cold as from the thought of the screams and the rivers of blood that had been shed less than a decade ago only a few hundred meters ahead. Sometimes in such a place, the human cruelty was so visibly inhuman that the mind's eye was forced open, condemned to seeing evil everywhere. Out of the corner of his eye, Alexei thought he glimpsed those fabulous angels, ravenous for wasted human dreams, feeding on the dying, jittering brains. Oh, it was a good thing that Nemo Klein's words had never reached the NKVD.

Being left to his own devices for the last stop on his journey was the most annoying of all his frustrations. When he'd first surfaced in the clamor of Jaffa Road and been promptly snatched by his bodyguards, Alexei had feared that he'd be punished for failing to record a single word or provide a single scrap of intelligence. But what if Sretensky heard this tale about music-loving angels and, interpreting it literally, decided to see if the seraphs' immaterial asses could withstand a couple of nuclear bombs? No, it was better this way; their ignorance was preferable to his own. If only they'd agreed to drive him to the gate and stay there, his grim but comforting guards! If only he had the solace of their giant steps crushing the pebbles, the wheezing of their powerful lungs as a sort of amulet against this modern-day Golgotha! And if only they hadn't fastened this accursed recording device onto his chest, this so-called "bug." Its adhesive bandage, extending in a cross from his sternum to his groin and across his ribcage, pulled at his chest hair and plagued him with an infernal itch. If only Sretensky hadn't specified that if Alexei dared to lay a finger on the damn thing, the Colonel would personally supervise the digging of Alexei's grave at the remotest corner of Siberia!

This time Alexei told himself he would prove himself worthy and maybe at the same time obtain some hard facts on the mystery of *Sixteen* from the last remaining person who'd helped create it in the first place. Oh yes, despite the gloom of the contact's chosen location for their rendezvous, Alexei had very high hopes for his imminent meeting with Isay Semyonovich!

As he'd expected, during his wanderings the arch-perpetrators of the *Sixteen* crime were being hunted down obsessively.

As Sretensky had informed him, of sixteen musicians, only one was still at large. The rest had either perished trying to defect or in police custody. Five had committed suicide. This left the elderly Isay Abramovich Semyonovich as the only link to the original musical traitors. Semyonovich was a retired violist, a prisoner of war in 1942 during the nine hundred-day siege and a death-camp survivor.

A letter from Semyonovich to the NKVD must have seemed like a supreme stroke of luck to Sretensky. With an old man's terseness, the musician asked to meet with "late Comrade Rabinovich's trusted assistant." The urgency of the letter suggested that perhaps its author sensed he wasn't long for this world. He was, after all, born in 1870.

Unbelievably, the octogenarian had managed to drag himself across Belarus and had been living in an abandoned storehouse near Poland's Vistula River. Taking into account his past, the local authorities had given him consent to take up residence in what was perhaps the most disturbing memorial in the world. None of this would have mattered if Stalin were still alive. In that case, a phone call from the Kremlin would have sufficed for the crazy old coot to be shipped back home with a bow tied around his head. But in the last ten months, Poland, the sassiest of the Soviet-orbit countries, had been steadily de-Stalinizing. Thus "those sons of whores blindly devoted to that idiot Gomulka," in the Colonel's words, had responded to the urgent request of their inquisitive neighbors with a refusal wrapped in acceptance. Why, yes, of course, Comrade Samoilenko was most welcome to enter their country, fly out to Kraków and even be driven to the outskirts of Oświęcim in the NKVD limousine. But if his escorts thought they might step out of the car for a second, they should think again. The place was a sad yet vital part of Polish heritage, and allowing two Soviet citizens to be there in a foreign-intelligence capacity was already a generous concession on their part. The gist of it was, "We see a gun, you see your agents in Hell."

Some preliminary ranting had followed on Sretensky's part, but in the end, he had to bite the Polish bullet and send, "the incompetent ass, Alexei," without escort. As the ominous gates ahead grew bigger, Alexei hoped the Colonel's fears wouldn't be confirmed. The letter was three weeks old. What if the old man had simply given up the ghost? This was not the time to be thinking of ghosts. The complex of human slaughterhouses was barely two hundred yards away and the air grew thicker with every breath. Perhaps it was full of the suffering spirits' essence or maybe it was Nemo Klein's angels he was breathing in. Wait...was that music? No, just the rusty gates swinging on moaning hinges. Above him were the horrible words, left as a bitter reminder, and far more bitter to him because Uncle Petya had been freed through his work. Uncle Petya's work had been music and music had finally freed him from the pain. A droplet ran down Alexei's cheek, and he thought he was crying from cold. It was a sprinkle of rain. A final joke since the sky was now white in the rising sun, and yet its whiteness came off, falling upon the earth in rapid drops, caustic as lye. Suddenly it was coming down thicker than the spirits, pelting Alexei in a shower. Within seconds, it had short-circuited the device strapped to his chest and was chasing him through the entrance gate into Birkenau.

Hunted by sheets of rain, Alexei found his way to the old man's quarters as if a guardian spirit voice guided his steps. A lonely viola's heart-warming call broke through the downpour's drumming with a song's chorus that to the Soviet Union signified panic and to Alexei a sacred balm. He followed the music through a maze of buildings which were no more real than Uncle Petya's death. This was the most precious gift of all. If Rabinovich had been a painter or a sculptor or a novelist, he'd be survived by only facsimiles, but music, each time born anew, was eternally alive. Alexei's heart beat frantically with the mad hope that Uncle Petya would be waiting.

He turned a corner, humming the words, as the viola grew louder:

For the moon never beams without bringing me dreams
Of the beautiful Annabel Lee;
And the stars never rise but I see the bright eyes
Of the beautiful Annabel Lee

Alexei bolted inside the black door yawning ahead. A lament of strings echoed in the dim concrete space where an old man crouched, his image fluttering and momentarily taking the shape of Uncle Petya, before assuming his own form. *Never rise.*

How old he is!

Isai Semyonovich didn't rise from the upturned crate until his drenched guest stood before him. Then he shook Alexei's hand with an old man's civility and disappeared into the shadows. He returned immediately with a second crate for his visitor. Looking around, Alexei saw that the old man's only earthly comforts were a cot in the corner, a small stack of books by its side and the picture of a little girl pinned to the wall where one would expect to see a mirror. Semyonovich didn't take Alexei's overcoat to dry or offer any sort of refreshment. He was anxious to talk, and Alexei, too, only cared for what the old man had to say.

How old he is! he thought again. A face like creased paper. The face of one already dead.

Semyonovich's voice sounded shattered, as though great violence had broken out inside him and the resulting rubble and smoke had never settled. Despite this he spoke loudly, ignoring Alexei's responses. Alexei recognized him as a man whose only passion is to tell the tale. He called Uncle Petya by the pet name *Petrushka*, as if Rabinovich were a little boy. Upon seeing his frailty, Alexei had feared that Semyonovich would ramble endlessly. Yet the old man, surprising him, began to talk at once about *Sixteen* and its curious birth. For days, weeks and months, the octogenarian violist had wound himself up like a music box, and, as happens with those boxes, it was difficult at first to recognize the exact tune. He had too great an experience to recount, too enormous an emotion to convey, and it was hard for Alexei to make sense of his disjointed speech.

Semyonovich began with Uncle Petya's re-use of the *Annabel Lee* setting for the third movement, which the old man only moments before had played on his viola. Did Alexei know this was Edgar Allan Poe's last poem? It was the saddest thing. She was thirteen when he married her and his first cousin. Virginia was her name, and she died at twenty-four, leaving the poor man barely alive for another two years which he'd spent mourning and drinking to forget her. Some say he'd never laid a finger on her, though, how could he not? Semyonovich shook his head in disbelief and confided that, even at his advanced years, he still shook with the memory of what it was like to have the beast inside! Ah, Petrushka, the sainted child, he sure knew what he was doing when he chose this poem! Why, it was life distilled, bearing its threefold curse—happiness-sorrow-happiness, or else, sorrow-happiness-sorrow. Hadn't Alexei noticed how Petrushka did it? So simple, really, the shift to a major arpeggio in the chorus. This was life: love, pain of love, bliss of those who will come next and read your poems and listen to your songs and rejoice in your love and in the pain of your love. But to the creator, oh Lord, to him it was usually the other way around. There was the loneliness before, then the glimpse of a life worth living and finally it would be taken from you, snatched from your loving hands by the envious seraphs and turned to dust. Oh yes, the moon never beamed, the kingdom by the sea was lost forever. Alexei, Semyonovich noted, would surely live long enough to see that it always turned out this way.

Then, eyes aglow with mischief, he asked if Alexei recalled the story of Odysseus ordering his companions to stop up their ears with wax so they would not to be driven mad by the singing of the Sirens. Odysseus was tied to the mast, so he could hear but not act on the madness that the singing produced. With a jolt, Alexei remembered the piece of beeswax the NKVD had found on the double-bass player.

Semyonovich went on. Petrushka used the same method throughout the rehearsals. The musicians had been the companions and Petrushka the only one listening, suffering through his symphony. Oh, what fun they'd had, him behaving like a proper conductor for the first time, forbidding them to glimpse at one another's sheets, though they all knew perfectly well by then what they were playing. Petrushka also had ordered identical shoes—with thin pieces of sheet metal instead of soles—made for all of them, allowing them to feel the vibrations through the floorboards of the stage and not lose their timing, since so many of them hadn't played in years...what with their ailments.

Alexei opened his mouth to ask about this. Could this be important? Had Uncle Petya selected these old people because they were dying, sick with some fatal disease and so less apt to care what repercussions *Sixteen* might bring for them? Then, with a violent gasp that sounded as if he'd taken a sharp blow to the chest, the old man fell silent and stared at the picture of the girl on the wall. As he talked, he'd been balancing his cherished instrument atop his knees, the fingers of his left hand clutching the bow tenderly, as though the viola were a sickly sort of pet. Now, looking at the girl, the withered hands that held the viola came alive, stroking the fingerboard with agitated passion. His unkempt fingernails scratched the strings and petted the bridge like a beloved's body, rising to meet his hands and giving a different kind of music.

When he faced Alexei, thick tears rolled down his cheeks in furrows worn by years of helpless crying. His lips trembled.

"I was dead for ten years, my boy. Ten years I spent in the ground. Then Petrushka, dug me out, reached down, gave me his hand and said, 'Don't lie there, not yet, come out, come play this music and you'll live.' And I did, I did!" He burst into a choked-up fit of laughing. His eyes swerved to the girl with a wide grin. "And now I'm waiting above ground—above this ground which her dust made holy. And I know she can listen to my music as surely as I've been listening to hers! It's not the Kaddish, my precious, my sweet, my pretty one. Oh no, no, no."

The rest of the old man's tale came out in spasms of blissful recollection, alternating with tremors of regret and shaking sighs of impossible love. All the while a river of tears ran down his contorted face until Alexei had to look away.

Her name was Lizaveta, and she was his granddaughter. She'd come into his life in 1929 and been taken from him in 1943, in a building not far from the one where they were now. How many times had he repeated those magical dates? Nineteen twenty-nine. Nineteen forty-three. Fourteen years old. As if the outrage of the numbers might finally annoy the Lord Himself and shake Him out of His celestial apathy to correct the mistake like an accountant, to raise the girl from her unknown burial place. Oh, a man as young as Alexei could hardly understand what it meant. The child of your child! It wasn't simply a matter of love magnified. No, it had a very selfish sense. A grandchild could become a passion like no child of one's flesh could ever be—that was why so many hateful parents were gods to their grandchildren.

"You see, my boy, your own child, for all the unimaginable happiness it brings, is like a whisper from the dead. No matter how young you are, the moment you hold it in your arms you hear that whisper: 'You're growing older by the day, and one day, sooner or later, you will die.' They're proof that you are growing older and precious consolation that your passage through this life isn't a lost cause. But they do remind you of time ticking by. That was why my Nina, a girl every bit as kind and beautiful as her own daughter, could never stir within me the love I felt for my beloved Lizaveta."

This little creature, he told Alexei, had been a miracle leaving him speechless with awe from her earliest days. He had come upon Nina pinning a fresh diaper around Lizaveta's supple bum. His granddaughter had turned and waved her tiny paws, giggling with babyish laughter. At that moment he hadn't felt like a Grandpa at all. He felt young as a boy again, aflame with a desire to coddle little Lizaveta and awash with feelings he'd never experienced when Nina had been an infant.

At the time, he'd been a widower for almost twenty years, a man meekly retired to the life of a relic. "After a certain point, your children treat your love like the sun. 'Oh, see? There it is, as always.'" Internally the unspent love had been accumulating and now it could all be unleashed on his granddaughter like a rain of gold, made all the more torrential by the spontaneous affection the baby showed him. He had an unfair advantage. Lizaveta's parents were still young and had promises to themselves still to keep, not to mention the tiredness of working and providing for a ravenously growing human being. But Grandpa, indulging her every whim and surrendering his young man's heart to her, became the person most cherished and most passionately hugged. "You could not count the number of kisses she gave me anymore than you could count the raindrops." And still outside it poured.

Then, in July 1941, in the midst of the Nazis' pogrom in the Zhetel Jewish Quarter of Dyatlovo, the twelve-year-old girl, came upon a Schutzstaffel officer shooting, one by one, her mother, her father and her six-month old brother. "She saw them fall right in front of her."

No child could remain entirely sane when such violent evil was perpetrated right before her. Lizaveta went quite mad. Now only Grandpa remained. The Grandpa whom she had started to outgrow was now the person she clung to as ferociously as when she'd been an infant. Now *Dyiédushka* had to hold her all the time, to comfort her and wipe away her tears. He had to coax her to eat and plead with her to bathe, until she had to be fed and bathed and put to bed by the old man, hardly ever letting go of his hands, her eyes refusing to look away from his and her lips unable to detach themselves from his withered cheeks. For all this reversion, not once did her grandfather's heart waver, not once did he view her as a burden, much less as an invalid. In his mind, her infantile state seemed a perverse gift. His beloved Lizaveta had magically returned to that dependent age. She was his alone to cherish and take care of, and so tremendous was his new surge of affection that he actually thought this frailty made her even more beautiful. "I remember looking at her as she slept, and her transparent beauty seemed not of this world. She looked like a fairy. I'd touch her and she seemed to be made of sunny air, of pure brightness."

Alexei fought hard against a wave of nausea but the old man's words betrayed only a kindness. After a certain point in this morbid cohabitation, he'd really forgotten that his granddaughter had an actual body made of flesh. Maybe Lizaveta had forgotten, too. But the body hadn't forgotten; if anything, the mind's devastation had left it entirely to its own devices. Lizaveta's body craved the solace that came from sitting on Semyonovich's lap, her arm wrapped around his shoulders and her face buried in his throat. Soon, she couldn't even sleep unless her thinning limbs nestled inside the sturdier ones of Grandpa. Who knew what soothing memories these embraces brought back? At any rate, the wind of those dark times shook them both. Jews all around them were being massacred. Then one day, or rather one night, the old man's body, which had become like petrified wood, brought forth an unexpected and shameful branch.

"I knew I was a monster," Semyonovich said, wiping the tears off his viola. "I knew it then, and I knew it again when they brought us here to die. I had created our own original sin which now only death could expunge. For more than a year, my baby suffered the same fate in the soldiers' hands that I had cursed her with. Still I was so insane with love that I rejoiced in our mutual punishment. I thought she had been guilty too. Death finally took pity on my precious and returned her to that special shining air of which stars, fairies and angels are made. And me, being too old, they stuck into the dirt as it befitted me. For ten years I was kept underground, unable to move and unable to die. Why Petrushka should have pitied and unearthed me, I'll never know. But that music he gave me to play, that song—oh God, my boy, the moment I touched it I heard her speak to me again!"

As if seized by a sudden desire to hear once more Lizaveta's voice, the old man, sniffing back the tears, took hold of the viola and the bow, steadied his hands and played *Sixteen*'s opening theme. Alexei, listening to the lilting sorrow of the waltz while the rain continued to fall, sobbed. His thoughts were a tangle of thorns. Faina, growing older and older, alone and unprotected, then, someday, gone. Gone like Uncle Petya.

And like Vittorio, gone too. Destroyed. Vittorio might as well be shining air and dust from a crematorium for all the happiness he'd ever be able to give him. And this pathetic shell of a man, this beast who'd fucked his own demented granddaughter, even this man Alexei couldn't bring himself to detest. Through these senseless tears, the old man looked so harmless.

A thought like a fiery nail drove through shame. If Vittorio were at the mercy of my love, I would fuck him; fuck him no matter if he were my own father or mother. I'd fuck him if he were my son or daughter, my own grandson or granddaughter.

Semyonovich, his eyes mercifully shut against Alexei's outburst, led the music to a dwindling glissando with his fingers, the chords whispering a final A-minor *arpeggio*. Still ignoring his guest, the old man dragged himself to the cot and placed the viola and the bow atop his threadbare pillow as if tucking a child in to sleep. He lingered above this sole companion, his face lit with a smile full of love as if he were gazing at his slumbering Lizaveta.

Shuffling back to Alexei, he once more took up his seat on the upturned crate and from the pocket of his ancient cardigan removed a key and extended it toward Alexei. At first, Alexei didn't even know if he were supposed to take it or simply admire it as another precious *memento mori*. It was a heavy, old-fashioned key made of tarnished brass. It bore no key ring or key chain. "Thank you," he said. "But what is it for?"

"Don't worry, you'll find it," Semyonovich said. "You can't miss it, anyway. It's on the outskirts of Petrograd, and, to misquote the poet, it looks like a small kingdom built by a private sea. It's yours now and you should go there at once."

Mad thoughts swarmed through Alexei's head. So this key belonged to Uncle Petya? What did it unlock? What could be so secret that he had to rely on a chance meeting between Alexei and the ancient musician? And what was this place in Petrograd? *A small kingdom by a private sea.* My God, why should the old, turn into semi-senile fools? Did knowledge itself do this to you? Was it just another of the angels' tricks, so that no human might ever know too much?

His abstracted gaze fell on the old man's hand. The skin was thin as parchment, the fingers as frail butterfly wings.

"Don't begrudge him his death, my dear boy," the old man said. "Sometimes love makes life and death equally impossible. You may manage to forget yourself, but every day hangs on a balance. Some may decide to linger or to throw it all away and sleep. Me, I'm still alive simply because of all the years I've lost. It would be too much to have been dead so many times to be in a hurry to die again. Surely not when the dearest thing in life has been restored, at last, to my heart. Petrushka had been so tired—so worn from dragging poor Katyusha around all these years. Katyusha weighed down on his heart. He thought of nothing but her. Maybe he simply wished to return to her or to forget her altogether and disappear."

Return to his mother? The earth like a womb? Alexei knew that the confidences Uncle Petya made to this man might finally shed some light on this senseless flight from darkness to deeper darkness. Semyonovich was old enough to have known Ekaterina and her son since they'd been babies, Alexei realized. His heart beat wildly as he pummelled the old man with questions. What did he mean? What was the exact nature of Rabinovich's torment? What unspeakable love had he harbored for his own mother? Was this key he'd given him the key to her home, the place where Uncle Petya had spent his blissful childhood and which had been lost in the fire of the Revolution?

But Semyonovich had withdrawn his hand and sat back, not answering a single question. The music box had played its melody and would bring forth no further sound. The old man stared at Alexei, his dry lips quivering and his entire face contorted in a sort of helpless eagerness and desperate politeness like some imbecile.

Semyonovich drew a deep breath and reached once more to take Alexei's hand. "Although you surely know, my dear boy, that, barring the lost ones, he never loved anyone as much as he loved you."

Alexei flinched, staring at the old man with disbelief. He realized that although the old man's fingers could still find the fingerboard of his viola, although his eyes could still discern some movement and his voice was able to shape familiar sounds, Semyonovich hadn't heard a single word he'd said.

Semyonovich was deaf as a stone.

CHAPTER FIFTEEN

Cursing the tangle of nettles, roots and branches, Alexei twitched each time he heard sound in the dark forest. He envisioned impaling himself on some phallic root—death by flora. Or perhaps he'd fall prey to the predatory fauna. Did wolves hunt in daylight? Did the Leningrad district wildlife include eagles and hawks? What about bears? They were supposed to hibernate during the winter, but what if he stepped on one?

Suddenly, his right foot met a partly concealed hole filled with stagnant rainwater, and with a splash and scream, Alexei was sitting waist-deep in the freezing pit. Well, I'd say I'm one with Mother Russia now, he thought, breaking into wild laughter. Alexei took comfort in the thought that the NKVD, Politburo, Party, Kremlin and the entire country were all in a similar state of panic, while men like Colonel Sretensky flailed and collapsed in a mire of their own creation.

As Alexei sat in an abandoned warehouse in Auschwitz, disaster had again struck in Moscow. Comrades Mikoyan, Molotov, Kaganovich and Voroshilov, four of the most powerful members of the 1953 Politburo, had gone missing. The NKVD had unleashed a nationwide manhunt to find them. Yet all four seemed to have vanished without dropping a hint as to the reason or a clue regarding their possible whereabouts. This, of course, stank of a coup. Not even the Americans had the power to abduct four ministers from their Moscow quarters within hours. But no matter how hard the General Secretary was taking the blow, he could no more produce the missing tetrad than raise Stalin from the dead. Even when Khrushchev threatened General Tito with a declaration of war, accusing him of kidnapping his men on the basis that "Tito" was a non-existent name in Slavic languages, the four did not appear. On that very same morning, a riot had broken out when a throng of Muscovites had charged *en masse* into the Mavzoley Lenina. They had overtaken the guards and were stopped by emergency military forces while attempting to smash the bulletproof glass casket containing Josef Stalin's embalmed remains in order to... To what? Tear the body apart and keep the bits as holy relics? Devour the formaldehyde-rich Corpus Stalini on the spot? Judging by their rabid state, anything was possible. Rumors spoke of more than sixty dead and even more wounded. The alleged havoc was so great that Alexei had almost felt a guilty excitement, like a child staying up late to see the searchlights trace a bomber-infested sky during a raid of his hometown. The state of emergency benefited him greatly. He'd been left on his own to wander through the woods, get drenched and perhaps be devoured by wild beasts. All agents had been recalled to the capital. As the Colonel had put it, "There's no time to dig up the shit of your shit-face Jewish son-of-a-whore. You can go fuck yourself for all I care, Samoilenko, but know this: if this whole mess turns out to be the work of your dead buddy, make sure you manage to defect before I get my hands on you." Not a soul had asked Alexei about his reasons for visiting the Leningrad Conservatory and going through the archives dating back to

Uncle Petya's youth. There were more pressing matters at hand as he learned while on the train skirting the Neva. The *Sixteen* pandemic was spreading abroad. Westerners were coming down with the same symptoms as well!

One could only guess at the delight of the higher Soviet echelons over these latest developments, even while caught in their own private Apocalypse. Let the world laugh at the rest of Europe for a change! After all, the reports from the Western bloc verged equally on the hilarious.

First and foremost came word concerning Winston Churchill. The ailing Prime Minister of the United Kingdom had apparently gone public about a series of strokes he'd suffered during the last two years which the British government had kept under wraps. Officials had explained the symptoms as a severe case of fatigue. But now Churchill, scorning his doctors, his country and his young Queen, had quit his Downing Street residence and was either holed up in his country estate in Kent or had deserted the British Isles altogether and fled to the Aegean Sea. There he might be hoping to die from cigars, ouzo and heat stroke, brought on by hours of reclining on a deck chair on his dear friend Ari's freshly christened luxurious *Christina O* yacht.

According to the rumors, the madness had then swum across *La Manche* and was now afflicting the French. Although days away from his succession by René Coty, Jules-Vincent Auriol, President of the Fourth Republic, had fled the dubious comforts of the Élysée Palace overnight, as if the entire quartier had been struck with bubonic plague. From an Algerian aquatic resort he issued an official account, claiming that he'd rather be shot by a guerrilla warrior of the FLN than have to swear yet another prime minister before the *"succession de merde."*

Finally, it seemed that the Germans were also succumbing to this triple-time dance. At six o' clock Moscow time, urgent reports arrived from *Cominform* contacts in the Soviet sector of Berlin, claiming that an unprecedented crowd of people from the Western sector were crossing Checkpoint Charlie and marching into the eastern half of the city. Later, the reports became more frantic, speaking of a tide of West Berliners that had begun to cross the borders of the German Democratic Republic's capital heedless of passport control. Next, the reports ceased altogether, and after a while, the Kremlin received a panicked Telex from President and Head of State Wilhelm Peck that claimed the Democratic Sector was under attack by the Franco-Anglo-American bourgeoisie. The sea of intercity migrants had caused no damage. All they did was engage in an all-around feast of vociferous family reunions, amorous displays and an insane consumption of American alcohol and tobacco. At first, the Politburo didn't know what to make of all this, but then, to allay the terror of the jittery East Germans, they sent back word, assuring them that this sudden translocation *en bloc* could only mean that, at last, the imperialist West was conceding its defeat, drawn by the obviously superior quality of life offered by a democratic socialist regime.

Eventually, there were three possible interpretations of these strange, contradictory occurrence: a) the Soviet bloc was collapsing so rapidly that it was dragging along some of its neighboring nations; b) Europe was under attack by the Americans; or c) a new, unstoppable germ that sooner or later would cross the Atlantic and bring about Pentagon threats which would naturally have to be met with counter-threats by the People's Commissariat of Defence of the USSR resulting in a missile-launcher-trigger-happy World War III that would

bequeath the Earth to what animals and plants survived—in
which case the situation demanded less thinking and more
vodka.

So, while the people of the former Russian capital engaged in
exuberant public drinking as they braced for the world's end,
Alexei slipped unnoticed into the Leningrad District Registry.

There, in the basement office of the topography secretariat,
he was greeted by one of the strangest creatures he had ever
encountered in his life: a mad civil servant who wasn't mad
from years of alcohol abuse.

He was a tiny, ancient man, barely erect and extremely
eager to provide the esteemed comrade with a minute
description of all the natural features of the taiga bordering
the city. Perhaps he was a little too eager, for although he
bowed in deference and scuttled here and there, pointing at
maps and aerial photographs and a hundred different ledgers
and diagrams, he snatched back most of these things only
moments after showing them to Alexei. Like a gluttonous
squirrel hoarding more acorns than he could ever consume,
the old man rushed about picking up everything in sight,
until he was reduced to a swaying stack of paper floating in
the dimness of the office as though moved by a bureaucratic
poltergeist. Baffled and tired, Alexei was about to sit down
when he saw an empty can of sardines with a fork sticking
out on the seat. He jerked upright and, sniffing the rancid
air, noticed a pile of bedclothes lying in the corner. Scattered
around the room were crusts of bread, brown apple cores and
a number of cans. His eyes moved from the makeshift bed
and foodstuffs to the old man, who, panting and gasping, was
locking his cherished archives in a filing cabinet. His hair was
tousled, his cheeks unshaven, his clothes wrinkled and he

stank to high heaven. It appeared that the registrar had been living in his office for quite some time.

Nevertheless, Alexei managed to extract some general knowledge of the nearby countryside. Yes, certainly, there were a number of inland lagoons from the Neva estuary to the Lake Ladoga outlet. The civil servant advised the esteemed comrade to look in the vicinity of the Pontonnyy, Ivanovskoye or Lobanovo riverside. What was more astonishing was that the old man referred to the city as *Sankt-Petersburg*, a crime that could easily land him in a Gulag.

Alexei left the old man clinging to the filing cabinet like a human padlock, his ferret eyes darting as if burglars were after his papery treasure.

On the train, many passengers were tonguing and groping one another. From the few who weren't, Alexei acquired more information about his destination. An obese woman told him of a magnificent private residence a few kilometers outside Kolpino built in the center of an artificial lake. It sounded just about the ideal place to stash an illegitimate princess. The estate belonged to a member of the *nomenklatura*. The sound of the word put a smile in his heart, as he recalled Uncle Petya's mock rage at being termed a luminary of the Party elite. "I tend to think of myself as more of an *apparatchik*," he used to say. "You know, a human tool, like a musical cock the Party strokes to ejaculate jaunty Soviet tunes."

That must be it! Alexei thought, immensely relieved that finally, at the end of this arduous journey, he was rewarded with a piece of good luck.

However, after four hours of wandering in impenetrable woodland, he began to question this luck. The Neva riverside wasn't quite as friendly up close as on the map, and his imagined serene walk to Ekaterina's vanished dacha was proving desperate. Just now, he'd stepped into a steaming pile of animal shit. For all his love of Uncle Petya, Alexei wanted this *Sixteen* scavenger hunt to be over with once and for all.

As his exasperation was on the verge of erupting into a sobbing fit, he stepped out of a pine grove and came upon the lake.

Like an image out of Poe or a dreamy Böcklin landscape come to life, a great mass of cypress trees rose from the center of the lake. The conifers stood in perfect aquatic isolation, their suspended roots as magical as the soles of Christ's feet must have seemed to his disciples when He walked on water. A boat was tied to a small pier on the shore of the lake. Alexei held his breath, drawn to the motionless boat. The water surrounding its keel was oily and dead to the eye—a lonely Underworld ferry minus Charon. Alexei had never rowed, and he was a poor swimmer, yet the eeriness of the scene disarmed his fear. He stepped into the frail-looking boat, unused for God knew how many years.

He clutched the oars and rowed. The water offered no resistance. It was as if he were transported by sheer will. Halfway to the dark-green islet, his thoughts turned to the ruins hidden by the trees. He envisioned the black husk of Uncle Petya's childhood, the private tomb of his lost, unsung mother. He held the key to this tomb, a doubtlessly pointless key at the end of a pointless journey. Only now, in the utter stillness of the lake, did Alexei realize that his entire hunt to solve the enigma of *Sixteen* had been an elaborate exercise in pointlessness, a painstaking lesson of surrender. With his last work, the spirit of Uncle Petya had taken him by the hand, revealing to Alexei the pleasure and the delicate despair of surrendering. Uncle Petya had led him through soliloquies which led nowhere else than to the same passions which had haunted the composer—the beauty of art and love, the unfathomable nature of existence, equally imponderable.

Yes, there were angels among us, even if most of them were ill and drew us toward their obscure routes. If a man could love his mother as he would any other woman and still this horrible desire filled him with songs of astounding beauty, if even motherhood, death and loss could be transformed, then they were pointless too and all one could ever hope to do was to submit.

The boat bumped against soft soil. The islet was breath-taking. Alexei was reminded of a description he'd read of the Hanging Gardens of Babylon. There appeared to be a series of terraces upon which the cypress trees grew, forming an al-most solid cone of evergreen. The space between the trunks was thick with cypress bushes. Cypress cones covered the ground. Stumbling through this thick stratum of seeds, Alexei walked along the islet's perimeter, looking for an opening.

He came upon a narrow passage between two sturdy trunks. Something metallic winked. Alexei wormed through the buoyant trees and reached a granite wall, taller than the trees, with four concentric tiers. This astonishing infrastructure was holding the forest afloat! Who provided for these trees, other than the rain? What hand had planted them? How many years had they stood here like sentinels of the dead?

It had to be the same hand that had erected the massive four-meter-high solid-steel door, which Alexei now unlocked and entered.

* * *

From day he stepped into night, for the towering trees bent toward one another and obscured the sky. Alexei took out his lighter and peered through wavering flames. He gasped. Instead of the sad ruins he was expecting, he saw the lovely place intact, as if the violence of recorded history had not laid a finger upon it.

It was a typical luxurious dacha, no different than those that had been destroyed thirty-six years ago.

Alexei saw that the swing on the porch was the same as the one in the photo. Seated on the polished wood, her hands grabbing these thick ropes, Ekaterina had been swinging obliviously at a time when her secluded home hadn't yet been cast by the cypresses into perennial gloom. And when she'd returned from America with her pianist husband, this place couldn't possibly be the prison she had left, Alexei thought. No, the water must have come later on. He stood at the carved wooden door. Behind it, Ekaterina had lain in bed, screaming and pulling at the sheets until, with the same undignified plop that we all make, Uncle Petya had been born. Alexei felt faint.

He snapped on a wall switch, and the parlor flooded with blinding light. Alexei slowly took in the garden, the swing, the low fence over which he'd nearly tripped, the chestnut and apple trees he'd overlooked, the cypress tight against the sun—all magnificent.

A man could lose himself here, thought Alexei, and the moment he stepped into the parlor he realized that was exactly what had happened to dear Uncle Petya. While he had rested his heart here, his heart became overgrown as well, until he finally had to rush head-on into the blackness of death to reclaim it. Alexei saw traces of Uncle Petya everywhere; all left from his last visit a year ago. There was the empty pack of American cigarettes, overflowing ashtrays, blackened dregs in a wineglass and the missing sleeve of a record Alexei had searched for in Uncle Petya's apartment. It was a 1937 record of Arthur Schnabel playing Schubert's penultimate sonata, which Rabinovich would listen to over and over until each note turned into a hammer beating against Alexei's skull. Treading this sacred space, Alexei concluded that the chairs, tables, vitrines, chandeliers, mirrors, paintings and carpets gracing this turn-of-the-century country house were only copies. Nothing original had survived the Revolution's fire and brimstone. Rather, the interiors he passed through had been selected so to convey that age and environment. This was not so much a home as an obsessively created and maintained shrine.

The thought of Uncle Petya secretly haunting antique shops and auctions, hungering for duplicates of a cherished youth gone up in flames, was a blow. The next was worse. Alexei imagined Rabinovich when the reproduction was finished. Imagined him traveling to this recreated bliss and being confronted by more silence. Imagined him dreaming of his mother tip-toeing into the room to wake him, then striving to see her face and hear her voice. He saw and heard nothing. Alexei averted his eyes from the meticulous forgery. As he mounted the stairs, Alexei's hand skimmed the dusty banister. Uncle Petya claimed to have never seen a dust cloth in his life.

More rooms were to be examined, more wounds to be probed, and for all the sting of sadness, Alexei knew the unveiling of this pain was his inheritance.

Here, he first fed off her breast; here was planted the seed of awful desire.

Alexei stood at the doorway of the dacha's main bedroom, his mind a blank. The room, even if destroyed and reproduced like a backdrop, was overwhelming. Within these walls, or rather their originals, Uncle Petya had been created.

Like the cosmos extending and shrinking at the same time, the son had returned to his birthplace. The vast four-poster bed had been occupied, the gleaming silken bedding and the pillows drawn to the left side. Alexei sat on the bed, making believe it was still warm.

He could barely take in the framed drawing of the Rabinovich family tree hanging on the wall, the work of some loving amateur, all rosettes and curlicues, and beneath it a photograph of Uncle Petya, no older than twenty. Both had clearly been salvaged from the ruins. They were badly charred, the curved blackened paper severing half the family tree, while Uncle Petya's face looked as if he suffered from a rare disease, which he did. The pox of history.

Alexei opened the drawer of the night stand and removed a parcel of letters. Ashes smudged his fingers. Many of the letters were scorched and the singed paper crumbled at the gentlest touch as though the recorded sentiments preferred disintegration over being read by anyone other than the intended.

Not that his eyes could focus anymore. Alexei cried for every particle of soot, so that all he managed to read were incoherent snatches from a young woman's enthusiastic fountain pen. The woman was writing to her cherished son, a student abroad, her yearning watering down the ink.

[...] so hard, my love! Sometimes I awaken with [...] in the middle of the night, feeling like a traitor [...] remember the shape of your fingernails and toes!

[...] and Papa, too, is so anxious to see you, it almost [...]

the dearest man [...] of our most secret love, our bond
that over – [...] And who wouldn't be je –

Inhaling sharply, Alexei looked away. Along with "marriage," he'd seen the word "nuptial" out of the corner of his eye. *Our nuptial night, my love, for which the sun itself goes to sleep,* wrote Ekaterina. Despite his determination, Alexei couldn't face such a revolting truth in the heart of such delicate a beauty.

Then, studying the carved mahogany bedstead, the brocaded wallpaper, the golden tassels hanging from the curtain rope, his eyes strayed once more to the family tree and Uncle Petya's photograph. Then, it hit him.

What fancy ancestral roots could be claimed by a former shepherdess? How could a girl raised in poverty have become such a master watercolorist? Turning on the bedside lamp, he noticed two shocking things. Uncle Petya was conspicuously older in this portrait than the boy in the photograph Alexei had found in his study. The corners of his eyes and lips already bore a premonition of worry lines which were to deepen in years to come. According to the fable, his mother never lived to see her son become a man of twenty. The fire that had devoured half his face betrayed the inconsistency, its lost part now another misleading touch in the Rabinovich riddle. Then, Alexei noticed the last branch of the family tree, connecting *Yekaterina (1901 – 1917)* with the boy Papa was so anxious to meet and so jealous of, the man to whom she'd promised herself and for whom the Sun went to sleep: *Pyotr Anastasevich (1897 – 1953)*. The dates were noted in Uncle Petya's calligraphy.

The weight of this untruth was so unbearable, it drove him instantly wild. He had to know, he had the right to know, goddamn it! With shaking fingers, he pulled at the drawer's knob so violently it clattered to the floor. Lying on top of the striped silken lining was another letter, a recent one as neither paper nor ink had aged. This, too, was written in Uncle Petya's best hand and was part of Alexei's rightful legacy. For who would read if not he, even if it were addressed to another? No, this had been left explicitly for Alexei. It contained the missing words of farewell.

> *Katya,*
>
> *There are no words to place before your name you do not know already. You know these other words beforehand too, yet I must write them nonetheless, as you've been long in the plane of complete and restful knowledge while I still struggle, restless in my ignorance and blindness.*
>
> *You see these poor words also through my eyes, as you grow old inside me and share whatever I give to myself and to you. In fact, I wonder if it's not your sight and senses you bestow upon me as a mercy, so the wax of pain won't seal me up completely.*
>
> *You were guilty, my love, as all life is guilty. You trespassed into existence, and it was only fair that you should bear its load. Should an eagle resent life if the rodents it feeds on were to revolt and climb upon his nest and set him on fire? You demanded from fate and fate demanded back, you were greedy for happiness and fate was greedy for your death. And I, stupidly, was greedy for, and guilty of, both.*
>
> *Though it is hopeless and idiotic to think such thoughts, sometimes I can't help wondering whether some nether part of me, capable of such dark transactions,*

didn't give you up for the music—since your loss filled me with music, so much so my body could never contain it and I had to regurgitate it, to vomit scalding chunks of my soul on the black-and-white keys. If I hadn't grown so weary, my love, if my insides hadn't turned into such a seething mass, I honestly believe that I could sing your passing to no end of time, until the sun and the earth cooled off and froze and turned me into a silly stooping statue seated at the piano.

And yet, forever insatiable as your death had made me, I stole even more from the exquisite treasure of your loss than music: I took everything, left you with nothing. And I know you've forgiven me because no insult could be greater to our love than to see it distorted, raped by the banality of other people's minds, and you, beloved Katya, perverted into a heroine of bad melodrama. A child-widower is always a comical creature; the world looks down on the heartbreak of youth. One is supposed to outgrow one's own heart like a shirt, but losing you left me stunted, a dwarf. I could never grow, and neither could my heart.

And also, there was no one left to claim you, no one to protect you against the forces of historical stupidity and oblivion. So, I made it my lifelong task to swallow you whole, and as you lived in me so did I slowly understand what should be done. It was I, the living and the weak, who must curl up and live inside you, because if there's one thing humanity can't help holding as sacred it is motherhood. A mother is holy; she can't be touched, nor can she be erased by others. Her body, having once contained her son's cock, can be allowed to command it forever.

I took your name along with everything that hadn't died with you. In the bitterness of the years thereafter, I often came to believe in this lie and feel its comfort—I, who had no particular affection for my actual birth mother. For if in love we find a better version of ourselves, why shouldn't we also seek a second mother thus?

I turned you into my mother, Katya, because your love bore me anew, because to this day I am the lonesome offspring of your absence, the orphan of your death.

Alexei bolted out of the bedroom. He was running down the stairs when the lights flickered and extinguished, shrouding the dacha in darkness. Like a hunted animal he froze, then descended in tiny, fearful steps.

What scant sunlight had made its way through the cypress trees earlier had since been obscured by clouds. Not even a wildcat's eyes could penetrate such a thick absence of light. He thumbed the wheel on his cigarette lighter, a gift from Uncle Petya, and now a key out of this gloom. The flame caught. Alexei was startled by his own reflection in an ornate mirror extending to ceiling. The glass was heavily tarnished, more black than silver. As Alexei's eyes focused, some of the tarnished places began forming regular patterns. Coming closer he realized that someone had written on the glass with thick finger-strokes of black paint.

Raising the lighter he read the message, and the fury and grief and remorse and the bitter, bitter, bitter feelings of unfairness, irrelevancy and betrayal that had chased him out of the bedroom in a panic were suddenly nothing but dust on his heart. Dust on which Uncle Petya's finger traced his parting words.

You gave my music and my life a shape that they could never have hoped to master on their own. And for this, my boy, you'll always have my deep, undying love.

CHAPTER SIXTEEN

Ultimately, common sense prevailed in the USSR and abroad. The human race had paid too dear a price in the last global war to react rashly to such an indeterminate threat. After a while, it subsided on its own. In the end, the planet didn't go up in smoke, and even the Soviet rulers, who had sustained the gravest damage and were known for their brashness, realized that they'd been after the wrong scapegoat. Thus, began an era that would later be known as the *Khrushchovskaya Ottepel* (Khrushchev's Thaw) during which the General Secretary of the Communist Party and Leader of the People, like a warm gust of reason and comradely dignity, began to blow upon the persistent glacier of Stalin's personality cult, unfreezing the Russian people from fear of pointless persecution...at least this was the general principle propagated by the authorities and the press. In truth, the former reign of terror had merely quieted a bit, as a boa constrictor might after ingesting a calf. This did not mean it would be safe for any frail creature of the jungle to frolic around the dozing snake. Demotions, displacements and terms of imprisonment or exile continued to be liberally administered, although it was true that the Russian people were treated more humanely.

In this spirit, Alexei Mikhailovich Samoilenko's failure in his mission and his late mentor's close association with Stalin were treated with relative leniency; that is, if the State's seizure of all your inheritance and drastic reduction of your salary can be termed lenient. The worst case had befallen Colonel Sretensky, who'd been transferred to an Archangel Gulag as a warden, where he perished along with his prisoners. Losing the royalties from Uncle Petya's works put an end to many of his and Faina's creature comforts. He continued to be the Moscow Conservatory *bête noire*. But his life was by no means a black pit of despair. Uncle Petya's apartment had been bought by Oleg, Prokofiev's younger son, a highly accomplished sculptor, painter and poet. Oleg promised to keep Rabinovich's old studio and use the late composer's home solely for his poetry. He also insisted, despite Alexei's sincere refusal, to pay the young man a small monthly amount as a sort of unofficial rent. And there was also the varying income from Alexei's recent and quite successful "special and private" piano lessons.

The matter of *Sixteen* never received official Party closure, though the overall consensus was that it had been a minor disturbance caused by the Russian people's exaggerated love for the late composer and his music. Alexei accepted this as a version of the story not greatly removed from the truth. An obsessive love was given as the root of the public's disobedience, and, well...love had everything to do with it.

A few months later, the ban on Uncle Petya's music was lifted. There was too much money at stake, and besides, if Stalin could be rehabilitated, then so could his pet composer. In the case of Rabinovich, the *sine qua non* was that, by silent universal agreement, no recording of *Sixteen* was ever made. Not even the American-based record companies seemed to mind. There was so much gorgeous stuff by this Russian guy as it was; who needed the trouble?

What Alexei did regret, was that all the people who had come into contact with him during the *Sixteen* quest were plagued by bad luck.

Thomas Mann, to whom Alexei had written, expressing his deepest gratitude and respect, had not replied. Two months later, Alexei received a courteous missive from Katia Mann in which she apologized, saying that the novelist's health had taken a turn for the worse during the winter.

Alexei's letter to Vittorio, two sober pages distilled from about a hundred wild ones, was left unanswered for a long time. Then, on the anniversary of Uncle Petya's death, he received a registered envelope at the Conservatory, whose sender stated his name as *V. A. Alessandrini, Nuntius Equador*. For reasons he couldn't specify, but which had obviously left him embittered, Vittorio wrote of his transfer to the alarmingly altitudinous Quito as part of his Holiness' overall plan to tighten the Vatican's relations with the pious if governmentally unstable Latin Americas. To Alexei's hint about the *"castrati,"* their once favorite joke, Vittorio replied that it was great they really existed after all. But since they, too, were most likely on the Holy See payroll, would it be too much to ask for them to whisk him away from that godforsaken place where the centipedes were big enough to carry you off while you slept?

Nemo Klein had also fallen victim to this series of ominous developments. Early in April, Alexei received an official note from the Israeli embassy in which he was informed of the Mossad agent's horrific death. A Palestinian man in Jericho had thrown a Molotov cocktail that had exploded in Klein's face. A letter addressed to Alexei was found among Klein's personal effects. Shocked and intrigued, Alexei went to the embassy and obtained the letter. Klein revealed that the explosion had blinded, not killed him and that, relieved of his spying duties, he'd decided to go underground and invest himself full-time in his angelic quest. Moreover, Herr Klein included a small treat for Alexei in his letter: some twenty-odd bars of an E-minor barcarole that he claimed would prove the presence of those intervening alien creatures beyond any doubt. A second sealed envelope, which was to be opened only after the music was played, contained the proof. Alexei decided to indulge the man and played the barcarole on the piano. When he finished, he went to the kitchen, poured himself a glass of red wine and returned to his desk where the small envelope was lying. Inside was a sheet of paper reading RED WINE. He was taken aback, though no more than he would be by some conjurer's act. He couldn't make much of Klein's revelation because he happened to love red wine. It was one of the many tastes he had developed out of affection for Uncle Petya. Drinking red wine reminded him of his mentor and produced a sweet tranquility. It eased his smoker's cough, and as of late, he'd drink nearly a half-bottle of dry red wine every evening. To Hell with how much it cost. It made things easier, so why shouldn't he indulge himself?

Of poor Isay Semyonovich, Alexei heard no more, but that was for the better. He hoped the old man was finally at peace, reunited with his beloved Lizaveta. If Alexei needed more tales of human heartache, all he had to do was sit with Faina while she consoled Irina Ivanovna. The intrusive neighbor, whom he'd once suspected of being an NKVD snitch, had been utterly ravaged by fate. Within a month's time she'd lost her daughter to breast cancer and her son to vehicular manslaughter. As if this weren't enough, the old woman had suddenly found her hands full of bitter in-laws and grandchildren. She had aged horribly, so she'd become Faina's adopted wretch, hovering constantly in their living room and making Alexei feel doubly terrible, as if he had condemned her to this tearful state.

Alexei often thought of Uncle Petya's "kingdom by the sea," and during the onset of his sudden financial hardship, he had actually contemplated selling it. Which, of course, he'd never do. Even if he weren't certain the Party would snatch up every part of Uncle Petya's estate, he would not reveal the existence of such a place to a living soul. He also knew that he would never travel there again. He was determined to let the house be claimed by the cypress trees until their dark limbs closed around it completely, concealing its secret forever.

As for *Sixteen*, Alexei knew he'd always be in its debt. For one thing, it was a haunting story. Out of his tremendous love and pain, a man had single-handedly brought an entire nation to its knees to avenge the death of his beloved. Despite Uncle Petya's fear that his private tragedy should fall prey to banality, Alexei couldn't help marvelling at the near-superhuman genius of what was essentially twelve minutes of sorrowful music. What power must that music contain if its performers had to be deaf or have their ears stopped up with wax to prevent them from violently seeking at once what each of them loved most? Alexei was now convinced that this was *Sixteen*'s influence: it commanded you to go after your heart's most passionate desire, be it person, animal, object or place. It compelled you to assert your love with death-defying madness. Whoever listened to this music would no longer accept, no longer know, loss and defeat. Rather, the listeners would scorn any power, including the course of history and time itself, and obey only this drive to seek the heart's desire.

This is not to mention *Sixteen*'s potential as a breadwinner. Initially, Alexei had felt guilty exploiting the music's power but in the course of days and weeks began to see it as a propagation of Uncle Petya's will and a supreme mercy to Alexei's dozens of devoted private pupils. There seemed to be no end of demand for a live piano version of the forbidden symphony. People approached him at the Conservatory, even people he thought disliked him. They'd stop him on the stairs of the apartment building or come up to him in the street and implore him for a private performance. This astounding source of income, which he carefully designated as "piano lessons" on his tax forms, could amount to anything. It ranged from a poor woman's cooking him a meal while he played the piano, and she sobbed and sniffled over her pots and pans for her dead son or daughter or grand-niece, to amounts of money Alexei couldn't possibly accept in good conscience without feeling he'd taken advantage of the petitioner's need. He had no fear of being found out, for each listener survived the wild feelings *Sixteen* had awakened. They could handle their love without getting themselves killed. It was enough that there now existed a magical means of forcing unshed tears to flow again and bruised hearts to flower.

Alexei spent more time thinking about Uncle Petya. How did he stand such a crippling life? What darkness fed his mind over the merciless years? To imagine himself, even for a second, hurled into such an abyss (to have Vittorio as a youth of sixteen pledge his heart to him and to lose him) made Alexei grateful that Vittorio had never been his own to take away.

Alexei would also wonder about the nameless thousands. Who was luckier after all? Was it the people who had died, their hearts brimming with love, or those whom *Sixteen* had left unaffected, men and women who apparently loved nothing so much as to give up their lives for a glimpse of it? He felt equally sorry for both. But he was puzzled by the unmoved ones, by their undisturbed perseverance and their monstrous strength. Whatever in the world kept them alive?

If the mystery of *Sixteen* hadn't received closure, Alexei had. He often went two or three days at a time without once thinking of Uncle. Then, grief surfaced again, protesting in its nagging voice. What would Uncle Petya think of this, what would he say to that, or react to this-and-that situation? Now all Alexei had to do to silence the pain was to remind himself that he knew perfectly well how any and all of these things would unfold, because he thought and spoke and reacted in the same way as Uncle Petya. He had been molded by Uncle Petya's '*deep, undying love.*'

Alexei also supplied the same soothing wisdom to his mother. He was no longer terrified of Faina turning grayer. He had made peace with the fact that death was slowly but surely weaving its web around her. Because Faina had no other living relatives, he was already the sole heir to her essence. The same way he'd learned to devour the comfort of her love, he'd have to ingest her death as well. He would swallow her whole, and she would live and grow inside him thereafter. What looked like sorrow was a simple siphoning of Faina's soul into his. Although she was diminishing as a separate being, her loving substance had become heavier and stronger in his heart.

One morning, as Alexei was wandering the streets relishing a Russian spring unprecedented in its mellowness, he passed a hardware store and, on a whim, bought two buckets of very bright red paint.

Once home, he emptied his room of all its furniture leaving nothing but the paint and the mahogany box containing Uncle Petya's ashes. He locked the door and spread old *Pravda* editions on the floor. He tipped the box into the paint canisters, mixing the thick white dust into the pigment until it vanished smoothly into the redness. Then, he painted his room.

In the nights to come he'd lie on his bed and look at the walls, and into the walls. The bright red paint would sing a song, and listening, he'd fall asleep.

Books from Etruscan Press

Zarathustra Must Die | Dorian Alexander
The Disappearance of Seth | Kazim Ali
Drift Ice | Jennifer Atkinson
Crow Man | Tom Bailey
Coronology | Claire Bateman
What We Ask of Flesh | Remica L. Bingham
The Greatest Jewish-American Lover in Hungarian History | Michael Blumenthal
No Hurry | Michael Blumenthal
Choir of the Wells | Bruce Bond
Cinder | Bruce Bond
The Other Sky | Bruce Bond and Aron Wiesenfeld
Peal | Bruce Bond
Poems and Their Making: A Conversation | Moderated by Philip Brady
Crave: Sojourn of a Hungry Soul | Laurie Jean Cannady
Toucans in the Arctic | Scott Coffel
Wattle & daub | Brian Coughlan
Body of a Dancer | Renée E. D'Aoust
Aard-vark to Axolotl: Pictures From my Grandfather's Dictionary | Karen Donovan
Scything Grace | Sean Thomas Dougherty
Areas of Fog | Will Dowd
Romer | Robert Eastwood
Surrendering Oz | Bonnie Friedman
Nahoonkara | Peter Grandbois
The Candle: Poems of Our 20th Century Holocausts | William Heyen
The Confessions of Doc Williams & Other Poems | William Heyen
The Football Corporations | William Heyen
A Poetics of Hiroshima | William Heyen
September 11, 2001: American Writers Respond | Edited by William Heyen
Shoah Train | William Heyen

Etruscan Press Is Proud of Support Received From

Wilkes University

Youngstown State University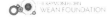

The Raymond John Wean Foundation

The Ohio Arts Council

The Stephen & Jeryl Oristaglio Foundation

The Nathalie & James Andrews Foundation

The National Endowment for the Arts

The Ruth H. Beecher Foundation

The Bates-Manzano Fund

The New Mexico Community Foundation

Founded in 2001 with a generous grant from the Oristaglio Foundation, Etruscan Press is a nonprofit cooperative of poets and writers working to produce and promote books that nurture the dialogue among genres, achieve a distinctive voice, and reshape the literary and cultural histories of which we are a part.

etruscan press
www.etruscanpress.org
Etruscan Press books may be ordered from

Consortium Book Sales and Distribution
800.283.3572
www.cbsd.com

Etruscan Press is a 501(c)(3) nonprofit organization.
Contributions to Etruscan Press are tax deductible
as allowed under applicable law.
For more information, a prospectus,
or to order one of our titles,
contact us at books@etruscanpress.org.